MAURETANIA

MAURETANIA

Book II, The Middle Empire

CONN HALLINAN

Ballingarry Press

To Anne

My wife, my champion, always my first reader. And one of the best things that's ever happened to me.

Characters in Mauretania, in order of their appearance

Aelia Dasumi, the richest woman in Hispania taken in the
   Mauri slave raid
Himilco, second-in-command of the Mauri
Bogud, Mauri raider who first encounters Aelia
Xanthippus, commander of the Cretian archers for the Mauri
Cassius Cornelius, cavalry officer, Ala II Flavia Hispanorum
   Romanorum
Rachel, slave taken along with Aelia
Marcus Favonius Facilis, centurion of the First Century
   of the First Cohort
Titus Valens, Legate VII Legion at Legio
Quintus Junius, tribune of the VII Legion at Legio
Demaratus, signifer, First Century
Flavius Priscus, optio, First Century
Sextus Aelius, tesserarius, Second Century
Manlius Valeranus, centurion of the Second Century
Publius Fulvius, centurion of the Third Century
Aulus Junius, centurion of the Fourth Century
Cerficius Nonius, centurion of the Fifth Century
Timotheus, Greek doctor for the First Cohort
Cleomanes, Cretian archer officer, VII Legion

Julius Dasumi, brother of Aelia

Cleomanes, Cretian archer officer

Domitius Antonius, governor of Mauretania Tingitana

Salvius Getha, secretary to the Governor

Quintus Titius, former optio of the III Legion Augusta

Macro Lucilius, former tesserarius of the III Legion Augusta

Contents

Prologue

250 A.D.

It is 300 years since Julius Caesar conquered Gaul and made it one of Rome's wealthiest provinces, but once again the Empire's legions are fighting desperate battles in the dense forests of the north. Victories no longer signal the end of a war, instead presaging future wars. The myriad tribes Rome once so easily defeated or manipulated have banded together into great confederations that contend almost as equals on the field of battle. While the Empire strains to hold back the floodtide of Goths and Franks pouring across the Rhine and the Danube, fierce Parthian horsemen press on Rome's eastern borders. Assailed from without by invasion, the Empire is shaken from within by inflation and political upheaval.

The year 250 AD is the heart of the "Middle Empire," that period between the conquests of Julius Caesar and the last stages of the empire. "Mauretania" opens in the fifth year of the reign of the Emperor Philippus "The Arabian," who seized power following the murder of Emperor Gordian III, who in turn had become emperor following the murder of Maximinus. From the reign of Caracala (211-217 AD) to the Emperor Diocletian (284-305 AD),

Rome will have 12 emperors. All but two die by violence, five by murder. Civil war becomes the norm. Rome is still immensely powerful, but a careful listener might hear the first whispers of decline and fall.

The first book in this series, "Hispania," followed the lives of its three principal characters. Centurion Marcus Favonius, the younger son of a politically ambitious family, fled the enmity of the Praetorian Guard that has marked him for assassination. Accompanying him was his Optio Flavius Priscus, Marcus's second in command, and a street fighter from the tough slums of Rome. The third member of the trio is Demaratus, the centurion's third in command, a former sailor from Athens, and a man with a keen sense of history and an outsider's view of the empire he serves.

Pursued by the Praetorians, the three fled to Hispania, only to be caught up in the complex politics of Rome's oldest and richest province.

As instability grows and trade declines, the Empire shifts from conquest to defending its borders, and the once all-powerful Roman economy begins to falter. For hundreds of years, Rome's economy had depended on the millions of slaves captured through war. But by the Middle Empire those days are a distant memory: The era of cheap slaves is over and, as slaves grow increasingly expensive, slavery's inefficiency and instability accelerate.

In 250 A.D, Hispania was a land of vast mineral wealth, and Rome's oldest and richest province. It was here that the empire began. It is here that Rome first confronted an enemy as powerful as itself: Carthage. It was here that Caesar defeated Pompey in the civil war that ends the Republic. And it was here that the western empire makes its last stand.

Hispania was also home to one of the most interesting units in the Roman Army, the VII Legion Hispania Gemina Pia, the legion that is the centerpiece for this book. The VII Legion, the oldest serving legion in the Roman Army, had an unerring knack for picking the winning side in a civil war.

Mauretania begins where Hispania left off. It will take our three principal characters across the straits south of the Pillars of Hercules in pursuit of Mauri slave raiders who have seized a woman that Marcus feels deeply about. The expedition will embroil the VII Legion in the complex politics of North Africa and confront a plot to destroy Marcus and his men.

I

The ships moved ghostlike over the swell; silent, almost invisible. Their masts, struck to the decks, etched no silhouette against the moonless sky. The tholes, filled with cloth, dampened any sound of the oars. With the tide approaching flood, the raiders would have several hours before they would find themselves stranded with the ebb.

One of the eight ships edged forward, feeling its way toward the beach, where small combers advanced and retreated on the sloping sands. Beyond the dunes were the lights of a town, but the night was advanced, and most of the small villas were dark. Near the water's edge a light gleamed, disappeared, then sparkled again.

A large man in the prow of the first boat whispered to a companion, and the oars dipped into the water, driving the ship toward the beach. The other seven ships followed. The man wore a long robe with half armor. He carried a small, rounded shield and a long, slightly curved blade. As the ship nudged the beach he slipped over the side into waist-deep water and waded ashore.

Another man loomed out of the darkness.

"Are there soldiers?" the large man asked.

"Only half a century," the man on the beach answered.

"Has the gate been silenced?" asked the large man.

There was no response for a moment. Then the man on the beach said, "No. You will have to take the gate yourself."

"You have failed me," rebuked the large man.

"I am a merchant, Juba, not a soldier," the man on the beach said, his voice muted but sharp with anger. "I said there were slaves to be taken, and rich looting as well. It is not my job to provide them to you on a platter. You have more than enough men to take this town."

The large man glanced to either side. Men were pouring off the ships and gathering in a ragged crowd just below the crest of the dunes. They had been instructed to remain silent, and for the most part they were, though there was an occasional "clank" as a shield collided with a breastplate or a helmet.

A small, lithe man carrying a bow appeared at his elbow.

"Xanthippus, go with your archers and take the main gate. This man here will show you where it is. I will send Matho and soldiers with you to take it. Make sure no one escapes to give a warning. Hold the gate until I call for you," Juba said. "Now go!"

But the lithe man remained standing at his shoulder.

"The loot will be divided equally," said Juba. "You and your men will not be the poorer for this. After me, you will have the pick of the first five slaves."

The lithe man nodded and vanished.

By now all the men were ashore and tension was building. The large man strode up the beach and plunged into their midst.

They gathered around him and he waited until there was absolute silence.

"Hear me, brothers," he said. "This is a town filled with rich Romans and their slaves. There are only a handful of soldiers. But we must strike quickly. Take young women and children. Kill the men and the old. They have no value as slaves. Gather all the women and children. And take only what you can carry. Everything will be divided equally when we return home, so don't get greedy. Pay attention to the sky! When it turns gray, head back to the ships. We wait for no one. Go!"

The mass of men turned and trotted toward the small resort town.

Aelia Dasumi woke briefly. A noise—probably drunken vigiles carousing on the beach—had wakened her. She stretched on her couch and sighed. How had she ever let herself be talked into coming to this dreary and boring little town? Because she was a good friend, she reminded herself. Her cousin Faustina was in deep mourning for her latest failed love and had written a tearful letter asking her to visit. So she came, and here she was, counting the days until she could return to Corduba and being awakened by a bunch of drunken men.

She turned over and composed herself to fall back to sleep.

But the shouting only grew louder.

Angrily, Aelia rose from her couch and called for the night slave. The woman appeared dressed in a light shift, looking confused. She had been sleeping. If Aelia said anything about her transgression to Faustina, the woman would be beaten. Aelia stared at her for a long moment, a look that brought the woman fully awake. She looked terrified.

"Go find out what that noise is about," Aelia said, "and explain to them that they have awakened a Dasumi and have placed their futures in grave peril."

The woman curtsied and, throwing a shawl over her shoulders, called for a slave boy to bring a lamp. Both left quietly by the front door.

Aelia sat for a while in the atrium and watched the fountain, but she was restless and upset and she began to pace the front entrance. As the noise escalated, so did her rage. Finally, she flung open the front door and stalked through the small garden, with its ugly little bench and sad looking pots of flowers, and marched into the street.

The house was in the middle of a long block that led to the sea, and a crowd of men was moving closer, making a terrible racket. She crossed her arms and tried to think of exactly the right words delivered in the tone of imperious anger that would send them slinking away.

Suddenly she saw an older man dragged into the street from an open door. The man was trying to say something when one of the men grasped him by his hair and lifted him off the ground. Another swung a sword and cut the man's head from his body. The headless corpse collapsed in the road, one of its arms twitching for a moment. A cheer of laughter went up from the men.

Aelia stood transfixed by the scene, trying to put it in a context that made sense. Gradually the noises and crashes came into focus, as did the men. They were not vigiles, nor were they soldiers. Neither would be dragging citizens out in the middle of the night and murdering them. That might happen in Rome, but not Hispania, where everyone had learned that killing enemies was bad for business.

The man holding the head glanced up the street, and he and Aelia locked eyes. He was tall, with a full beard, a helmet, breastplate, and a long robe. He flung the head over his shoulder, leaned forward, and with an enormous smile, beckoned her to him.

She sprinted for the door of the villa, slamming it behind her and bolted it. "Household," she cried, "we are under attack."

Within moments slaves crowded into the atrium. Aelia took a deep breath. It was important not to show panic in front of slaves. The armor that walled off slave from master was thin.

"The town is under attack. You male slaves must arm yourselves. The women and children should go out through the back entrance and flee to the barracks," she said calmly.

The men looked at one another. "There are no weapons in this house, my lady," said one, "we are not allowed weapons."

At this moment her cousin Faustina appeared, looking disheveled and hung over, wearing a thin linen shift. "What is going on, Aelia, why have I been wakened?" she asked.

"The town is being attacked, cousin. I think they are slavers from Mauretania," Aelia told her.

"Slavers!" Faustina shrieked. "They will murder us all."

"They will only kill the men, Mistress," said a slave woman reaching out to comfort her.

"How dare you speak to me without permission," Faustina screamed, lashing a backhand across the woman's face, drawing blood from the slave's nose and upper lip.

The woman quailed, touched her bloodied face and fled toward the back of the house. Several of the other slaves looked at one another and silently followed.

"Come back here, you swine!" shouted Faustina, "I will have you flogged to death! You will hang crucified on our doorstep!"

Suddenly there was a thunderous pounding on the door.

Faustina made small gulping sounds, putting her hands over her cheeks. "What will we do?" she whispered to Aelia, as if somehow talking quietly would make the pounding go away.

Aelia was terrified as well, but she reminded herself who she was and what was expected of her. "Quickly, help push this chest in front of the door." But the chest that stood on one wall of the entrance way was as heavy as lead, and her cousin was useless for doing anything but whimpering.

While they were futilely trying to wrestle with the huge piece of furniture, there was a sharp crack from the door. Aelia watched with horror as the bar across the double door bent and then split, the doors bulging inwards from the pressure of the men outside.

Faustina turned to her; her mouth contorted with fear, and let forth an unearthly sound that would have frozen the Medusa in her tracks.

"By the Gods, woman, run!" Aelia ordered. "Out the back."

Her cousin stood frozen for a moment, and then fled toward the back of the house with a parting wail.

At that moment, the doors gave way, and several men smashed their way into the front entrance.

Aelia dashed to follow Faustina, tipping over a large vase as she went by. She heard a crash behind her, and a man cursed.

The hallway had four rooms opening off it, one of them Aelia's bedroom. She raced down the hall and pulled on the door that led to the back entrance to the house.

It wouldn't move. Her idiot cousin had bolted it, trapping Aelia in the corridor. She turned and ran back the way she had come, heading for her room, but a man was coming down the hall. Either her pursuer had recovered his balance or another had taken his place. He was closer to her room than she was. Her only hope—if there was one—was to barricade herself in her room.

A household shrine to the goddess Carna was set into the wall near the locked rear door which held a small statue and some candle stubs. Snatching the little goddess, she ran straight at the man. Her charge drew a look of surprise from him and he stopped, cautiously raising his sword. Women do not normally run at armed men, particularly such a willowy specimen as Aelia. The hesitation gave Aelia just enough time to hurl the statue at him. He raised his left hand to protect his face, but the little figurine was stone and Aelia's long limbs lent it considerable force. It slid by his guard and smashed into his nose with a satisfying "thunk."

As he staggered backwards, she whipped by him, slammed her door and threw the bolt. Almost immediately men began assailing the door, which soon began to give way under the siege.

Aelia looked desperately for something to defend herself with. She flung open a chest and grabbed a dagger she had purchased for her brother two days before. It was more ornamental than practical, with an intricate, inlaid handle, but the blade was long and sharp. She looked at it for a long moment. She knew what she should do: avoid dishonor at all costs, and plunge it into her breast.

But Aelia Dasumi was, above all things, a practical person, although one would not know it by looking at her. Men said she was the most beautiful woman in Hispania, and Aelia did not debate them. Since she was also wealthy beyond imagining, she spent vast amounts of money on clothes, jewelry, and make-up. All of this made her intensely fond of her life and, since she was not certain that there was anything on the other side, she was not eager to depart this one.

Slipping the dagger behind her back, she tucked it into her belt. Then she closed her eyes for a moment, composed herself, and said a short prayer to Fortuna.

The door shattered in pieces and a broad-shouldered man forced himself into the room, a sword in one hand, and a small round shield in the other.

"Who is it that dares disturb Aelia Dasumi?" she said, frostily.

The broad-shouldered man grinned, and made a mocking little bow. "Himilco at your service, lady, and we have come to make a good deal of money out of those skinny limbs of yours."

Another man pushed past Himilco, blood running down his face and staining his robe, clearly the man whom Aelia had struck with the statue. "No money out of this one. I am going to fuck her like a dog and then skin her alive. That will take some time, bitch, and you'll be begging for death all through it."

Aelia saw the man meant it. Without a moment of hesitation, she whipped out the dagger and drove straight for his heart. The move was so quick that the man who had issued the threat had no time to react. The only thing that saved him was Himilco, who whipped up his shield and deflected the dagger. Reaching across her, he clamped her wrist in a grip of steel and twisted it until she gasped and dropped the knife.

With a roar of rage, the man she had struck with the statue reached for her, but Himilco shoved him aside. "This one goes back with us. She will bring a fine ransom or sell for a fortune in the south," he said.

"She is mine! I saw her first," screamed the man.

"Yes, Bogud, and you would be dead if I hadn't stopped her from running that pretty little blade though your heart," said Himilco mildly.

Bogud started to protest again, but Himilco cut him off. "Break down that door at the end of the hall," he said. Bogud hesitated, looking for a moment as if he were going to continue the argument, but Himilco had a quiet authority about him. The two stared at one another and finally Bogud broke eye contact and turned to go. At the door he glanced back at Aelia with a look of pure hate. "You will pay for this, Roman whore."

As Bogud left to begin the assault on the hall door, Himilco turned back to Aelia. "If you don't behave, Roman, I will give you to him," he said. "Now, you wouldn't have any other surprises concealed about you, would you?"

Aelia shook her head.

"Let's be sure, shall we," said Himilco, grabbing the front of her silk shift and tearing it from her body. For a moment she thought to cover her nakedness, but she instead put her arms out and slowly turned to show she was concealing nothing.

Himilco grinned. "Well done, Roman. Juba will want to have

a look at you. Who knows, he may even keep you for himself. You could do a lot worse than that."

"May I put on some clothes," Aelia asked coldly.

"That thing you were wearing will do fine," said Himilco, calling back over his shoulder for one of his men. When the man came in, Himilco told him to take Aelia directly to the beach. When the man protested that it would cut into his time to loot, Himilco said, "I think this one is worth more than anything you could carry in a sack. You'll get your cut. We pool our loot in any case."

The man started to grumble again, but Himilco cut him short. "This one is valuable. Anything happens to her, you answer to me, is that clear?" The man nodded unhappily.

Aelia had put on her shift and was waiting to see how all this would come out, resigned that there seemed to be no way out.

"And you, lady whoever you said you were, are not going to give anyone any trouble at all," said Himilco. "If you do, Adhubal here is going to give you to Bogud, and that will a bad thing for you. Do we understand each other?"

Aelia nodded resignedly and quietly followed the man out of the house. She heard several long, agonized screams from the house. The voice sounded like her cousin.

Xanthippus the archer was deeply angry. The fools that Juba had sent to take the main gate had botched the whole thing. When Xanthippus urged stealth, they laughed at his timidity. "Cretians should stick to their bows and let men do the fighting," the leader said, and instead of trying to surprise the soldiers at the gate, they had charged the eight men.

Even outnumbered five to one, the soldiers formed a quick ring with their backs to the gate and held off the attackers. While the mob of slavers was slashing away, the Romans were using their short swords with lethal efficiency, stabbing through their shields, and using the latter to keep the attackers off balance.

With the crowd of attackers blocking their view, it was almost impossible for the archers to get a clear shot. But finally, the combination of numbers and the few arrows that got through to their targets started to tell, and the ring of Legionnaires contracted.

A Roman officer broke off from the rest of the soldiers and sprinted up the stairs. At first, Xanthippus thought the legionnaires were running for it, but instead, the four remaining soldiers attacked, driving their enemy back. By the time Xanthippus had shifted his target, the officer had reached the ledge surrounding the wall and, swinging his sword rang a great strip of iron that hung down from a tripod. He hit it three times before Xanthippus's arrow struck him in the back. The man staggered, but kept ringing the alarm.

Several other Cretians added their shafts until the officer went down, his back pin-cushioned with arrows.

A combination of exhaustion and numbers had finally overrun the Romans at the gate, and one by one they fell, the last flinging himself at his tormentors, taking one of them down with him.

The attackers were cheering—although Xanthippus noticed that there were fewer of them than when they had initially charged the gate. Ignoring the celebration, the archer ran up the stairs to the wall and put his hand on the iron sheet, which was still reverberating. In spite of half a dozen arrows in his back, the officer was still alive. Xanthippus ignored him.

Notching an arrow, he moved toward a small watchtower that overlooked the gate, but it was deserted. When he returned, he found the leader of the attackers cutting off the officer's head and holding it aloft to the cheers from his men below.

Idiot! He had lost close to 10 men, the entire town was alerted to the attack, and the fool was celebrating. Xanthippus's gaze swept to the east and froze. In the middle of the blackness, a red spark stood out, slowly growing in size as he watched it.

The leader approached him holding the officer's head aloft, grinning. "That's how men fight, Cretian."

"You will soon have another opportunity to demonstrate your skill at battle again, Matho," said the archer, pointing toward the red spark.

The man looked out to the east. "Afraid of fire, are you?" he said.

"That's not a fire, you fool, it's a signal. A Roman Army signal. We will soon have a lot more of those fellows you fought at the gate to contend with," said Xanthippus

"I don't like your tone, little man," Matho said, tossing the officer's head over the wall, and delivered a backhand blow that staggered Xanthippus and drove him into the wall. Grabbing the Cretian by his tunic the Mauri said, "You archers are not real fighters, just girls with bows. Call me a fool again and I will toss your head over the wall as well."

Xanthippus controlled his response but decided at that moment that Matho had to die. No Cretian could absorb a blow like that and not exact revenge. But not just then. Carfully keeping the rage and humiliation out of his voice, he changed the subject. "Juba has to know that there may be Roman soldiers on the way. He will be very unhappy if he is surprised."

That gave Matho pause, and he dropped his grip of the archer's tunic. Leaning over the parapet, he bellowed to one of his men. "Maharbal, go tell Juba that the Cretian girls think that there might be Romans on the way."

The man hesitated. Bringing bad news was dicey, but a look from Matho killed his protests and he ran back toward the main part of town.

"There, happy now, Cretian?" the leader said.

"I think I should put my men on the wall up here in case there is an assault on the gate," replied Xanthippus.

"Do whatever you want," said Mathos dismissively, and went down the stairs to his men.

Xanthippus waved for his men to come up, and the 12 bowmen came up the stairs Mathos had gone down. They had all seen the blow and their faces were carefully neutral. He took them aside near the deserted watchtower and explained the situation.

"We should leave," said one. "We can't fight legionnaires. Let these asses hold the gate against the Roman Army."

"If we try to leave they will kill us," said Xanthippus. "We must bide our time. But each of you pick a target and keep your eye on him. Once they send their wounded away, the numbers will not be so uneven." The men all nodded and spread out along the wall.

Xanthippus examined the odds. The attackers' losses numbered eight killed and a dozen wounded, some probably fatally.

That left the archers outnumbered 20 to 13. On the other hand, Juba might send reinforcements. It was time for patience.

II

Cassius Corneloius, tesserarius of the 2nd Quingeniaery of the Ala II Flavia Hispanorum Romanoruim, rolled out of his bunk at the first sound of the alarm bell, still half asleep. It was as black as a cave in his small room, the oil lamp having exhausted its fuel sometime in the night. But he knew where his long cavalry spatha sword was, and his armor and helmet hung from a hook near the door. Opening the door let in a little light from the hallway. He shrugged into his mail shirt and buckled on his sword as he strode briskly toward the door to the parade ground.

He shared a room with Tiberius Curtius, his optio, but Tiberius was somewhere between Capria and Corduba bringing down a herd of fresh horses from Lusitania. Until he returned, Cassius was second in command. Not that second in command meant much here on the quiet western edge of Hispania. The cavalry quingeniaery, normally 500 men at full strength, was fewer than 300, and many of those were scattered in towns throughout the area. Cassius's unit was down to four turmae squads, and not even those were at their full strength of 30 men apiece.

In any case, this was sure to be a drill. The new commander, Fabius Germanus, was big on drills. He rousted the unit on a regular basis to keep the men in shape, dashing them about the countryside to fend off imaginary foes. All in all, Cassius approved, even though he found Fabius to be distant and cold.

By the time he got to the stables, the grooms were leading out the horses, and men were already throwing on four-horned saddles and slipping bridles over their mounts. Cassius shouted out orders: "Form your turmae. Move it!" A groom was leading out his mare, a sweet creature that combined speed and endurance. It whickered recognition at him as he stroked its withers. As a tesserarius, he would normally have a groom saddle and bridle his horse, but Cassius liked to do it himself.

The gate of the fort was opened already and Cassius glanced out as he set the saddle on his horse. He sucked in his breath. There was a bright spark several miles to the west. Someone had set a signal fire. Signal fires were not much used this far from the Empire's borders, but since the slaver raids from Mauretania had started, a system of signaling had been established.

It was possible the signal was part of the drill, but Cassius found that unlikely. The Roman Army—at least in Hispania— did things increasingly on the cheap, and setting a signal fire for training purposes didn't fit with the budget.

Fabius ran briskly down the stairs leading from the top of the wall.

"Form them up, tesserarius," he said, as his groom brought him his horse. Fabius never addressed him by name, only by rank, which annoyed Cassius. The commander was from Gaul, where apparently discipline and rank were more rigid than in Hispania. But for all his rigidity, Cassius respected the man's skills as a commander. He had learned a good deal from Fabius about how to maneuver cavalry.

Cassius was hoping Fabius would fill him in on what he knew about the signal fire, but the commander mounted and silently took his place at the head of the column. Cassius swallowed his resentment. After all, it was unlikely the commander knew any more than he did.

The quingeniaery formed up, each turmae in line, keeping a short distance from the squad in front and behind. Cassius did a quick count: 107 men, almost half a squad short. Cassius gave them a once-over. Each man carried a rounded shield and was armed with a spear, two javelins, and a long Spatha sword. Given it was the middle of the night, they looked pretty presentable. Cassius felt a little surge of pride. They were good men. Turning his horse to Fabius, he saluted. "Ready, sir."

The commander ran an eye over the unit, gave Cassius a nod, and led the way out of the gate at a brisk trot.

It took a half hour for the cavalry to reach the signal tower where the auxiliary officer in charge said they had heard an alarm bell from Ambis. The officer had immediately sent a messenger to alert an auxiliary unit in Gades, but it would be at least four hours before the infantry could reach the town.

Ambis was only two miles from the signal tower, but Fabius kept them at the same trot. There was no sense in arriving on horses too exhausted to fight. Cassius loped forward to pull alongside Fabius. "What deployment will you want when we reach the town, sir?" he asked.

"We will have to see the situation, tesserarius," Fabius replied, and did not elaborate.

Frustrated, Cassius dropped back to make sure all of the squads were keeping up.

After what seemed an eternity the wall of the town loomed. The gates were shut, and the watchtower looked deserted. Fabius brought the cavalry unit to within a hundred feet of the gate and hailed the town. There was no answer. He turned to say something to Cassius, and the arrow caught him right below his helmet line, just above his mail. He swayed for a moment, reaching for his neck. Whatever he was going to say turned into a gurgle and he fell sideways out of his saddle.

"Shields!" shouted Cassius. "Keep your mounts moving. We are under fire from archers. Turmae II, III and IV get out of range. Turmae I cover me while I help our commander."

Turmae I moved up to screen Cassius while he jumped from his horse. He could hear the other three squads galloping out of range. Fabius was on his face, his head slightly raised. Cassius realized that the arrow shaft had gone right through the spine. The man was dead, probably had been before he struck the ground.

Cassius lifted him and called for help. Two squad members broke off wheeling maneuvers and each leaned down, taking their commander under his arms. The horses shied from the body, but the men kept them under control and, with Fabius's body between them, they carried the dead commander out of range.

"Turmae I," called out Cassius, now hearing the whisper of arrow shafts through the night air as he mounted his own horse. "Retreat and reform out of range."

The cavalry broke off its maneuvers and dashed back the way it had come.

Except for Fabius, the casualties were minor. Two men had been struck, but their wounds were not major. Several horses had also suffered arrow wounds. The men gathered silently, looking to Cassius for direction.

Mentally, Cassius took a deep breath. Start with the easy stuff, he told himself. "The wounded men and those whose horses are hurt remain here with our commander's body." There was a shuffling as the wounded men dismounted and exchanged horses with those whose mounts had been struck by arrows. All told, he was only five men down, not bad for an ambush.

Now the hard part.

"Who here knows this town?" he asked.

A voice called out from darkness. "I do, sir. I have a cousin who lives here."

"What is on either side of the town?" Cassius asked.

"The wall runs on three sides, sir. The beach side doesn't have a wall. It's good ground on the south, sir, swampy on the north," the man replied.

"Why would you build a wall with only three sides?" asked Cassius.

"It wasn't so much to defend the town, sir, but to keep out"—the man paused, and chuckled—"to keep out people like us."

Roman hierarchy was something Cassius knew about, but as a Lusitanian, he could never understand it. The town had built a wall essentially for privacy, to separate the wealthy from the surrounding countryside. It now trapped the residents inside with whoever was in there attacking them. Would that amuse the Gods? Cassius couldn't imagine it wouldn't.

"All right, I want the VI Turmae to divide in half. Arruis," he said to the turmae commander, "you take half your men to the south and make it look like you are scouting the town's defenses. Make sure those people at the gate see you. Is that clear?" said Cassius.

Arrius nodded.

"Merge the rest of your squad with the Ist Turmae, "Cassius continued. "Now, make it look good. I want whoever was shooting us to be paying attention to the southern wall," said Cassius.

"Yes, sir," the man said, saluting. He called out a dozen names to go with him. The men gathered around him, and he led them back toward the gate, but then turned south just out of range of the archers. They were shouting and making a racket.

Cassius turned back to the rest of his men. "Lucius" he called to the man who was familiar with the town. "Ride with me."

The man pulled out of the ranks and joined Cassius.

"Can you lead us to that swampy ground?" asked Cassius.

"Yes, sir," replied the man, "But I am not sure we can cross it with our horses, sir."

"I don't intend to cross it with our horses, Lucius," he said. "Just bring us to a spot that is as close to the wall as we can get."

The darkness had begun to come off the night, and there was just a hint of gray in the east. It would be light in an hour, and Cassius needed darkness. He pushed the quingeniaery.

Lucius had to stop and look around a few times, but he

eventually led the unit to a level piece of ground several hundred yards from the wall. A medium size stream meandered before them, its banks heavy with tule and brush.

Cassius ordered the men to dismount and gathered them around him. "We are leaving the horses here, men. Each turmae, appoint two men to picket them. Take your shields, swords, and one lance. We are going to fight as infantry this morning. Any questions?"

A voice called out from the back," Do we get a pay raise?"

Cassius grinned. Cavalry was paid more than infantry, but they had to provide their animal's fodder out of their pay. It was a sore point with mounted troops, who resented the fact that the Roman Army was so dominated by foot soldiers.

"No, but you can eat your horse," which raised a ripple of laughter. When on short commons, legionnaires always ate horses before mules. Mules carried the infantry's supplies, while horses were just for cavalry, which the infantry held in contempt.

Cassius was nervous about his strategy. He was banking on the enemy not considering that cavalry might dismount and fight on foot and, further, that with the swamp guarding the northern flank, the north wall would be unwatched. It was a gamble. Dismounted cavalry might be effective fighting in the streets of a town, but if they had to assault a defended wall with fewer than 100 soldiers, the chances for repulse and failure were high.

His first instinct was to try to cut off the raiders from their ships—he assumed they had come by boat—but the stream was likely to be deeper the closer one got to the ocean, and even if he could ford it, his men would be fighting in soft sand. It would be almost impossible to maintain group cohesion in such bad footing and, given that he had no idea how big the force was he was about to assault, the last thing he wanted was to face superior numbers with his only lines of retreat the ocean or a swamp. At least in a town they could defend a street, even barricade themselves in some houses, and hold out until auxiliary reinforcements arrived.

He led the way toward the swampy ground, plunging down a brushy bank and into a stream whose coldness surprised him. The bottom was mixed mud and sand; while there were places he could easily move across, others sucked at his boots. The stream grew steadily deeper, finally reaching his lower chest, and he feared that if it got any deeper, they would have to turn back. You can't swim in chain.

But the streambed leveled out, and got shallower. Grunting and puffing he pulled himself up the bank, fighting his way through a thicket of tules. The wall loomed less than 100 feet away. He mentally cringed from an expected assault by archers, but he could detect neither movement on the wall nor the telltale whisper of arrow shafts.

Gradually, the cavalrymen staggered out of the stream and reformed around him. There was no need to urge quiet. Everyone had seen Fabius fall. Setting off at a brisk trot, Cassius led his men toward a small gate set into the wall. Since gates like this one were used mainly for exiting the town, he hoped it would not be barred. But no amount of shoving could budge it. It was bolted fast. It would have to be opened from the inside.

He could climb on two men's shoulders, but the top of the

wall would still be just out of reach. He cast off his mail shirt and helmet, and unbuckled his sword, keeping only his dagger.

He called out the names of four men. "Each of you grab a leg and an arm," he instructed them. Cassius was built small, and he had chosen the biggest men in the unit. He laid stomach down, facing the wall and each man took hold of one of his limbs. "Now swing me back and forth until I tell you to pitch me over," said Cassius.

The men looked at one another, some of them grinning. If their commander wanted them to pitch him over a wall, they would oblige. They began swinging him back and forth, "Higher" he instructed them, and they complied. "Let me go at the end of this next swing," said Cassius.

Judging exactly the right moment was largely guesswork, and Cassius was afraid that he would not have enough force to reach the top of the wall. Instead, they pitched him a good two feet higher than the crest of the wall and he found himself hurtling toward the street on the other side. Having been thrown innumerable times from horses, Cassius instinctively tucked himself into a ball, which put him into a spin that allowed him to hit the ground butt first with a tremendous thud.

The fall stunned him for a moment. He heard one of the men ask—sotto voce—if he was all right. He flexed his legs and found them intact and, while his backside would make sitting on a horse a considerable trial for a while, nothing was broken. He could hear sounds from the town, shouting, crashing, and an occasional scream. With a groan, he picked himself up and turned to the gate.

The sky had grown gray, and there was enough light for

Cassius to see the bolt that barred the sally port. He threw his weight behind it and the bolt slid aside with a screech of rusted iron. Grasping the door, he flung it open and beckoned the men inside.

The gate opened on a long, deserted street that ran parallel to the wall, and he lined up the men along its axis. Lucius, who had guided them to the wall, said that a street one block to their right would connect with a main street into the town's center.

Cassius donned his mail and took his sword and shield from one of the men. Then he addressed them.

"Comrades, we have never gone into battle fighting on foot," he told the men. "We do not know who we are fighting, although it is likely to be slavers. Stay together and when we meet resistance, try to envelop them. Turmae commanders, pay attention to your flanks. If the enemy is fighting without spears, toss your javelins and close with them. If they have spears, keep your shields up and use your javelins to keep them from closing with you until we can get around their flanks."

It was a lot of instructions, maybe too many. Most of them were so nervous or excited that they probably didn't hear a word he said, but hoped the turmae commanders would follow his orders.

"Comrades! For Hispania and Rome! Follow me," cried Cassius, turning and leading the men into the street Lucius said would lead them to the heart of the town.

Xanthippus watched the cavalry retreat into the darkness. His men had done some damage, but how much was not clear. Once again, the soldiers began cheering as if they had won a great battle, though the bowmen had done all the fighting. Mathos joined him on the wall just in time to see a unit of cavalry again approach the gate, then suddenly veer to the south.

The Mauri leader leaned over and called out to one of his men. "Take a message. The Romans have been defeated at the main gate, and they are gathering to attack the south wall." A man detached himself from the gate and ran back into the town.

"This could be a ruse. We strip the main gate, and the Romans make another assault," Xanthippus protested.

Mathos gave him a look that one reserves for children or the feeble minded. "Cavalry can't take walls, Cretian. It is very hard to get horses over them. Juba knows that. He will put a few men on the south wall to remind the Romans of that fact, and while they mill around, we will strip the town and be home by tomorrow night."

"What about the north wall?" said Xanthippus "This attack on the south could be a feint."

"There is an impassable swamp on the north, Cretian. We scouted this town thoroughly," replied Mathos dismissively, turning his back and strode down the stairs to his men.

Xanthippus did not like this. The Roman unit that rode south was too small to do anything. Where is the main body? He glanced up at the sky. It was turning from dark to gray, the colors that Juba said meant it was time to head for the boats. As much as it vexed him, he followed Mathos, catching him at the foot of the stairs.

"The day is coming. We are supposed to return to the boats," said the bowman.

" I thought the Romans were going to assault the gate,

Cretian. Make up your mind," said Mathos. "We will leave when I say we leave. Now get back up on the wall."

Xanthippus glanced around. The force at the gate was no longer 20. Some had been sent off, and a handful seemed to have slipped away to do some looting. The odds were almost even.

The bowman ran back up the steps and drew an arrow from his quiver. His men had already nocked their arrows. There was no need for orders. Each one had been stalking one of the men at the gate for the last 10 minutes. They watched Xanthippus until he nodded, then turned and drew on their targets.

Xanthippus's arrow caught Mathos as he was glancing up. The shaft went through his lower neck and into his chest. He coughed, staggered, spun around and dropped. He soon had lots of company. Only two of the soldiers had not been hit, but they were so surprised that they stood there looking up at the archers. The Cretians made short work of them.

The Cretian leader ran down the stairs, drawing his dagger. Several of the men were badly but not fatally wounded and he quickly cut their throats. He motioned to his men. "To the boats."

Things were suddenly going badly.

Juba had placed himself in the town's center with its ornate fountain and was overseeing the movement of slaves and loot to the ship. As the sky lightened, he urged his men to hurry. He heard the report that cavalry had been repulsed at the main gate and was massing for an attack on the southern part of the town. He sent soldiers to the south wall, but kept a core of disciplined Libyan infantry with him. He was suspicious. It was not like the

Romans to give up so easily after an initial repulse even if they were only cavalry.

He had just sent off for a report from the south wall when a flood of armed men came bursting into the main plaza, falling on the guards escorting slaves to the beach. It took him a moment to figure out who these men were with their round shields and long swords. Then it dawned on him that they were dismounted cavalry. So much for the attack on the south wall. The fools at the main gate had been tricked, and the supposed attack to the south had been a ruse.

He immediately threw his Libyans at the cavalry. The heavily armed infantry with their big shields and heavy spears stopped the cavalry before they could get all their men out of the side street and into action. Cavalry did not make good foot soldiers but there were a lot of them, and they kept trying to work themselves around the Libyans' flanks. If they succeeded, their numbers would offset the infantry, and the raiding party would be in trouble.

Juba sent out runners to call in his men, and to summon reinforcements to fight the cavalry. The Cretians appeared and their leader, Xanthippus, reported that the soldiers had deserted and gone to loot, but since there was no threat to the main gate, the archers had decided to return to the boats. "Without soldiers we cannot defend ourselves," the Cretian told him.

There was something about the bowman's story that didn't ring true. Mathos was not the brightest of soldiers, but he was loyal and stolid. He would not desert to go off and loot. But Juba's attention was drawn to more pressing matters.

"Have your men target the Romans, particularly those trying to work around our flanks," Juba ordered him.

Xanthippus nodded, and gathered his men. They deployed and sent shafts into the ranks of the cavalry. This slowed the Romans down, but it was clearly time for the raiders to go.

The Libyans and the reinforcements began a fighting retreat toward the beach. Juba instructed the Cretians to give the rear-guard cover fire from the prows of the ships, and the bowmen made a dash back toward the beach.

The cavalrymen were courageous, but they fought as individuals, and their long swords were better for slashing than stabbing. Slashing was effective if you are fighting other cavalry or cutting down soldiers who had broken and run. Mounted, the cavalry would fight as a unit, but, in the close quarters of a town and without any coordination of movement, the dismounted horsemen were too disorganized to take advantage of their initial surprise. As long as the Libyans held, the cavalry would be more an annoyance than a serious danger.

The streets and the sands leading to the ships were covered with abandoned loot, and the raiders were still hauling slaves on board. But Juba saw that the ships had pushed off the beach and were floating free.

Fighting on the sand was harder on the more heavily armored Libyans than the lighter cavalry, but the latter were flinching under the continued rain of arrows, and the Libyans were retiring in good order, slipping away by threes and fours, wading out to the ships and climbing aboard.

As the raiders' numbers diminished, the cavalry attacked with renewed fury, and several of the Libyans fell. But again, the steady "thrum" of bowstrings kept the cavalry from pressing their advantage. Juba waded out to a ship, reached up an arm, and was hauled aboard.

"Back water," he commanded, while the last of the Libyans scrambled aboard. The boats moved deeper into the bay, and began the long pull out to where they could raise their masts and set their sails.

Cassius stood thigh deep in the small waves and screamed his frustration at the ships. An arrow shaft hummed by his ear, and he quickly raised his shield. Backing up he warned his men to be careful of the arrows. They needed no reminding; all kept their shields up.

His men had fought well, and he was proud of them. It wasn't their fault that they had to engage with trained infantry. He wondered who those soldiers were. They were good.

A turmae commander touched his shoulder. "Several raiders were taken trying to get to the ships. Should we kill them?"

"No," answered Cassius. "We need to know what they know. Bind them and put them under guard. I will deal with them later. I also want a casualty report."

"Yes, sir," answered the man.

Aelia watched as the Roman soldiers fought their way down the beach toward the ships and her hopes leapt. But then she felt the ship float free and saw the oarmen pull the ship away from the land. She was huddled with a group of some 30 women and children, all in various stages of shock and terror.

The guards were looking back toward the beach, and some

had gone to the sides to haul their comrades aboard. Sensing an opportunity, she sprang up, clawed the face of the guard next to her, and made a dash for the ship's side. She was tantalizingly close when one of the men helping others aboard saw her. Almost casually, he punched her in the face.

Darkness descended on Aelia.

III

Aelia came slowly and painfully awake. For a moment she felt like she was going to be sick, but she took a deep breath and held her gorge. It was light enough now to see the entire ship, which was packed with armed men, loot, and captives. Her head spun whenever she moved. She felt a large knot above her eye where the man had struck her.

She was surrounded by women and children who were huddled in the bow of the ship. Aelia did not recognize the people around her, but then she was not a resident of Ambis. She finally saw a familiar face, one of her cousin's slaves, the woman Faustina had struck just before the slavers had burst into the house.

"You, slave," said Aelia, "what happened to your mistress, my cousin?"

The woman looked puzzled, then recognized her. The slave's lip was still swollen from where Faustina had hit her. The slave sat up and punched Aelia in the face. Aelia was as much stunned by the act of striking a master as the blow itself. With an angry yelp she launched herself at the slave woman, clawing at her face. "How dare you, you dog," she screamed.

Suddenly Aelia's head was snapped back. A guard had grabbed her by her long blond hair and pulled her away from the woman. "Here, here, bitch. Sit quietly or I'll beat you good," growled the man. Aelia struggled and the man cuffed her ear so hard that her head was set spinning again.

Slowly the world stopped turning and Aelia put her fingers to her lips, which were bloodied and starting to swell. The woman who hit her was looking at her with a grim smile on her face. "Slave? You call me a slave? Well, you are no different than me, Dasumi. As for your cousin, the last I saw of her they were raping and murdering her."

Aelia gathered herself to attack the woman again, but another woman leaned forward and pushed her back. The woman was tall and slender, with muscular arms and shoulders. He skin was olive, her hair black and cut short. "Don't be a fool, woman. Next time the guard may not be so gentle. Make trouble and they may toss you overboard."

"Not her, they won't," said the slave who had hit Aelia. "She is as rich as an emperor, aren't you Dasumi?" Then turning to the tall, slender woman she said, "They will ransom her. No hauling water and being fucked in the dirt for her."

"Maybe, maybe not," said the tall woman. "Slaves have no past, nor future. We stand together because that is all we have." Turning to Aelia, she said, "I am Rachel, of the house of Levi."

"A Jew?" answered Aelia.

"Yes," the woman smiled. "A Jew. You Romans can't seem to get rid of us, can you?"

"I meant no offense, Rachel of the house of Levi," said Aelia.

"None taken, and Rachel will do," she answered. "And your name?"

"Aelia Dasumi."

Rachel reached over and touched her arm. "I am sorry about your cousin, Aelia," she said quietly.

Aelia nodded, still in a state of shock. Before she could reply, there was a commotion near the mast, which caused the women and children to huddle together more closely.

Xanthippus, his arms bound at his side, stood before Juba. His men were similarly restrained, each held by two men.

"This is how you repay our service?" asked the bowman. "You would not have made it to the boats but for my men."

"That may or may not be true, Cretian, but I want to know what happened to Matho and the men I sent to the gate," asked Juba.

"I told you. They left us and went to loot," answered Xanthippus.

Juba raised an eyebrow. "Really? Tanit, come and show our friend what you found when you went to the gate to warn Matho that the boats were getting ready to leave."

A burly man in a long burnoose and half armor stepped forward and handed Juba an arrow shaft.

"Tell me, Cretian, do Roman cavalry use bows?" he asked the bound man quietly. "Tanit pulled this out of one of the men at the gate."

Xanthippus said nothing.

"It is said that Cretians are the best swimmers in the world,

Xanthippus," said Juba softly. "Let's see, shall we?" He nodded to the men holding the other bowmen. The men picked up the Cretians, dragged them to the side of the ship and casually tossed them into the sea.

"But what do we do with you, Xanthippus?" said Juba. "It is true you gave service, even if you murdered my men. And I repay my debts."

"Mathos was a fool," hissed the bowman.

"Yes, he was. But he was a Gaetuli, and my tribe takes care of its own," Juba answered. "Because of your service, I will give you a chance for life, Cretian, which is more than you gave my men."

A man pulled a small, round, skin boat toward the side where the men had thrown the other bowmen over board. Lifting it, he dropped it over the side, tying it up to a small grommet.

Juba nodded to the men holding Xanthippus, and they quickly unbound him, keeping a tight grip on the bowman's arms. The Mauri leader drew his knife and nodded again to the men holding Xanthippus. They grabbed the bowman's right arm and held it out.

"Now here is your chance, snake," said Juba. "I am going to cut off your string finger so that you can never again kill a Mauri with a bow. Then I am going to drop you over the side into that boat, and you can return to the sea that spawned you, Cretian."

Xanthippus stared straight into Juba's face. "Cut it off, Mauri dog."

Juba grinned at him. "If you weren't a murderer, I might even come to like you, Xanthippus," he said. With a quick downward stroke, he cut off the bowman's right index finger. The appendage flopped to the deck. The whole time the Cretian never took his eyes off of Juba.

The Mauri leader pointed with his knife, and Xanthippus was dragged to the side, dropped in the small boat, and cast off.

The scene riveted the women huddled in the bow, drawing together and shielding the children from the amputation.

"The Mauri may come to regret that act," whispered Rachel.

"Why?" Aelia whispered back.

"Cretians live for vengeance. Not even the Romans and Greeks can match them," she answered.

"May the Gods give him life, then," said Aelia.

IV

Marcus Favonius, Primus Pilus Centurion of the First Cohort of the VII Legion Gemina Hispania Pia, stood facing his commander, Legate Titus Valens, and the Tribune, Quintus Julius. Titus, tall, slim, and gray, sat stiffly behind a small desk, covered with a scatter of letters and orders. Quintus, older and fatter, relaxed in a chair to one side, his feet crossed at the ankles.

"When was this raid, sir?" asked Marcus.

"Six days ago, Centurion," replied the Legate.

"How did we find out so quickly?" asked Marcus, looking puzzled.

"Money overcomes all, even distance, Marcus," put in Quintus. "One of the citizens taken in the raid was the sister of Julius Dasumi. Corduba and Gedes are in an uproar. It seems the town of Ambis is a retreat for the rich and powerful. A string of horsemen rode night and day to get this message here. These Mauri slavers have gored a formidable bull this time."

Titus pushed a letter at Marcus, who was trying to absorb the news that Aelia Dasumi, a woman with whom he regularly corresponded, had been seized in a slave raid. "This is from Julius Dasumi, Marcus. It is addressed to you. You know him and his sister, I believe?"

Marcus nodded an acknowledgement, unrolled the scroll and quickly read it through. Aelia had been taken in the raid, and her cousin murdered. Julius was offering a ransom that would be delivered to Marcus when he and his men reached Gedes. It was presumptuous for the man to assume the VII Legion was at his beck and call, but Julius Dasumi was nothing if not presumptuous. Wealth does that to people, Marcus thought.

The letter said several raiders were captured and identified who led the raid and where the slaves were bound. It also included a personal appeal for Marcus to move with as much speed as possible. The news that Aelia had been seized in the raid unbalanced him and he took refuge in asking questions.

"Mauretania Tingitana, sir?" said Marcus.

The Legate nodded. "The Mauri have been restive of late, and there have been several raids on Hispania near Malaca, Sexi, and Abdera. But never this far west. Whoever did this is a bold man."

"And maybe a foolish one," said Quintus. "It is one thing to plunder towns, quite another to enslave the powerful. This will reverberate all the way to Rome."

"Maybe," said Titus.

"Sir?" said Marcus.

Titus leaned forward, rubbing his temples and closing his eyes. "As you know, Marcus, the military situation in Mauretania, both Tingitana and Caesariensis, as well as Numidia and Africa Proconsularis, is complex right now."

"I know that the III Legion Augusta was dissolved by the

Emperor Gordian III following the murder of Emperor Maximinus Thrax," said Marcus.

"Emperor Gordian," snorted Quintus. "a 13-year-old boy who was dead before he was 20. What they did to the III Augusta Pia Vindex was shameful."

"It was," agreed Titus, sitting back. "They not only dissolved the legion, they dismissed all the officers, transferred many of the men, and everyone lost all their privileges and pensions."

"And don't think the Mauri didn't notice," added Quintus. "If Rome is upset about slave raids in Hispania, they have only themselves to blame. Dissolving an honorable legion like the III Augusta is as dishonorable an act as that benighted body called the Senate ever conceived."

Titus looked at his Tribune with a somewhat pained expression. "The III Augusta was indeed an honorable legion, Quintus, but they got involved in politics. The Senate declared for Gordian because Maximinus ignored them. We cannot flaunt the will of the Senate. The senators re powerful and proud and could not stand being ignored. So, they turned against Maximinus."

"And which Gordian was that, Titus?" asked Quintus. "The old man governor of Africa who hanged himself, or that whelp of a son of his who died at Lambaesis? The men of the III Augusta were not rebels—they supported the rightful emperor who was simply tired of listening to those old women in the Senate."

"That will be enough, Tribune," said Titus quietly. Quintus subsided. Marcus knew that there was very little that intimidated the old Tribune, besides maybe hard work.

"Sir, I take it there are only auxiliary troops in Tingitana?" asked Marcus, trying to defuse the tension.

"Correct, and not many of those," answered Titus. "Our border in Tingitana does not go very far south in the province, and communications with Caesariensis are mostly by sea. There is a road that runs through Volubilis to the coast between Russadir and Portus Magnus. But it is not as secure as it was a few years ago, in part because the III Augusta was dissolved. The VII Legion has responsibility for Tingitana, so we will have to do this with our own resources and whatever you can put together locally."

"When we say 'we,' Marcus, we mean you," put in Quintus. "This is a job for the First Cohort."

"'We' are not in command, here, Tribune," said Titus coldly.

"Quite right, sir, I spoke out of turn," said Quintus.

Marcus was glad that Publius Felix, the other Tribune, was off in Barcino. Marcus had a tense relationship with Publius, and while Quintus was fonder of books and wine than war, the old man had been friendly to Marcus since his arrival in Legio, the headquarters of the VII Legion. He was also well informed, and kept up with events in Rome. And since he loved to gossip, that information was spread liberally.

Titus turned back to Marcus. "I am sending the First Cohort. I am afraid we cannot spare more than that. There is still tension around Capera with the Lusitanians."

Marcus had fought a battle with the Lusitanians after the latter had overrun the First Century of the First Cohort. Indeed, Marcus owed his present position as the number one centurion in the VII Legion to that battle and the death of the First Century's centurion.

Following the battle, Marcus discovered that the unrest

among the Lusitanians was the result of illegal land grabs by Roman landlords, and not simply a matter of local tribes rebelling against the authority of the Empire. The army was not particularly anxious to start a war, so Titus was trying to shift the problem to the local vigiles, but the landowners wanted war so they could confiscate all the lands of the Lusitanians. The Legate had tried to bring Rome into the dispute, but the Emperor Decius was off campaigning against the Goths and Rome wanted no part of it.

The situation in Lusitania had become more a war of words than swords, which suited Marcus just fine. He secretly sympathized with the Lusitanians, although the soldiers of the VII Legion still wanted revenge for the destruction of the First Century. Marcus was not unhappy to be sent to Tingitana, in part to distance himself from the tensions in Capera, and mostly because Aelia was involved. He quickly suppressed his image of her. There would be time for that later.

"Are you at full strength, Centurion?" Quintius asked.

The question brought Marcus back from memories and images of Aelia to the council of war.

"No, sir. Only the first and second centuries have a full complement of 160 men. Three weeks ago, the third had 140, but it may have recruited more in Barcino and Tarraco. The fourth and fifth are at a little over 130 apiece," replied Marcus. He knew the shortfall in men could draw a rebuke, but it was difficult to keep the cohorts up to full strength out here on the edge of northern Hispania. He had also sent some of his more experienced men to work with some of the greener cohorts.

"Almost half a century down," said Titus, the tone more

thoughtful than critical. "You will need to fill out your ranks from other centuries. I will give the orders, but don't take all the best men."

"No, sir," said Marcus, "but I would like to take the Cretian archers and arrange for some cavalry."

"The archers are rather unhappy in this cold place," said Quintius, "I think they would consider returning to their Mediterranean a gift from the Gods."

"I agree," said Titus, "and they may be useful. As for the cavalry, there is quite a lot of it where you are headed, Marcus."

"So I understand, sir, but the men who served in Tingitana last year did not think highly of it. I will use the local auxiliary cavalry, of course, but I would feel more comfortable if I had a core of good Hispania cavalry," adding, "I have developed a great deal of respect for them."

Marcus had fought Lusitanian cavalry last year, and had only managed to save his century by the unorthodox use of javelins. The battle had been a near thing, and he owed his present position to a young Lusitanian cavalryman who alerted the century and allowed it to survive the attack.

"Show him the report, Titus," said Quintus with a smile. "I think Marcus will find in it a note of familiarity."

Titus lifted a rather thick scroll from his desk and handed it to Marcus. "You are going to need this anyway, Centurion. It includes the information that we got from the captured raiders."

Marcus unrolled it, but put off studying the document until he had a chance to sit down and do it at his leisure. He quickly skimmed through the information until a name jumped off the page at him: Cassius Cornelius.

He looked up to find Quintus grinning at him. "Your young cavalryman managed to save the day at Ambis, or at least stop it from being a complete disaster."

"He did much the same for us, sir," said Marcus. Turning to the Legate, he asked, "Might it be possible to assign Cassius to me, sir?"

"Hmm," replied Titus. "There is pressure on us to maintain a cavalry presence in the south and the west. I should tell you that while the young man is presently the toast of Ambis and Gedes, he managed to create a number of powerful enemies in Capera."

"That had nothing to do with him, sir. If there was any fault in that matter with the decurions at Capera, it is mine," said Marcus.

"Oh, people like Arrius Granius do indeed find fault with you, Marcus," said Quintus, "but the wealthy and the powerful have long memories and wide arms. If Arrius had his way, he would have fed your whole century to the lions. On the other hand," he said, turning back toward Titus, "sending him off to Tingitana might be good for all concerned."

The young cavalryman had humiliated a rich and powerful merchant at the provincial council at Capera last year, and exposed the land stealing that had driven the Lusitanians into revolt. Arrius Granius, the senior decurion at Capera and the main instigator of the land grab against the Lusitanians, had accused Cassius of treason and demanded that Marcus arrest him. Marcus refused and the commander of the VII Legion had backed him up. But the affair was still simmering. By exposing Arrius, both Marcus and Cassius had earned a powerful and dangerous enemy.

Titus leaned back, considering the matter. "You will carry an order shifting Cassius from the Ala II to your command, but I can only let him have four turmae. You will have to make do with 120 cavalry. You can add to your cavalry forces once you are in Tingis."

"Thank you, sir," replied Marcus.

Titus rose and began pacing, a sign that something complex was coming.

"You will have a delicate mission, centurion," he said. "You will have to serve multiple masters and that is never an easy task."

Marcus said nothing because at this point he did not know enough to ask questions.

"The First Cohort will be the most disciplined military force in Mauretania Tingitana, but you are only a cohort, even if you have double the strength of any other cohort in the VII Legion. You will need the cooperation of local auxiliaries," said Titus.

Marcus was not sure where this was going. Of course, he would need the support of local forces, but the word "cooperation" suggested that such support was not automatic. Normally, a regular legion had automatic control over auxiliary units.

"Yes sir, I understand," said Marcus, "Will that be a problem?"

"It might," put in Quintus, who had poured himself a goblet of wine even though it was only a short time after breakfast. Titus frowned slightly at the older tribune, but went on.

"The tribune is correct, centurion. The local civilian authorities in Tingis have..." he paused, "an 'agreement' with the local tribes not to bother them in return for peace, and a steady supply of slaves, and animals for the games. The governor of the province, Domitius Antonius, is also embroiled in a dispute with the Christian Bishop, Nicias. I do not think the governor will look with much favor at the VII Legion arriving to stir up a Mauri hornet's nest, particularly as it will distract him from his quarrel with the Christians."

"It may also cut into his profits," added Quintus.

Marcus digested this for a moment. He could foresee trouble unless his orders were clear and explicit; in particular, what powers he would have when he arrived in Mauretania.

"Doesn't this raid suggest that the Mauris have broken that peace?" said Marcus.

"Not with Domitius, centurion," said Quintus, turning his goblet in his hand.

"An attack on any citizen anywhere in the Empire is an attack on the Empire itself. Surely the governor sees that," answered Marcus.

"Governor Domitius Antonius sees what he wishes to see, centurion. And I am confident that he is not going to like seeing you and the First Cohort," said Quintus.

"Am I authorized to pursue the slave raiders, sir?" Marcus asked Titus.

"Yes, of course," answered Titus, "but you must also work with the governor, as he controls the auxiliaries, particularly since the III Augusta was dissolved."

"Do I have authority to command the auxiliaries?" pressed Marcus. He had to be clear on this issue if the expedition was to have any hope of success.

"You can command them, centurion, but unless you secure their cooperation, such command may count for little," said Titus, still pacing. "Mauretania is much like Hispania, Marcus.

There is only one legion for four provinces, and now that legion does not exist. The civil authorities wield great power, much like they do in Hispania, and military commanders ignore them at their peril. The VII Legion answers only to me, and I answer to the Emperor. No one can command you, centurion, but that does not mean you command all men."

Marcus nodded slowly. "I understand, sir. I will do my best."

"I am sure you will, centurion," said Titus, stopping his pacing. "You have much to do and little time to accomplish it. The First will march day after tomorrow to Brigantium. Ships will be waiting to take you to Gedes to pick up supplies and cavalry."

Marcus's stomach heaved at the thought of a week at sea. He could almost manage to make himself seasick in a bath, and he quailed at what awaited him when they cleared the mole at Brigantium and headed south into the Atlantic. But there was no choice in the matter. By land it would take the cohort almost three weeks to reach the harbor at Gedes, and the men would be tired out from the march.

He was so deep into thinking about what he had to accomplish in the next two days that he stood for some time, ignoring his two superiors. Finally, Quintus said in a friendly tone, "Well, Marcus, you had best be about your business."

"Of course, sir," he replied, saluted and left the principia.

There was indeed much to do.

V

Marcus surveyed the group of men gathered in one of the larger rooms in the Principia. Around the table were his other centurions, the men who made up the Primi Ordines, the commanders of the First Cohort: Aulus Junius of the 4th Century, Certuicius Nonius if the 5th, and the newly appointed Manlius Valeranus of the reconstituted 2nd Century. Its predecessor was ash in a meadow south of Capria, where it had been overrun by Lusitanian cavalry. The 3rd Century was scattered between Barcino and Tarraco in the East. A message had been dispatched to its commander, Publius Fulvius, to gather his men, put them aboard ships, and meet up with the rest of the 1st Cohort at Tingis.

Aulus and Certuicius were both young, owing their command more to the wealth of their families in Gedes and Corduba than any great military skills, but neither was stupid and, under Marcus's tutelage, they had made progress. How much would be tested in the weeks and months ahead. Neither had ever drawn a sword in battle.

Manlius was a former optio, solid and dependable. His experience as a former second in command had prepared him well for handling a century. Marcus had no worries about the veteran.

Behind them were the other officers, the optios, the signifers, and tesserarius. His own junior officers stood with their backs against the wall; Flavius Pricus, the invaluable optio who had served with Marcus for almost a decade; the signifer, Demaratus, a Greek and former sailor who had saved his life in Gaul; and the Hispanian tesserarius, Sextus Aelius.

Marcus had spent almost an hour laying out their orders and explaining their mission. He kept the complex political situation to himself, although he planned to explain it to his own officers.

"Questions?" he asked.

A flood of inquiries followed:

Would the cohort have cavalry? Some.

Would there be auxiliaries to back them up? Yes.

How long would the cohort be in Mauretania? Until the Roman citizens were freed and the slavers punished. In short, no idea.

The two young centurions asked the most questions, the bulk of which indicated that they hadn't quite mastered their jobs. Manlius only asked if the archers would be included and suggested that the cohort request a unit of Baleric slingers as well.

"I assume the slavers are Mauri, sir. If that's the case it will be infantry against some of the best cavalry in the Empire. Archers and slingers are handy at keeping them out of javelin range," he said.

Manlius had fought the Mauri when the First and Second centuries had served in Mauretania Tingitana the previous year.

He had been appointed an optio in the Second Century because of a particularly courageous defense of a small outpost the Mauri had attacked. The two centuries had been badly knocked about by the Mauri, whose light cavalry was effective at dashing in, hurling their javelins, and quickly getting out of range. Roman infantry was designed to fight other infantry, not cavalry, and certainly not the lightning-fast horsemen of the Mauri.

"The archers will accompany us, Manlius, and I will request a unit of slingers as well. An excellent suggestion," said Marcus. "And now gentlemen, we have much work to do and little time to do it. Cancel all liberty. I want a full inspection tomorrow morning. Dismissed."

The crowd of officers scattered purposefully, leaving only his three officers in the room. They were a contrasting lot.

Flavius and Sextus looked much alike, stocky and broad shouldered, with strong noses, short legs, and long torsos. While Flavius had been born in Rome's hard-edged slums, and Sextus in Emerita Augusta, one of Hispania's oldest Roman cities, they were unmistakably Roman.

Demaratus was slim, handsome, and elegant in his uniform, a man who hid his emotions behind a watchful demeanor.

Marcus waited until he was sure the others had gone, then gave his officers a quick sketch of the complex political situation they would soon find themselves in.

"This relationship with the auxiliaries sounds uncertain, sir," commented Flavius.

"They are not worth much, sir," put in Sextus. "They showed up when they wanted to, and that was generally when there was no fighting to be done." Sextus had served with the Second

Century in Mauretania last year. Marcus had taken him out of the ranks and appointed him to his present position as third in command.

"Whatever the situation is, we will have to make it work," said Marcus. "And we don't have much time to do it in."

"Do you know the nature of the dispute between the governor and this Bishop Nicias, sir?" asked Demaratus.

I do not, nor was I offered an explanation," answered Marcus. "I think the Legate does not know."

"The bishop's a Greek?" asked Flavius, looking at Demaratus.

"Not a surprise," answered the signifer with a slightly annoyed edge in his voice. "There are more Christians in the African provinces than in the rest of the Empire, and Greeks and Jews make up much of their numbers."

Marcus caught the edge in Demaratus's comment and felt a certain sympathy. The Greeks were a complex people, and Marcus had discovered that they did not think of themselves as "Greek," but rather as citizens of the city-state they hailed from. Demaratus was an Athenian. The cohort's doctor, Timotheus, was apparently from somewhere else in Greece. But to the Romans they were simply all "Greeks."

"Well, Christians can be trouble," said Flavius.

The comment was unnecessary. Marcus, Flavius, and Demaratus had originally been assigned to Hispania because a Christian centurion in the 2nd Century of the 1st Cohort had been arrested for refusing to honor the emperors, thus challenging the state religion.

"So can emperors," said Demaratus quietly.

"Aye, but we work for them, signifer, not some bishop,"

Flavius snapped. He was annoyed that Demaratus would make such a comment in front of Sextus, who was a new officer who Flavius thought would have difficulty with the cynicism of the more veteran officers—or all Greeks. But Flavius had forgotten his own roots in the ranks; loyalty and cynicism were bread and cheese for the legionnaires. Sextus would never voice his thoughts around his superiors, but he was much of the same mind as the signifer.

Demaratus was not intimidated. "The emperor is in Rome," the Greek shot back. "I doubt he thinks much about a province like Tingitana, optio. One can ignore a Christian bishop in the heart of the empire. That may not be possible on its margins. We should proceed with caution."

Flavius reddened and flared at Demaratus. "Who said anything about not being cautious? I said they were trouble. You Greeks take a man's words and...."

"Enough," said Marcus quietly. "What we need is a plan, not an argument."

Sextus had watched this interplay before. Flavius and Demaratus argued constantly, but as hot as some of their exchanges got, the two were close. In fact, there was a triangle of intimacy between the centurion and his two officers that Sextus could not quite work out. He had never seen such a free exchange between superior and junior officers, and he found it disconcerting. It also annoyed him because he was not invited into the inner circle. He felt the urge to challenge his superior officers on a number of occasions, but since he did not know how it would be received, he reverted to the standard obedience of the Roman army.

"The Legate has given us permission to fill out the centuries with men from other cohorts," said Marcus. "Sextus, I want you to come up with enough names to make sure we leave here at full strength. Run those names by the optio. Then see to the First Century's equipment."

Turning to his optio, he said, "Flavius, I want you to assemble a meeting of the other optios. Some of them looked like they wanted to ask questions this morning, but held their tongues. Find out what they need."

"And Demaratus," said Marcus, "I need you to sit down with Timotheus. I want to find out as much as I can about what we can do to avoid the health problems the two centuries had last year. And he may know more about this dispute with the bishop."

The string of orders had quieted his officers. "Let's pull together, comrades," he finished.

The three saluted and scattered.

Demaratus and Timotheus were doing what Athenians and Corinthians had done for at least six centuries: arguing.

"In truth, I do not understand you, doctor. I was the medical officer on board our ship, and while my knowledge is not as extensive as yours, I have read Hippocrates quite carefully."

"Which one?" asked Timotheus. The doctor was slighter than Demaratus, but built like most Greeks: high cheekbones in a well-formed face and long limbs, very different than the short-legged, long-torsoed Romans. The two men were drinking wine in the legion's hospital and discussing Marcus's request.

Demaratus frowned. "I don't understand."

Timotheus rose and went to a library set along one wall of

the clinic. Pulling two scrolls out of their holders he returned, took a sip of wine, and unrolled them.

"You must distinguish between a disease that can be treated and those that are terminal. You must avoid attempting to treat those whose outcome is almost certainly fatal," the doctor read. Putting it aside, he took up the second scroll, and continued: "The relationship between a doctor and his patient is one of trust and high moral certitude. As a patient puts his life into his doctor's hands, so must that doctor do everything in his power to cure a patient. Even if a condition appears fatal, a doctor must do everything he can to effect a cure."

Putting down the scroll, the doctor smiled. "So, my friend, which Hippocrates should I follow?"

Demaratus's frown deepened. "Both of those scrolls cannot be by the same man."

"You may be right," said Timotheus, his smile broadening, "but then which is the real Hippocrates who should guide my hand"

"Corinthians are impossible," grumbled the signifer.

Timotheus laughed and poured more wine. "None of what we read was written by Hippocrates, Demaratus. What he wrote is long dust. We know very little about him. He was from Cos, that's about it. What we do know is what his students, and his students' students, wrote down, and everything they wrote down they added to."

"Then the words of Hippocrates have been adulterated?" asked Demaratus.

"And many times to our benefit," replied the doctor. "It was Praxagoras, not Hippocrates, who taught us about arteries and that the pulse we feel in a man's wrist can predict disease. Praxagoras gives credit to Hippocrates for his knowledge, but it was he who discovered it. Hippocrates makes no mention of it."

Demaratus frowned. "But surely you do not challenge the foundation of the great man's knowledge: that disease is an imbalance in the natural state of the body between blood, phlegm, and yellow and black bile. I have seen a patient improve from being bled. Do you question that as well?"

"To question is the essence of Hippocrates," replied Timotheus. "He gave us two great truths, Demaratus. First, that disease has a cause which we can understand. Even when the Gods send disease, it takes an earthly form, not a divine one. And the second most important thing: 'observation is the basis of prognosis,' and its dictum that 'hypothesize nothing you cannot test.'"

The signifer was quiet for a time, turning his cup in his hand. "But then is disease the result of imbalance of the four humors, or is it not?" he finally asked.

"I do not question that imbalance is the source of disease, but I am not certain that such imbalances have an internal source. We have both seen our cities ravaged by disease. How could a city's population all be unbalanced at once?" said the doctor.

"Deadly miasmas are the cause of such things," replied Demaratus "Hippocrates says such miasmas throw the humors out of balance."

"If the source of disease can be an external miasma, how do we know that there are no other sources as well?" asked Timotheus.

"How do you mean?" said Demaratus.

"Have you read Herodotus?" asked the doctor.

"Of course," replied Demaratus a little stiffly, offended that Timotheus would suggest a literate Athenian would not read the greatest historian of all time.

"There is a passage on Egyptian fishermen that I find most interesting," said Timotheus, who had indeed intended to annoy Demaratus; the Peloponnesian wars were long dead, but not the sense of competition between city states. "It appears that the fishermen wrap themselves in their nets each night, and few of them come down with disease we attribute to bad air, malaria."

"Surely such nets do not keep out the air," said Demaratus.

"Surely not, which suggests that malaria may have a different source than bad air," said Timotheus.

"But what?" asked the signifer.

"I do not know, but in this I intend to follow Hippocrates: observe," replied the doctor.

Demaratus digested this for a moment. "What of the flux that plagued the two centuries the last time they were vexillated to Tingitana?"

"The cause of that was the water the men drank while we were barracked in Tingis. I warned our commander, Gnaesus, that the sanitary conditions in the city made the water unsafe. But the governor insisted the centuries stay in the city because he thought it was threatened by the Mauri. I think he had another agenda," said Timotheus, rising and putting the scrolls back in their slots.

"Which was?" asked Demaratus.

"Tingis is much like Athens: a plot in every tavern," said the doctor with a grin that took any sting out of the words.

"Yes, well, plots are complex things, so I can't imagine that Corinthians have much experience with them. Possibly you are the wrong person to ask this question of?" replied Demaratus with an answering grin.

"In truth, I do not know what was behind the governor's designs, except that it was at a time of great upheaval in Rome," said Timotheus in a serious voice. "I suspect he was more concerned with keeping an eye on the VII Legion than he was about the Mauri. My recommendation is that, regardless of what the governor wants, the cohort should avoid quartering itself in the city. Since the Mauri slavers are likely to be south of Lixus, that should present no problem."

The two men had been speaking Latin, but Demaratus asked his next question in Greek.

"What do you know of this Greek bishop in Tingis, Timotheus?" he asked.

The doctor pursed his lips and rubbed his temples. "He is a careful man who is drawn to power," he finally said.

"We are told that there is a dispute between Bishop Nicias and the governor, Domitius Antonius," said Demaratus. "If he is drawn to power, why is he fighting with the governor?"

"The word you must pay attention to, signifer, is 'told.' What we are 'told' may bear little resemblance to what is actually happening. Applying Hippocrates to politics is not a bad idea. Observe, don't accept the hypotheses of others. What is done in public may not be what is afoot in private," answered Timotheus.

"There are many Christians in Africa, are there not?" asked Demaratus.

"Yes, but they are still few in number and mostly keep to

themselves, although they preach in the markets," replied the doctor.

"And yet they have power?" said Demaratus.

"They have power because they do not challenge those who presently hold it, Demaratus. They flaunt the gods of Rome, but they have no quarrel with the Empire itself. Indeed, I think they want to run it," the doctor said.

"But didn't the centurion of the 2nd Century challenge the Empire?" replied Demaratus.

"You asked about bishops, not Christians," replied Timotheus. "There are many kinds of Christians, and they hurl more abuse at one another than they do at governors and emperors. And bishops cannot always control what the members of their church do. No bishop instructed our centurion to challenge Rome. He did that on his own."

Demaratus left the clinic with much to report and more to think about.

VI

The ships rounded a rocky headland and drove in toward a long beach at the head of a broad, curving bay. Tree-covered hills rose in the distance; a great purple smudge indicated a range of high mountains beyond. Aelia's jaw hurt from the blow that had knocked her unconscious, and her lip throbbed from the slave woman's punch. Her shift was filthy, and she felt grimy. Her skin was covered with a light coat of dry salt from the spray that had come aboard once the ships entered the Atlantic.

Aelia had expected a short trip across the Pillars of Hercules, but it was now early morning of the second day out from Hispania. She had only a vague notion of the geography of Africa, but it would seem the ships had avoided the city of Tingis and instead headed south along the coast of Mauretania Tingitana. She felt a wave of panic. This was not a simple kidnapping that would end with a hefty ransom. Aelia Dasumi was a long way from home and how she would get back was not obvious.

She looked around at her companions, most of whom were

still asleep. The woman Rachel, who was quieting a child, arched an eyebrow at her. Aelia gave her a wan smile.

The ship was beginning to stir. Men were rising and stretching and pointing toward the shore. Huddled in the bow, Aelia could not see much, and when she tried to stand and look over the side, the guard shoved her roughly. "You'll see our land soon enough, woman," he growled. She sat back down, hugging her knees and marshalling all her discipline not to cry or give in to despair.

The crew began pulling down the sails, and the rowers, who had until then sat with their backs to the sides, sleeping or playing dice, unshipped their oars and pulled. The pitch of the boats increased, which Aelia imagined must mean they were driving through surf and closing on the beach. Eventually she felt the ship ground, slide off, and then ground more firmly. Men dropped over the side, while others handed them bales and vases and an enormous variety of loot. Two men gingerly slid a large bronze statue of a boy over the gunwales to curses and shouts on the other side. She hoped the men below were crushed and drowned.

"All right, slaves, up you get," shouted one of their guards. Prodding them with the butt of his spear, he woke the few who were still sleeping and pushed them all toward the side of the ship. "Up we go," he shouted, pushing at the women and children who hesitated when they saw the drop of several feet and water below them.

Another guard grabbed a young girl and hurled her bodily over the side. She screamed in fear as she disappeared. The others climbed over and, one by one, dropped into the gently surging

surf. Aelia and Rachel were among the last to go, Rachel clutch-
ing a small boy in her arms. When one of the guards attempted
to pull them apart, Rachel shoved him away. "Fool, do you want
lose a slave to the sea? What profit is in that?" she said, her face
fierce, her arms tightly enclosing the child.

Aelia expected him to strike her, but instead he backed off
with a grin. "Full of vinegar, are we? All right, over with the
both of you, and don't drop him." Rachel, holding the child to
her breast, threw her legs over the side and vanished.

Aelia was next. The guard reached for her, but she pulled her
arm away, gave him an icy look, eliciting a laugh, and jumped.
Several men were waiting to catch her and hand her along to the
beach. The other slaves were being driven up the sands toward a
flat, scrubby plain.

Slaves were joining them from the other boats, until there
were well over 100 crowded together. Aelia only recognized a
few people, but that was hardly surprising. She knew very few in
the town outside of her cousin. Most of the people looked like
slaves, although there were some well-dressed adults and children, clearly free residents. One woman had dried blood on her
ear lobes, which Aelia suspected once held expensive earrings.

The slaves look resigned, their previous owners terrified. It
was beginning to dawn on the Romans that they were no longer
citizens of an empire, but at the mercy of people they had no
power over.

Aelia looked around until she located Rachel and joined her.
"Can I be with you?" Aelia asked, and then thought about how
the world had suddenly turned upside down. Here she was, a
Dasumi, asking a slave if she could be with her. She felt like

giggling until she realized she was on the verge of hysteria. She once again brought all of her discipline to bear.

Rachel, sitting with the child she had taken over the side of the ship—Aelia wondered if he was from the house she served in—moved to one side and made room for her. As Aelia sat, Rachel patted her arm and gave her a brief smile. For one of the first times in her life, Aelia Dasumi felt a wave of shame engulf her.

"I don't know what is going to happen," Aelia said in a whisper.

"None of us do," said Rachel. "We are not in control of our lives. This must be unusual for you, Roman, but all slaves know the feeling. We can do nothing but wait." Turning to the child in her arms, she said, "Antonius, this is Aelia."

The boy was no more than six or seven, with salt-fringed, matted curly hair. His eyes widened, and he nodded, but said nothing, just pressed more closely into Rachel's breast.

"Hello, Antonius," said Aelia, dragging up at least the hint of a smile.

The boy said nothing, burying his face into Rachel.

"Antonius was our neighbor. He played with Valeria, didn't you, Antonius?" said Rachel, stroking his hair. "He is a little sad right now, Aelia."

Aelia did not know what to say, but she brushed the child's shoulder with her fingers.

"Up, slaves," came a command from outside the ring of women and children gathered above the beach. Slowly people got to their feet, instinctively huddling closer together.

Aelia was taller than most of the people around her, so she could see what was going on. A group of men had gathered to address the slaves. Among them she recognized her captor from the town. Next to him was a very large man with a full beard and a sharp, hawk-like nose. He had a long scar on one cheek and stood with his hands at his waist. He waited until the crowd had fallen silent.

"I am Juba of the Gaetuli, and you are my slaves," he said. He spoke Latin with an inflection and his voice, while not loud, carried. "If you obey me and my men, you will have long lives. If you do not, you will die."

"If you do not give us food and water, we will not last long enough for you to kill us, Juba of the Gaetuli," called out Rachel. "These children cannot be without water for much longer."

Aelia cringed. Rachel had just committed suicide.

"Maybe we will use you as an example," said Juba quietly.

Rachel shot back. "You have invested money and blood to bring us here. Would you throw it all away because I point out the obvious?"

Juba walked slowly toward Rachel, the crowd of slaves parting in his path. The Jewess stood watching him. Finally, Juba stopped a few feet from Rachel.

Aelia stood frozen for a moment. If this man killed Rachel, Aelia realized that she would be utterly alone in the world. She knew none of the town residents, and she now knew she could expect nothing but hostility from the slaves. She stepped in front of him.

The Mauri looked her and up and down. "It would seem we have a revolt on our hands, Himilco," he said to his companion.

"This is the one I told you about," said the other Mauri. "I think you can weigh her out in gold."

"Get her out of my way so I can cut this other one's throat," said Juba.

"She is my slave," said Aelia. "Kill her and I guarantee you will never see a coin of ransom."

"And how would you arrange that, Roman? said Juba mildly.

"I will drink no water," said Aelia.

"And how long do you think you could keep that up?" asked Juba.

"To the death," said Aelia.

Juba turned to Himilco, who responded with a shrug. "She beat up Bogud," he said with a grin.

Juba laughed. "So, this is the one who gave Bogud that swollen nose. What would you do to me, slave?"

"Nothing, I would just die," replied Aelia softly.

Juba stared at her for a long minute while Aelia marshaled every ounce of discipline not to faint. Finally he nodded. "Tell your slave to keep a civil tongue in her head, Roman." Turning to Himilco he said, "and get the slaves some water." Turning, he walked away.

Himilco gave Aelia a wink and followed him.

Aelia's legs gave out and she collasped, her head spinning.

VII

The transports slowly nosed their way in toward the long mole at Gedes, while the men gathered up their equipment and prepared to disembark. The cohort would spend only one day in the great port before heading south to Tingus, but the men would have an opportunity to stretch their legs and help take on supplies for the coming campaign.

Marcus watched the mole with grim determination. He had been violently ill the whole time the expedition was at sea. Indeed, he had felt the first qualms of seasickness while the transports were still tied up to the dockside at Brigantium. He concentrated on the land, willing himself not to let his stomach heave, but there was nothing in it but air. His face, normally rounded, was drawn and lean, and its color a combination of sunburn red mixed with green and white. He silently cursed the sea, ships, Neptune, slavers, and life.

Flavius and Demaratus kept a discreet distance from their commander throughout the voyage. Both were well aware of Marcus's affliction and the illusion that he successfully hid it from the men. But as they closed on the mole, Demaratus pointed out sections of Gedes to Flavius. A former sailor, he had visited Hispania's main seaport in the west many times. A bad-tempered glare from Marcus silenced him.

A small crowd of officials and military officers were gathered to meet the convoy, and Marcus realized that he would have to be polite and in control, although he would be happy if he simply avoided throwing up on them.

The sailors tossed heavy cables to slaves on the shore, who pulled the ship closer to the mole and wrapped the cables around stone bollards. A gangplank was wrestled off the deck and dropped into place. As the senior officer, Marcus stepped up to it and carefully crossed the short distance to the dockside. A covey of civilians had gathered, and Marcus did his best to look interested in meeting them, nodding at things they said while he tried to find his land legs. The military officers in the crowd at dockside recognized a superior in trouble, and discreetly backed off, although one seemed unable to contain himself.

"Welcome to Gedes, sir," the officer said, barely containing his excitement.

Marcus tried to focus on the officer, although the man's enthusiasm was annoying. He was vaguely familiar, and then memory broke through the fog of seasickness. "Cassius, Cassius, good to see you," he said, and forced himself to smile, an expression that came out looking more like a death head's grin than a friendly expression.

Just as Cassius was changing his expression from eager to disappointed, Flavius stepped forward, grabbed the young cavalryman by his shoulders and picked him right off the ground. "Look what we have here, Demaratus. Cassius and the cavalry are here to save us again."

Flavius's remark brought a wave of friendly laughter from the men disembarking from the ships. The Lusitanian was well liked in the First Cohort, where it was recognized that the horsemen's courageous ride and timely warning saved the Second Century from annihilation in the battle of the meadow. It was also well known that Cassius had upbraided one of the most powerful men in Hispania, the man who bore a good deal of blame for provoking the war that led to the destruction of the First Century. Added to that was the fact that Cassius was friendly, enthusiastic, and not much concerned with status. It was a combination that would make any officer popular in the rigid hierarchy of the Legions.

"Let us hope he is not pursued by an army of enemies this time," said Demaratus, embracing the cavalryman. Sextus pushed forward and gripped Cassius's right arm, threw his arm over the man's shoulders. Whatever disappointment Cassius might have felt in Marcus's distant greeting dissolved.

While Marcus pushed on with the civilians, Flavius discreetly explained to Cassius that the centurion was sea sick. The crowd of officers and men pushed in toward the town, while gangs of slaves passed by, already beginning to load the transports for the voyage the next day.

Demaratus contemplated the small chest and letter that had been delivered to the cohort's headquarters less than an hour before. The slave who brought it told the duty officer it was money, so the duty officer had it delivered to Demaratus. As signifer of the First Century, he was the primary financial officer in the cohort.

He had broken the seal on the chest, assuming it was for the extra expenses the cohort would encounter in Tingis. The chest was filled with silver denari, although of the kind that was mostly lead. Demaratus frowned. Why was a small chest of standard silver coin being sent to the cohort? If it was for expenses, it should have been much larger, and the coins would have had a larger silver content. It was a considerable outlay of money, but not enough for the entire cohort's requirements.

The letter might explain things. Glancing at it, he saw the seal was private—a boar with crossed spear—and that it was addressed to Marcus, not the cohort or the VII Legion. He set both aside and turned back to his payment rolls.

He had just finished enrolling the new men transferred from the VII Legion's other cohorts into the 4th and 5th centuries, when Marcus came into the headquarters looking considerably better than he had several hours before.

"Sir?" said Demaratus, "There is a letter for you, along with a chest of coins. I opened the chest before I realized that the two might be related."

Marcus casually picked up the letter, and then focused on the seal. Breaking it, he quickly ran through the contents. "How much was in the chest, Signifer?" he asked.

"I haven't had a chance to count it, sir. But I would imagine around 1,000 denari," replied Demaratus.

Without a word, Marcus handed Demaratus the letter. The Greek read it through, frowned, and read it through again. The letter was from Julius Dasumi, Aelia's brother. The chest was ransom money.

"I don't think it is enough, sir," said Demaratus, looking up from the letter. "And it should be in gold, not silver, and certainly not silver that is mostly lead. I don't understand. Isn't the Dasumi family wealthy? The men who stole Aelia Dasumi will find that out, and they will hardly free her for a small chest of diluted silver."

Marcus took the letter back. "Keep the chest separate, signifer," he said. "And keep this between you, me, and Flavius," said Marcus.

"Yes sir."

"Is everything else in order?" Marcus asked.

"I am waiting for the money we will need over and beyond the cohort's usual expenses, sir, but otherwise we are ready to leave," answered Demaratus.

Marcus nodded, looking preoccupied. "I will see the local authorities about the extra money and have it sent here before dinner. You will need to be here to sign for it, so you had best take care of whatever other errands you need to now."

"Thank you, sir," said Demaratus, rising to leave. He actually had no errands to run, but he did have gossip. True, Marcus had told him to keep this between the three senior officers, but Romans didn't enjoy gossip like Greeks. Demaratus wanted to talk this over with Timotheus. It would break Marcus's admonition, but the doctor, a friend of the Dasumi family, and of Aelia in particular, might give him some insight into the ransom matter. Demaratus told himself that he was not gossiping, but gathering intelligence, and that was more important than a vow.

Demaratus found the doctor in the clinic surrounded by piles of boxes and rolls of linen. He looked harassed and not at all enthusiastic about a visit from the signifer.

"Demaratus," he said, forcing a smile of welcome. "Is there something I can do for you? Are you feeling ill?"

"Why would Aelia's brother send a chest of diluted silver to ransom his sister?" asked Demaratus knowing that the question would evaporate Timotheus' irritation at being interrupted.

The doctor put aside a scroll he was packing and for a moment said nothing. "How diluted?" he asked finally.

Demaratus shrugged. "Like the normal coins that the men find increasingly difficult to get merchants to accept. And a small chest of those at that. It can't be more than 1,000 denari. I can only assume he does not want her back."

The doctor nodded slowly. "I am not completely surprised, but I am astounded by his boldness."

Demaratus waited, letting his silence do the interrogating.

The doctor rose and began pacing. "Aelia and Julius were the only children in the Denari family, and Aelia's father doted on her. And as much as he doted on Aelia, he denied Julius. When he set up his will he divided his wealth between the two."

Demaratus frowned. "Under normal circumstances the inheritance would go to Julius. How did he manage to bypass the male heir?"

Timotheus smiled. "Oh, Septimius Dasumi did pretty much what he pleased. No magistrate could be appointed without his approval, no governor could rule without his support. In this case, he went to the Senate in Rome, and when the Senate resisted, he got the Emperor Severus Alexander himself to agree to the will."

"And if Aelia..." started Demaratus, and then stopped.

"Yes," said the doctor. "She has no husband or children. If she were to permanently disappear, then her half of the Dasumi fortune would revert to Julius."

"Why did you say Julius was bold?" asked Demaratus.

"Julius must know this story will eventually come out, and it will be scandal. Particularly since Aelia is well liked and has a wide and influential circle of friends. Julius is respected, and even feared, but not liked. He will be accused of abandoning his sister," answered Timotheus.

"But there is nothing in the law that says a man must pay gold, not silver, for his kin. Indeed, Julius does not have to even send a chest of lead coins," said Demaratus.

"I am sure Julius is thinking along those lines, but he is also a careful man. I think he may have an in with this new emperor, Decius. I know that a number of his associates were opponents of Phillip, although Julius was careful not to take sides in the recent civil war. The will could be seen as a threat to primogeniture, and a new emperor might reconsider the act of his predecessor," said the doctor, "particularly if the plaintiff made a substantial donation. And Julius Dasumi has more money than he knows what to do with."

Demaratus was silent a moment, spinning off the various implications this news engendered. "I am instructed to keep this between the three senior officers," he finally said.

"This conversation is between the two of us," Timotheus said simply. "But you might consider passing the information about the will on to Marcus and let him draw his own conclusions. You can say it came up in a conversation we had about the Dasumi family."

Demaratus nodded, and then changed the subject. "You have enough linen here to wrap us all at our deaths. Do you imagine you will need to bury the entire cohort?"

Timotheus smiled and returned to his sorting. "Do you remember our conversation on Egyptian fishermen?" asked the doctor. "Well, I intend to test an idea of mine about malaria."

"By wrapping the men in linen? Exactly how do you imagine they will walk, let alone fight?" asked Demaratus.

"It is not for the men, signifer. It is for the barrack windows, in case Marcus does not follow my advice about avoiding Tingis," Timotheus answered.

Demaratus looked at him blankly.

"On some barracks I will put linen, on others not," explained Timotheus. "If there is a difference in the incidence of malaria between those with linen in their windows and those without, then that will tell us something, won't it?"

Demaratus started to argue, "I don't see how the presence of linen will tell you"--then stopped. "Oh. Your theory that it is not bad air that causes malaria. But what will the linen do?"

Timotheus shrugged. "Maybe nothing. But it will allow me to test a hypothesis. If all the men get equally sick, then we can assume it is the air, because air passes through linen. But if the men in the barracks without linen become sick, and the men in the barracks with linen on their windows do not, then we can hypothesize that there is something else that causes malaria besides bad air."

"What would that be?"

"I don't know," answered the doctor, "but eliminating one cause allows us to search for another."

"Suppose all get equally sick, or no one gets sick," asked Demaratus.

Timotheus grinned. "Well, then we shall just have to devise another experiment to test another hypothesis, won't we?"

"And if Marcus does follow your advice and we do not stay in Tingus?" asked Demaratus.

"Why, then I will have enough linen to wrap all of us when we die," replied the doctor.

Demaratus shook his head, even though he found the whole idea of an experiment intriguing. "Doctors talk in circles," he said.

"Life is a circle, my friend. We begin helpless, we end helpless," said Timotheus, "and now as engaging as this conversation is, I have much to do before we leave tomorrow, signifer."

Demaratus left, turning the information on the Dasumi family over in his mind. His first job was to fill in Flavius on the situation.

VIII

Domitius Antonius, governor of Mauretania Tingiatana, was worried, and worry made him foul tempered. He was a big man, both in height and girth, and his anger filled whatever room he was in. Opposite him sat a man so plain and diminutive that he seemed less a person than an afterthought.

"Does that fool Juba understand how much trouble this is going to cause us all?" he thundered at the man, who blinked but said nothing. "We are about to have a cohort of the VII Legion in our midst. A slave raid on one of the wealthiest towns in Hispania. Did he think Nuevo Carthego would not react?"

"I am not sure that Juba much cares about what anyone in Hispania thinks, sir, and if you are going to organize a raid, it seems sensible it ought to be on someplace that has a great deal of wealth," replied the slight man mildly.

"When I care to ask for your opinion, Salvius Getha, I will ask it," roared Domitius.

"You asked me a question, sir. I replied," said the man, absently adjusting a bracelet on his arm.

"Don't talk back to me!" thundered Domitius, pounding both fists on the desk that separated the pair. Salvius adjusted an ink well that looked in danger of falling off the table, and said nothing.

Domitius was on his feet, pacing. "Juba has brought the wolf to our door with this raid. The VII Legion will arrive in a day, and they will be looking for trouble. Trouble means the peace in the south unravels, and that will put an end to slaves and coliseum beasts coming north. It also means tension with my auxiliaries. It means war, and war is bad for business, not to mention expensive."

Whirling on Salvius, Domitius growled out, "Well?"

"Do you wish me to talk, sir?" asked the secretary.

"One day you will take your insubordination too far, you miserable excuse for a human being. I will replace you with someone who knows his place, and then I will feed you to something most unpleasant," said the governor, leaning forward on the balls of his feet.

"Yes, sir," answered the secretary. "You will give me time before my demise to explain our tax rolls and records to the authorities in Rome?"

Domitius glowered at the little man but looked slightly uncomfortable.

Salvius continued: "We must consult history in this matter, sir."

"Be so good as to enlighten me," replied the governor.

"This is not the first time we have played host to the VII Legion, sir. As I recall, things did not go well for them the last time, and they left after only a few months," continued the secretary. "Why do we assume this will be any different?"

"This is different," said Domitius, resuming his pacing. "All we had to do last time was to negotiate a secret treaty with the Mauri and there was no longer a reason for the VII to remain. That, and make sure that they drew their water from the well in the barracks. This time they will not go home until they get our citizens back."

"Yes, the water in the well," commented Salvius. "That was an intelligent move."

"I am an intelligent man," said the governor, absently picking through a bowl of fruit on a side table.

The secretary said nothing. The well had been his idea.

"Salvius, I want you to make contact with Juba and arrange for him to hand back the citizens he took," said Domitius, finally selecting a fig and a date.

The secretary frowned. "That might not be easy, sir. Juba is much stronger than he was when the VII Legion was here last year. He has recruited several new tribes and hired some formidable Libyans. I would not care to match our auxiliaries against them."

"Is the man blind? Doesn't he see that Rome will not tolerate this? That he may find himself facing a full legion, maybe two, if he does not take a reasonable approach to this?" asked the governor.

Salvius pursed his lips for a moment. "I am not sure he feels the need to be 'reasonable,' sir. Rome would have to send another legion besides the VII. There is talk about reestablishing the III Augusta in our sister province, Mauretania Caesariensis, but that will take time. Rome might send the II Traiana Fortis from Aegyptus, but that province is always restive. I think we can write off the legions in Syria. They are busy enough with the Parthians. Rome could always ship a legion from Pannonia or Gaul, but with the Franks and the Goths gathering on the borders, I doubt that the Senate or anyone else would consider it. Defending citizens is a fine thing, but not if it unleashes the barbarians to threaten Rome or overrun a province."

"I had no idea you were such a tactician," said Domitius dryly.

"One does not have to wear a legate's red to understand that, as much as we are fond of our Tingitana, it does not weigh much in the balance of empire, sir," replied Salvius. "Juba is an intelligent man with a good understanding of politics. Even if Hispania were to send the entire VII Legion—a doubtful prospect given the recent unrest in the west among the Lusitanians—Juba would merely retreat into the Atlas Mountains or the desert and wait until Rome had exhausted its soldiers or its purse."

"Then Juba has grown too strong," said the governor.

"Agreed," said Salvius, "but there is little we can do about it, Plus, he has no designs on Tingis. For the time being, I doubt he is much interested in anything north of Volubilis."

"Is this all leading somewhere, Salvius?" asked Domitius.

"Yes, I would think so sir."

"And that would be?" said the governor impatiently.

The secretary paused for a moment to straighten a perfectly aligned pen. "The VII Legion is not a legion, it is a single cohort, although admittedly larger than your standard cohort. Even if they were all demi-gods, however, they are fewer than a thousand men. Many of them will sicken while they are here, thanks to a certain water source. They will find our auxiliaries difficult to co-ordinate with, and their enemies will be well informed as to their plans and movements. They will grow impatient and impatience breeds carelessness. They will march out to finish off this Juba and Juba will be waiting."

The governor glanced around him, though no one else was in the room. "Are you suggesting we send a Roman cohort into an ambush? Do you know what would happen to us if that were ever discovered?"

Salvius shrugged. "Probably not much more than if our tax rolls were ever closely examined or if it were known what our role was the last time the VII Legion was in Tingitana."

"This is different. We are talking about destroying part of a legion. Rome would have to respond," whispered Domitius.

"You may be right, but I doubt it. Again, sir, we should have no illusions about our importance. But in any case, it would take time for Rome to do all that, time enough for us to retire to some more congenial climate," said Salvius.

"You are bold, Salvius, too bold I think," said Domitius.

The secretary said nothing.

The governor resumed his pacing. "I am not ready to make such a decision, Salvius. We will quarter the cohort in the barracks and then see what we will see. In the meantime, use our contacts to find out what Juba is up to. We need more information."

The secretary bowed, keeping his thoughts to himself.

"And Salvius, get that Nicias in here. His people are driving me to distraction. They preach in the market and openly flaunt their refusal to pay taxes or follow the laws," added the governor, flinging himself onto an enormous chair.

"Yes, sir. I will inform the Bishop of Tingus that he is to wait on you," said Salvius.

"Bishop," rumbled Domitius. "A pig-headed atheist is what he is, and if he doesn't watch his step, I will flay the skin off his back."

Salvius bowed and left.

Domitius waited until his secretary was gone and then slipped a small scroll out of his desk. He had broken the seal—crossed spears and a boar—and read it quickly when it had first arrived, but he now reread it carefully. The contents brought to mind Salvius's scheme involving the First Cohort. He slipped the scroll into his toga. This was a letter no one but he must ever see.

IX

For Marcus, the passage across the Straits of Hercules was unpleasant but blessedly short. Once again a delegation was on hand to welcome the cohort, only this time Marcus was in better shape to return the formalities. The governor, Domitius Antonius—a large, bluff man with calculating eyes—was surrounded by a cloud of officials and auxiliary officers. He embraced Marcus (who did his best not to look as stiff and awkward as he felt) and introduced a flood of people whom the centurion promptly forgot. He did notice with some relief that Flavius and Demaratus were paying attention.

By the time the introductions were finished, the cohort was forming up on the long, stone quay. Flavius stepped away from the officials gathered around Marcus to see that everything was proper, but Sextus had things well in hand. The tesserarius shot him a quick look that signaled "what now," but Flavius shrugged and indicated with his hand, "wait."

The optio returned to the conversation at the dockside, which had taken a slightly argumentative turn. Timotheus had lobbied Marcus to avoid the city barracks where the 1st Century had stayed last year. He was convinced that there was something in the buildings or the water—he suspected the latter—that had sickened the men. Sextus, who had been a legionnaire at the time, supported him. So it was decided that the cohort would not remain in Tingis but move south of the city where Timotheus said there was good ground for a marching camp and a clean supply of water.

"Centurion, we have the barracks prepared for your cohort," the governor was saying to Marcus, "and the town is looking forward to extending its hospitality to the VII Legion."

"We are not here to visit, sir," replied Marcus. "We do not intend a long stay, and the Mauri are to the south of us."

"They are indeed, and this slave raid has unhinged the whole city. Our people were looking forward to the protection the VII Legion can provide. If you refuse our hospitality, this will cause great unrest in Tingis," the governor argued.

Marcus smiled politely. "Then you will assuage their fears, Domitius. If the Mauri are to the south, the VII will be between these raiders and Tingis. And if any residents wish to visit our camp, you can assure them that we will be delighted to host them."

The governor's jaw tightened with anger, but he mastered himself. Another emotion flitted across his face that Marcus could not quite catch. Fear? But why would the governor be fearful of the cohort building a temporary fort? That made no sense. Most cities are not overly enthusiastic about quartering troops, who tend to get drunk and smash things up. He assumed that the governor was used to having his way, a sentiment that the man would have to get over when it came to the army. If Timotheus said avoid garrisoning the cohort in the city, Marcus would avoid the city.

Domitius bowed. "Of course, centurion. You can be assured that the city will provide fresh meat and fruit for your men."

"That is most generous of you, sir. I wonder if you might arrange a meeting with your auxiliary officers? We have much to discuss. I would also like to have whatever information you might have on this Mauri who led the raid. Juba is his name, I believe," said Marcus.

"He is a harpy, centurion. He plagues us all. But we know little about him as he stays in the high mountains and the great desert to the east of us. But I will see what I can find out," said Domitius. "And I suggest a meeting tomorrow morning at the forum with my commanders."

"That will do fine," said Marcus.

By this time the cohort was drawn up. Marcus nodded to his officers. Demaratus took his place at the head of the 1st Century. The men would focus on the cohort's signum he was carrying and move when it moved. Flavius walked to the rear to make sure there would be no stragglers, and then signaled Marcus.

Marcus turned back to the governor. "It is an honor and pleasure to meet you sir. I look forward to working closely with you over the next several weeks."

The governor bowed stiffly. "Until tomorrow, centurion."

Led by Demaratus, the men of the 1st Cohort shouldered their packs, dressed their lines, and marched through the city, as curious crowds gathered at street corners and cheered them.

Tingis was an orderly town, not overly wealthy, and not very large. Within a short time, the cohort was outside its walls and marching south. To the east loomed a high escarpment, to the west the sweep of the broad Atlantic, white combers running up long stretches of white beach.

The doctor was in front with Demaratus and Marcus acting as a guide and pointing out some of the local terrain. Five miles south of the city, the cohort came to a broad, flat meadow, cut by a clear, rocky stream on its southern edge.

"This is what I had in mind, sir," said Timotheus. "There is a breeze from the west to keep the insects away, and the water is clean and fresh."

"Good spot," said Demaratus, surveying the ground.

Marcus agreed. "We are close enough to the city to make supplying the camp no problem. In a pinch, we could fall back on Tingis. This will do. Hopefully, our stay will not be an extended one."

Once the spot was picked, the cohort went into action. The engineers laid down string for the placement of the ditch and wall, and the men broke out their Dolabras and chopped away at the ground. Others gathered the sharpened stakes the cohort had been carrying, while small squads went into the woods that surrounded the meadow and cut down trees for more stakes and guard towers.

Flavius and Sextus wandered through the laboring cohort, but there was little need for orders. The Roman Army had built marching camps for 500 years, and many of the men in the ranks had done so hundreds of times. A fortified camp with a deep ditch and staked walls rose quickly out of the meadow.

When the camp was largely constructed, groups of men broke off and set up the tents for their contuberniums, the eight-man squads that formed the basic legion unit. Before the long shadows of early evening began to reach out of the west, the camp was completed, the tents lined up by their centuries, sentries posted, and cooking fires lit. Marcus had seen this happen thousands of times, yet it never failed to move him. He would have been hard pressed to put the emotion in words, however.

Flavius appeared, saluted, and gave his report, which was always the same: "Camp complete, sir, sentries posted. Do you have any orders, sir?"

Marcus grinned at him. "Move it ten yards to the east, Optio?

Flavius took his helmet off, ran his hand through his hair, and said with a straight face, "Would the Centurion like the pleasure of giving that order, sir?"

"Bring on a mutiny, would it?" asked Marcus.

"No, they're a happy lot, sir. Happy to be free of Tingis, I think," replied Flavius, "They would just build another."

"Well, let's not put them to the test. I want a staff meeting after dinner. Pass the word," said Marcus.

"Yes, sir," said Flavius and disappeared into the sea of tents that had sprung up around the cohort headquarters, a multiple-room tent that sat in the center of the camp.

Marcus sat on his cot, thinking through the staff meeting. Much of it had been routine. The doctor pointed out where he wanted the latrines placed. Sextus wanted to settle on a schedule for drills. Cassius wanted to purchase more horses in Tingis and start sending out patrols to locate the Mauri.

Marcus delegated most of this to Flavius, although he told Cassius to hold off on the patrols until after the meeting with the governor and the auxiliary officers in the forum. The mention of the auxiliaries had brought on silence. The only one who had any experience with these was Sextus, who was in the ranks when the VII Legion and auxiliaries had worked together.

"We didn't trust them, sir," Sextus said to a question from Marcus on their reliability. "They just never showed up when we needed them, but since I wasn't an officer, I don't know what the arrangements were."

"What about the cavalry, sir?" asked Cassius.

"What about 'em? We never saw them at all. And we didn't have our own cavalry then, Cassius, so we never knew when we were going to get attacked," answered Sextus. "We would get word that a unit was under attack, and out we would go to relieve it. And at least half the time it was bad information, and we would end up getting ambushed and having to fight our way out of it. They never overran us, but we lost a lot of good men."

Cassius nodded, then turned to Marcus. "We will need auxiliary cavalry, but I would like my men to do the scouting. I also want to use our cavalry as a screen behind which you can maneuver, sir. Maybe we can turn the ambush tables on them a few times."

The idea of using cavalry as a screen was new to Marcus. Cavalry always stayed on the edge to prevent an enemy from flanking a unit, and to spread panic once an enemy unit broke. The idea of a screen that prevented the enemy from knowing what the infantry was doing was inventive. Marcus had forgotten how innovative Cassius was.

Flavius frowned. "You can keep an enemy from knowing where we are?"

"Yes, sir. I think we can. My former commander was working on this before our last fight. If my men are aggressive enough, they can keep enemy cavalry at bay," said Cassius.

Flavius looked doubtful, as did Sextus, but Demaratus was thoughtful. "Can you match these Mauri horsemen?"

"Most of my men are Lusitanians, sir. We can match anyone," replied Cassius. From another man that might have come out as a boast, but Cassius was matter of fact. "We can use the auxiliary cavalry as flank protectors."

Flavius and Sextus looked more doubtful at that statement. "I don't much like leaving our flanks to unreliable cavalry," said Flavius.

The meeting—which was running late—threatened to descend into a debate on infantry vs. cavalry, so Marcus put a quick end to it. "I'll review your proposal later, Cassius. In the meantime, you can buy some horses after the meeting tomorrow."

Marcus was exhausted, more from the week of seasickness than anything else, but too restless to sleep. He tried reading, but found he was too tired to focus.

It was not the meeting that was keeping Marcus from going to sleep; it was the vague disquiet from his exchange with the governor. Going over the conversation, he could find no specific reason for his feelings, but there they were. An emotion that looked like fear had flashed across the Governor's face, but Marcus did not always read people correctly. Given the size of his force, Marcus could not afford to alienate the civil authorities. Nonetheless, he didn't trust the governor. He would have to be careful.

A few hours before dawn he finally fell asleep.

X

Governor Domitius Antonius glowered across a table at Nicias, the Bishop of Tingis. Nicias was tall—though not as tall as the governor—and slim. He was a handsome man, with deep-set eyes and a mane of silver-gray hair brushed straight back. He wore a simple, finely made toga of light wool and a modest gold bracelet on his right wrist, with a large signet ring on his left hand.

"You task me, Nicias," rumbled the governor, pushing a piece of parchment across the table in the direction of the bishop. The latter looked down, read it swiftly, and then smiled.

"The people who wrote this task me as well, sir. This has nothing to do with the church," he said with a smile and a slight shrug,

"Really?" replied Domitius. "Does your religion not claim that this criminal, Jesus of Nazareth, is the son of a god? Does your religion not claim that there is one god and this Jesus is that god, and that all other gods are false? Does your religion not claim that to die in defense of this Jesus is to have eternal life is this place called," he glanced back at the paper, adding "Heaven?"

"We do say that Jesus is the son of god, but we dispute that he was a criminal to any but the Jews. We believe there is only one god. We are not alone in this belief, sire. The Jews and the Zoroasters believe much the same thing. And we do not condemn the beliefs of others, and only wish to live quietly in our communities," Nicias answered smoothly.

"The people who wrote this document believe all those things, Nicias, and they also believe that if you are a Christian, you cannot pay your taxes because that is like believing in another god," replied the governor quietly. "That is treason."

Nicias frowned. "There are many religions and many beliefs in the Empire, sir. You cannot hold the true church responsible for everyone who calls him or herself a Christian. We have never failed to pay our due. Our Lord Jesus says that we should render up to God that which is God's and to Caesar that which is Caesar's."

"So you have said in the past, Bishop, but we are having the same discussion we had last year," said Domitius. "I have arrested several Christians for reading this out in the market and the forum, and I am losing my patience."

"Those are not followers of the true church, sir," protested Nicias. "They are heretics who do not look for the word of God in our sacred texts but within themselves."

"I am aware of those Christians who call themselves 'Gnostics,' but those I arrested for preaching this treasonous nonsense are not Gnostics. Indeed, they claim the Gnostics are heretics," answered the governor, "just as you do. More than that, they refuse to answer to the charges or recognize the authority of the Empire. They have asked to be crucified," continued Domitius, leaning forward on his elbows. "They call themselves 'martyrs,' and they say their death will send them to the place called 'heaven.'"

"Sir, I...." started Nicias.

"And is it not said in your church that those who die in the defense of their religion shall go to this place?" continued the governor, overriding the bishop's protests.

"Yes, sir, it is...." said Nicias trying to get a word in.

"Then it is your religion that has not only led to these arrests, but has put in my prison a group of people who are asking me to kill them," said the governor, brushing past the bishop's attempt to explain himself. "Under these circumstances wouldn't it make more sense for me to kill you and give you the opportunity to go to this heaven place instead?"

The bishop paled a bit. "I don't see how that will have an effect on these heretics."

"It might not," mused Domitius, "but what's the loss if it doesn't work? You get to go to your heaven, and after a bit you can welcome in these friends of yours."

"Sir, I wish to state that the true church has nothing but respect and admiration for the Empire, and these heretics are just as much a burden on us as they are you," protested Nicias.

"You, sir, are not the Empire and your 'burdens' are self-imposed," thundered Domitius. "How dare you compare your burdens to mine."

"I beg your forgiveness, sir, I meant no disrespect. I only meant that there are some heretics who seek this state of martyrdom, not only because they believe it leads to heaven, but because it gives them great power here on earth," said Nicias in a tone of outrage. "More than that, they claim they can absolve sins by laying hands on people, thus circumventing the episcopal authority of the church."

"My, my, my," said the governor, leaning back in his chair. "This church of yours doesn't sound all that different than the Empire, it's only that bishops make the decisions, not tribunes and emperors."

Nicias was silent for a moment. "We see no contradiction between religious and temporal structure, sir. I believe Christians and the Empire share common ground."

Domitius chuckled. "Scratch a Christian and what do you find? A love of power. You need a new religion for this?"

"We do not seek power in this world," replied Nicias stiffly.

"Which brings us back to the people in my prison," said the governor.

Nicias said nothing.

"I have a thought on this matter and I will see you tomorrow afternoon in the forum for their trial," said the governor.

Nicias bowed. "Of course, sir."

"Now get out of here, Bishop, before I change my mind about aiding your entrance to this heaven place," growled the governor.

Nicias rose, bowed again, and left.

Throughout the discussion, the secretary, Salvius, had sat quietly in the corner, taking notes. Domitius looked over at him. "Well?"

"Deftly done, sire," he replied. "Exactly what do you intend to do with those Christians?"

"Like Nicias, you will have to be patient," said the governor, looking pleased with himself.

"I shall be unable to sleep tonight in anticipation," said the secretary.

Domitius looked sharply at him, but there was nothing in Salvius's tone or demeanor that indicated anything but respect. The governor, however, knew better.

"Why this concern with the bishop?" asked Salvius.

"I want to keep him off balance," replied the governor.

"To what purpose?" said Salvius.

"There are some things even you should not know," replied Domitius, and then changed the subject. "What of Juba? Your first plan to disable the VII Legion was a failure. Let us hope you are not a failure in this matter as well."

Salvius knew better than to point out that the governor took credit for the plan to feed the VII Legion contaminated water until the scheme fell through. Then it was Salvius's plan. The secretary said nothing, but he did enter the observation in the ledger he kept in his head.

"Juba is rumored to be at his quarters south of Sala, sire. I am meeting with a"—Salvius paused here, looking for the right word— "local, trustworthy source to make the contact for us."

"Why a 'local'? You can't trust these Mauri."

"If we use one of our men, then there is a link back to us, sire. I think you agree that if it were known that we were in contact with men who had just raided a brother province, it would not go well for us," answered the secretary.

Domitius said nothing.

"What of the Dasumi woman?" asked Salvius.

The governor shrugged. "I understand her brother sent a ransom along with the VII Legion. It is not our business. What I want is information on what Juba intends."

"Yes, sir," said the secretary.

"I leave this up to you, Salvius. Just don't fail," grumbled Domitius. "I hope you are prepared for the meeting tomorrow with that cursed centurion?"

The governor was dumping the Juba matter on Salvius. That way if it went wrong, he had someone to blame. And, as for being "prepared for the meeting," the secretary would do all the work and Domitius would get all the credit. Another mark went down in the ledger.

"Of course, sir. It is all taken care of."

The governor wandered over to the fruit bowl. "That plan of yours involving giving certain information to our southern friends," he said, choosing a fig.

"Yes, sir?" replied the secretary.

"I am not convinced that Juba could destroy an entire cohort, particularly this cohort. It is, as you know, considerably larger than a standard cohort," said Domitius.

"I am aware of that, sir," said Salvius.

The governor turned and looked directly at him. "I am particularly interested in the First Century of that cohort, Salvius.

"The commanding centurion's century. May I ask why?" said the secretary.

"You may not," answered Domitius. "See to it."

Salvius bowed, and left.

The governor took a handful of figs and strolled to a balcony that overlooked a courtyard. There was danger in this, but also profit, a great deal of profit, if he could pull it off.

XI

Aelia's mouth was filled with grit, but she was too dry to spit it out. Her slippers, not meant for walking on rock, were in the final stages of disintegration. Her feet hurt, her legs ached, and she was filthy, exhausted, and feeling dreadfully sorry for herself. The procession had stopped after a long climb up from the beach, and captors and captives alike were resting under a stand of oak and juniper. A water skin was passed around, but it was at least half a dozen people away, and most of them were children. The children drank slowly and often, which Aelia found intensely annoying, a sentiment she suppressed, since in all fairness it was the children who had been responsible for getting them water at all, the children and Rachel.

She steeled herself to ignore her body. To keep her mind off her thirst, she studied Rachel. The woman was carrying the water skin and taking it from child to child. Only after the children had drunk did she begin passing it among the adults. Several more skins appeared, so it wasn't long until Aelia took a long pull from one. The water was warm and musty, but she could never remember water tasting so good. She had to discipline herself to pass on the skin after three long drinks.

Rachel was just finishing wrapping a woman's foot—her strength and endurance amazed Aelia—when she caught the Roman woman's eye. Aelia wearily rose to her feet, limped over to Rachel, and sat down next to her.

Rachel looked directly at her. "Thank you, Aelia. That took great courage."

Aelia shrugged. "I figured I was too valuable for him to kill over something like that."

Rachel smiled. "You did not, and you are a bad liar, Aelia Dasumi. But I am puzzled as to why you took that chance."

Aelia hesitated. She could say that she agreed with Rachel about the children or that she refused to be bullied by the Mauri leader, but in truth, she was too tired to construct a story. She also suspected that Rachel would see right through it, as she had seen through her statement about why she had taken the chance in the first place.

"You showed me kindness, Rachel. You are my only friend," she finally said.

Rachel put her hand across Aelia's. "We are all friends in this now, Aelia, because we are all slaves. Your act was still brave, and the others saw it. No slave loves his master, but there are those here who are grateful for what you did. You will have other friends."

"But I do not want to be a slave," said Aelia, summoning up a certain exhausted fierceness.

Rachel laughed quietly. "Do you think any here like being a slave? All a slave dreams of is freedom. It haunts our days, even when one is a favored household slave like myself. People are not made to serve others against their will."

"I have always been kind to my slaves," said Aelia defensively.

"The only kindness for a slave is freedom," answered Rachel.

Aelia was too exhausted for this conversation, but she was fearful of alienating the one person who had shown her kindness. She was trying to think about how to change the subject without looking too obvious. But it was Rachel who did so.

"I saw something in the exchange with this Juba that we should think about," said Rachel.

The shift in subject threw Aelia off balance. "With Juba?"

Rachel nodded. "The one who stood next to him and said you were valuable. He also made a joke that I did not follow about a man."

Aelia frowned. "His name is," and she took a moment to reach for it, "Himilco, I think. He was the man who seized me in my cousin's house."

"He mentioned another man," prodded Rachel.

"Yes, the man I hit with the statue," answered Aelia. "I did not remember his name until Himilco mentioned it. Bogud. A horrid man! He was going to rape and kill me."

Rachel raised an eyebrow. "And this Himilco stopped him?"

"Only because he saw I was more valuable alive than dead," said Aelia.

"Maybe, but maybe there is more. He intervened with Juba as well, and I thought I saw him wink at you," said Rachel.

Aelia narrowed her eyes in anger. "He is only protecting his investment. It was he who brought me to this place. He is a dirty barbarian."

Rachel grabbed Aelia by her arm and squeezed hard.

"Stop, you are hurting me," gasped Aelia.

"Listen to me, Aelia Dasumi," she said fiercely. "If we do not get free of these men, I predict our lives will be painfully short and brutal. You may or may not be ransomed. Many things can go wrong, and Juba looks to be a man who is less interested in gold than causing the Romans trouble. We have no power, no leverage, nothing. This man Himilco likes you, he admires your courage, maybe your beauty. You will be solicitous of him, do you understand? We need every edge if we are to get out of this."

Aelia recoiled. Rachel's' normally pleasant face was contorted, her eyes intense.

"What would you have me do, seduce him?" Aelia gasped, partly from the pain, partly from surprise.

"If it could get me back to Hispania, I would sleep with him and his donkey, Dasumi," whispered Rachel. "When you are a slave, you do not have the right to say 'no,' so as distasteful as such a union might be, we have no choice. I do not care what you do with him, but it is an opportunity we cannot pass up."

Tears sprang to Aelia's eyes and a wave of depression. Her one friend had turned on her.

Rachel saw the look in the Roman woman's eyes, reached across, and drew Aelia to her. "No, no, woman. You read my desperation as anger," she said. "I was a slave, but a favored slave, with a master who loved me." She loosened her hold on Aelia. "At least I think he did. He kept promising to free me, but never did."

"I am sorry," said Aelia, "I must seem a pampered bitch to you."

Rachel cocked her head. "Pampered, yes, but not a bitch. And smart, because you have me for a slave."

"I only said that...." started Aelia.

"To save my life, mistress," laughed the woman. "I was not insulted."

Both women sat back and studied one another.

"So, you think Himilco is a chink in Juba's armor?" Aelia finally said.

Rachel shrugged. "I don't know, but do we have anything else? I think..." Aelia saw the woman's eyes widen in fear.

Aelia was suddenly jerked to her feet by her hair. As she turned around to see her attacker, she was slapped across the face. The blow stunned her and she could feel blood in her mouth.

Bogud thrust his face into hers. His face was still swollen where the statue had struck him, and there was a black bruise surrounding his nose and upper lip. "Silence, Roman whore. Slaves don't talk unless they are told to talk."

Aelia recovered and tried to push away from him. He delivered another stunning open hand blow to the side of her head, jerking it upwards by her hair, so her feet were just touching the ground. For a moment she felt as if she would faint.

All of a sudden Bogud released her and she fell in a heap at his feet.

As her head begin to clear she could hear an argument going on above her. Hands pulled her clear—Rachel's hands—and she slowly focused on the two men in front of her. Himilco was standing toe to toe with Bogud, although the latter was much taller and broader. Bogud was shouting something about her, but her ears were still ringing from his blow. She could not hear Himilco at first.

Gradually she began to follow the argument, which had drawn a crowd of men who gathered around in a semi-circle. She did not see Juba.

"She is a slave and I will do with her what I wish, Himilco. Stand aside," said Bogud.

But Himilco stood his ground. "She is a valuable commodity, Bogud. I found her, and she is to be left alone."

"She is not yours, dog! The slaves belong to us all," roared Bogud.

Aelia noticed the crowd of men stepped back and searched her memory for what might have caused it. It must have been the word "dog."

"Dog?" said Himilco softly, so softly that Aelia almost didn't hear him.

Bogud said nothing for a moment, then blustered, "You have no more rights to that bitch than any of us," a sentiment that he clearly hoped would win him allies. But the crowd of men remained silent and watchful.

"Dog?" repeated Himilco softly, which only made it sound more dangerous. Rachel tried to pull Aelia back into the group of slaves, but she resisted. She wanted to see this.

Bogud shifted his eyes and mumbled something about Himilco that Aelia could not catch.

"Bogud of the Nasamones, do you call Himilco of the Gaetuli a dog?" asked Himilco.

Bogud did not reply, but he stepped back and put his hand to his sword.

"What's going on here," said a voice from the fringe of the men watching Bogud and Himilco, and Juba pushed his way into the circle. Neither of the two men acknowledged him.

Juba stood with his hands on his hips, looking back and forth between the two. "Well?" he asked.

Bogud spoke up first. "Himilco has let the slaves plot with one another. I stopped those two women from conspiring, and he intervened. He said the Roman bitch was his."

Juba turned to Himilco and cocked an eyebrow.

Himilco kept his eyes on Bogud. "This man called the Gaetuli dogs. He will take it back or he will die here and now," Himilco said quietly.

Juba turned back to Bogud. "Did you call the Gaetuli dogs?"

Bogud look uncomfortable. "I may have said 'dog,' but I did not say it about your tribe," he answered defensively.

Himilco stepped forward and slid his blade out of its sheath. "He will take it back or he will die."

Juba put his hands between the two men. "Both of you step back."

"This is a personal matter, Juba," said Himilco. "It does not concern you."

"All things concern me, Himilco," replied Juba, and he stepped between the men. By this time the crowd had grown to close to a hundred.

Juba turned to Bogud. "You will take back what you said."

Bogud started to reply, but Juba silenced him with a piercing stare.

"You will take back what you said," he repeated.

The scene had turned deathly quiet. Bogud's face struggled

with a variety of emotions until finally he said, "I do not consider the Gaetuli to be dogs."

"That is not enough," said Himilco quietly.

"It is enough," replied Juba. "You will put up your blade."

Juba and Himilco locked eyes for a long moment and the latter slowly sheathed his sword.

Juba turned to the crowd of men. "We leave shortly. Take up your things." The crowd began to disperse. With one poisonous look over his shoulder, Bogud left as well.

Juba turned back to Himilco, putting his hand on the man's shoulder. "My friend, we have worked hard to bring the Nasamones into our alliance. If we are ever to rid ourselves of these Romans, we will have to be one people, not a bunch of tribes at one another's throats."

Himilco looked Juba straight in the face. "If the Gaetuli allow themselves to be called dogs, we will lose not just the Nasamones, but the Musulamii and the Pharusi as well. No one will run with dogs."

"What we do is bigger than all the tribes, Himilco. Bogud is a bully and a blowhard. You would threaten all we have built because you take personal offense? The men saw that he did not want to fight you, that he backed down. Isn't that enough?" said Juba.

Himilco was silent for a while. "You are my leader, Juba. I will not quarrel with you."

"Nor I with you, friend," said Juba. Then turning to the slaves, he picked Aelia out. "You are trouble, Roman. It might be best to cut your throat and be done with it."

Aelia had been abused, kidnapped, and mistreated. She was

dirty and exhausted, and these men had talked about her as if she was a piece of meat hanging in the market place. All the humiliation and outrage in her heart boiled over. She pushed Rachel aside and climbed to her feet, shaking with anger. "Give me a rock, barbarian, and make it a fair fight. Maybe it will be your throat that gets cut." She clenched her fists and started toward Juba, her hair wild, her face red and contorted with rage.

Rachel scrambled up and attempted to pull her back, but Aelia fought her off, struggling to reach Juba. The two men looked at one another, and Himilco finally shrugged. "She is interesting, isn't she?" he said.

"Crazy is more like it," said Juba with a chuckle.

Himilco finally stepped forward and took Aelia by the shoulders, shaking her. "Roman, be still. Your outrage is misplaced. You Romans have enslaved more people than there are rocks in the hills. You will get yourself, and maybe someone else, killed if you continue to behave this way. Would you have your servant here die as well?"

Aelia stopped struggling. "Rachel has nothing to do with my behavior. She is only guilty of guarding her mistress."

"Is it not a Roman rule to kill all slaves in a household if one does violence to a master?" said Juba.

Aelia's shoulders slumped. "Yes," she said softly. "It will not happen again. If you kill me, spare her. You need her to help with the children in any case."

Himilco gave her a searching look but said nothing.

Juba stared at Aelia for a full minute. "See that you behave yourself. This is your final chance, Roman. Do you understand?"

Aelia nodded mutely. She felt beaten, humiliated, and, as the anger drained away, terrified. She let Rachel put her arm around her and lead her back to the other slaves.

XII

The meeting between the governor, the officers of the auxiliaries, and the leadership of the VII Legion had gone badly
from the start. The governor and his staff were late, the auxiliary
officers stiff and formal. There had been no disagreements, but
neither had there been any agreements. No, Domitius did not
know where Juba and his forces were, but he was investigating.
Yes, the auxiliaries were at the disposal of the VII Legion, but
most were manning small forts and key intersections to keep
the roads open for commerce. Of course, Tingis would supply
horses for the Legion's cavalry, but horses were in short supply,
and many were being used to cover the roads to the south.

Only someone who had spent years with Marcus would have
picked up the signs of his growing frustration, the tendency to
stand rather than sit, the slight shifts from one leg to another,
the hands locked behind his back. Flavius knew all the signs, and
by the meeting's end the centurion was a deeply frustrated man.

The meeting had broken up with promises of this and promises of that, all hedged with caveats and "we will do our best."
Marcus, Sextus, and Cassius had left to return to the camp, while

Flavius and Demaratus dallied in the great, sprawling market that surrounded the Forum. The signifer suggested that he and Flavius stay and watch the governor act as magistrate.

"Why would we do that?" asked Flavius.

"Would you say the governor was an ally or an antagonist?" answered Demaratus.

The two were strolling through a forest of booths idly eyeing the various wares. There was a profusion of pounded copper and bronze dishes and bowls, plus fruits and vegetables, some of which Flavius had never seen before; he eyed an oddly shaped melon warily. The displays distracted him for a moment, so he was not quick in replying.

Finally he shrugged. "Seems much like all politicians. Tells you what he thinks you want to hear, but never commits himself."

"Maybe," said Demaratus.

"When pigeons gather, Greeks see a plot," Flavius said, picking up a copper bracelet set with some kind of blue stone.

Demaratus smiled. "What makes you think pigeons don't plot?" he said.

"Well, they may, but do we care?" said Flavius, fending off the woman who was trying to slip the bracelet over his wrist.

"We care if the pigeons can do us harm. And this governor is up to something," replied Demaratus.

Flavius was tempted to keep teasing the signifer, but he resisted. It would not be the first time the Greek saw things he didn't.

"What makes you think that the governor's reluctance to do anything is more than simple laziness and incompetence?" asked Flavius.

Demaratus swept his arm in an arc. "Does this have the look of an incompetent?"

Flavius did a slow pan of the market and had to admit it was well policed, the forum clean. Indeed, the whole city had a scrubbed and orderly look to it. "Well, it could be he has an efficient administration," Flavius said.

"Have you ever known inefficiency at the top not to find its way down to the bottom?" asked Demaratus.

Flavius grunted non-committedly.

Demaratus continued. "What is Mauretania Tingitana's major export, Flavius?"

"Why do I think you know the answer to that question?" said Flavius with a slight tone of annoyance, partly in response to the signfer's didactic tone, and partly because Flavius had not the slightest idea.

"Sorry, sir, I meant no disrespect," said Demaratus a little stiffly, catching the annoyance in Flavius's voice.

The two men had rounded on one another and were face to face. The silence dragged on for a few moments. At last Flavius asked, "Well?"

"Slaves and animals, sir," replied Demaratus.

"This has a point?" said the optio, annoyed with Demaratus for shifting to his formal voice, and annoyed with himself for starting it.

"Both come from the south. Both are passed through the hands of the Mauri," answered Demaratus.

"I don't see what that has to do with the governor and...." Flavius stopped in mid-sentence.

Demaratus nodded.

"How can the governor not know where Juba is if the Mauri are the go-betweens for Tingitana's major export, indeed, just about the only reason Rome is interested in this place?" continued Flavius. "Alright, Demaratus, that's a good point. What else?"

Flavius's encouragement thawed some of the signifer's stiffness. Both recognized that they had backed themselves into an awkward corner, and would need to work on getting back to being civil with one another. Since a strong bond of friendship lay beneath the surface, a little goodwill on both sides usually resolved their quarrels.

"The governor seemed determined that we should stay in the same place that the VII Legion stayed last time," said Demaratus.

"Aye, I caught that as well. In fact, he was rather put out that we decided to camp out of town," agreed Flavius. "And I never saw a city that wanted troops quartered in it unless it was under siege. But I still don't see your point."

"If you are asking me why the governor wanted us to stay in Tingis and why he is likely lying about his knowledge of the Mauri, I don't know. But it seems prudent that we should watch our backs until we find out," answered Demaratus.

Flavius stopped and looked around him. "We should find a taverna."

"Your answer to everything," remarked Demaratus.

"Greeks are knowledgeable, but not overly bright at times," said Flavius. "If we need information, we have to know where to find it. Now, my philosopher signifer, where would we find such knowledge in a town where we don't know anyone?"

"Why do I think you know the answer to that question, Flavius? I haven't the slightest idea."

"And that is why you are a signifer and I am an optio," said Flavius.

Flavius once more swept his gaze around the plaza. "We look for a taverna that soldiers might frequent."

Demaratus frowned, "Why soldiers? Any soldiers would be from the VII Legion, and I doubt auxiliaries would know what the governor was up to, or tell us if they did."

"We are looking for ex-soldiers, Demaratus," replied Flavius.

"I still don't...oh," said the signifer.

"Right. Let's see if we can find ourselves some former members of the III Legion Augusta," said Flavius, scanning several small tavernas. "Like that one," he said pointing to a place set off a side street. The sign was too far away to be read, but it had a shield and crossed pila.

The two strolled in the direction of taverna, which suddenly erupted with shouts and crashes. A legionnaire from the First Century came flying out the entrance to land with a thud on his back. Rolling to his feet, he charged into the opening, his fists cocked.

"Petronius!" roared Flavius with a voice that set Demaratus's ears ringing. The signifer was always surprised at the volume the optio could produce.

The man turned, his face red and bloodied, fully prepared to set on whoever had called his name until he recognized Flavius. "Sir," he panted, staggering a little. "We were attacked."

"By whom?" asked Demaratus. "Civilians?"

"By some whores and dogs from a legion without honor, sir," replied Petronius.

"Your instincts are unerring, optio," said Demaratus with a smile. "After you," he said.

Flavius plunged into the taverna to find a full-scale melee in progress. Legionnaires and men dressed as civilians were punching one another or rolling about on the floor. One man broke a stool over a soldier's head and was in turn bashed with a wine beaker by another legionnaire. Two men in aprons—Flavius assumed the proprietors—were vainly trying to reestablish order. One legionnaire broke off from trying to throttle a man he had pinned to a wall and threw a punch at one of the men with an apron.

"Order," roared Flavius with a voice that froze the scene of battle. "Legionnaires of the VII Legion, I want you against that wall," he thundered, pointing to a side of the taverna that had no windows.

"But sir," one soldier started to explain.

"Silence!" roared Flavius. Even the men the soldiers had been fighting backed off. Demaratus was always amazed at how intimidating the optio could become at a moment's notice.

Both sides backed slowly away, although one of the civilians, bleeding from a cut over one eye, held his ground, his arms crossed.

"Their optio," said Demaratus to himself. The man looked much like Flavius: shortish, built like a block of wood, with an air of command about him.

Flavius waited until his men were against the wall, and then turned to the man with the crossed arms. "Flavius Priscus, optio of the First Century, VII Legion Hispania," he said, thrusting out his right hand. The man hesitated, but then gripped the optio's hand.

"Quintus Titius, former optio, Third Century, III Legion Augusta Vindex Pia," said the man.

Flavius waved at Demaratus. "My signifer, Demaratus."

Quintus nodded at Demaratus, then re-crossed his arms. "Your men started this," he said.

Flavius crossed his arms (Demaratus wondered if this was something optios learned at a secret optio school). "The VII Legion picking on the III Legion? So tell me, Quintus, these Augusta lads, quiet and polite are they?" Demaratus cringed at the words, but Flavius put his little speech in a friendly, joshing manner.

"Polite and quiet enough to give your lads a good thumping," replied Quintus with a similar tone.

"There is no truth in that, sir," called out one of the VII Legion soldiers from the wall, "and the III Legion isn't even a legion, and...."

"Silence," roared Flavius, glaring at the First Century men. "The III Augusta is an honorable legion. If there be a lack of honor, it lies in Rome, not Mauretania. If you want to mix it up with another legion, fine. It's good training all around." This comment drew grins from both sides. "No man in my century will say that the members of a brother legion have no honor."

Demaratus felt some of the tension drain from the room. It was likely that the fight had started because someone from the VII Legion had made a remark about the III Legion's status. Some of the First Century men were avoiding the optio's eyes and looking a little sheepish. Demaratus suspected that most of the VII Legion men had joined in to support the man who made the comment and things had escalated from there.

Flavius turned back to Quintus. "Well, the fight looks like a draw, but of course the III Legion wouldn't last long in a drinking contest."

"That's so," said Quintus. "And I say that the VII Legion will have to be carted home in a donkey cart."

Flavius untied his purse and threw it to one of the proprietors. "Wine for all, and we will see who goes home in a cart." Legionnaires were always ready for a fight, but given the option between punching one another and drinking for free, the choice was clear.

Flavius nodded to a corner table. "Will you join us, Quintus?"

The man nodded and signaled another lean, sharp-faced man to the table. "My tesserarius, Macro Lucilius."

The conversation started with professional matters, including rumors about reconstituting the III Augusta. Quintus and Macro exchanged glances. "We had heard some talk, but talk don't mean much," said Macro.

"Our centurion told us that the legate of the VII Legion mentioned it to him," said Flavius. "I am not sure if that is better than a rumor, but our legate must know something."

Quintus stared down at his wine cup. When he looked up his eyes had a dangerous glitter. "Shamed us, they did. Took our eagle, took our retirement. And since they disbanded the Legion, everything has fallen apart. The Mauri roam at will, and we are pushed back to the coast."

"The shame was on them, Quintus, not the III Augusta," said Flavius.

No one at the table said anything for a moment until Demaratus spoke. "Sir, the III Legion is normally based in Mauretania Caesariensis. How did you end up in Tingis?"

"The Third Century was sent to reopen the road between Volubilis and Portus Magnus," answered the optio. "Mauri cavalry had cut it south of Calama. We were in Volubilis for re-supply when the Legion was dissolved. They turned us out right there. Some of the men stayed in Volubilis, but a lot of us came to Tingis. There is some thought that we might go to Hispania, but if your rumor is true, we may just stick where we are, though we are sick of this place and that pasty-faced, fat fart of a governor."

Flavius and Demaratus glanced at one another.

Macro caught the exchange. "Oh, not to worry. Domitius Antonius is not about to rile up the VII Legion by arresting some officers. He wants you lot out of here and back to Hispania."

"And why is that?" asked Demaratus.

"The governor has a nice little business running slaves and animals to Rome, and that means keeping on good terms with the Mauri. Staying on good terms means letting them do what they want. I'm not sure he didn't have a hand in that slave raid that brought you all here," answered Macro.

"That's a bit much," put in Quintus, "but I don't think he wants you lot to stir up any trouble with the Mauri. Going after this Juba fellow will stir up trouble, so don't look for a lot of help."

Flavius and Demaratus again looked at one another. "We had worked out some of that on our own," said Flavius. "When it comes to plots, it's handy to have a Greek around." Both Quintus and Macro laughed, but it was friendly. Keeping the two men friendly was why Demaratus had called Quintus "sir" even though he was no longer a superior officer.

"Do you have any idea where this Juba is?" asked Flavius.

"He normally stays close to Sala. He has a good beach for his ships, a river that runs all year, and, if he has to retreat, he goes up into the Atlas Mountains and you can forget trying to get him out of there. If legionnaires were mountain goats, they couldn't do it," answered Quintus. "But I know someone who met a man who says he knows exactly where Juba lives."

"Can you help us find this man?" asked Flavius.

"As I said, I don't know the man. He is supposed to be a Cretian. The man I met says this Juba did something to him, and well, you know Cretians. You don't want to cross them if you can avoid it," said Quintus.

"You would do us a good turn if you could find this Cretian for us, Quintus," said Flavius. "You know where we are camped."

"We could do that provided we find both men," said Quintus. "Now is all this talk just to avoid going home in that donkey cart?"

Flavius smiled. Demaratus had once seen a panther smile like that. The signifer had taken a liking to Quintus and Macro, but he knew who would be going home in the donkey cart.

XIII

Marcus, Flavius, Demaratus, Cassius, Sextus, and centurion Publius Fulvius of the Third Century stood on the long, stone mole and watched a fleet of ships work their way into the harbor. The Third Century had arrived two days before, and this fleet was bringing in the Second, the Fourth, and the Fifth. In a few hours Marcus would have almost 800 men, plus the 120 cavalry. Even without the auxiliaries, he had enough force to go on the offensive. And given the constant stream of excuses coming from the governor, it looked like the First Cohort was pretty much on its own.

The ships pulled alongside the mole, disgorged their troops and supplies, and moved out into the harbor, letting the next line of ships dock. Optios and tesserarius moved about, forming the centuries into units while the centurions gathered around Marcus.

In theory, the centurions were co-equals. In practice, Marcus's title of Primus Pilus made him the leader of the Primi Ordines, the group of centurions that made up the First Cohort's war council. Marcus's authority was also enhanced by his membership in the VII Legion's council of officers, which included the two tribunes and the legate. Indeed, since no tribune had accompanied the First Cohort, Marcus informally inherited the mantle.

Marcus studied his centurions discreetly. Publius Fulvius had a sour look about him. He had been marking time until he could return to Rome and buy a senator's seat. Getting dragged off on an expedition to Mauretania Tingitana was not on Publius's career trajectory.

Aulus Junius of the Fourth and Certificius Nonius of the Fifth were eager and excited, like two big puppies. But Marcus found them competent officers. Neither, however, had ever been in a fight.

Manlius Valeranus, the newly appointed centurion of the Second Century, was a solid and experienced veteran.

Marcus gave the centurions a brief rundown of the situation, promising more details when they reached camp. The governor had begged off welcoming the rest of the cohort because he was holding court as the magistrate.

As the centurions went to get their centuries on the move, Flavius and Demaratus took Marcus aside and asked for permission to seek out Quintus of the disbanded III Augusta to see if he had been able to locate the Cretian who supposedly knew where Juba was.

Marcus told them to find out what they could, but be back by nightfall. He wanted all the officers at an expanded meeting of the Primi Ordines.

As the four centuries marched off for the camp, Flavius and Demaratus retraced their steps to the tavern where they had first met Quintus, but neither he nor any of the III Legion veterans were there. One of the owners said that normally the men from the III Legion did not show up until mid-afternoon.

Flavius and Demaratus left to talk it over.

"Marcus said we need to be back by nightfall. If we get into a long discussion with Quintus, we will be cutting it close," said Flavius.

"On the other hand, we need this information, Flavius," said Demaratus. "I suggest we kill some time in the market and see if the man shows up. We can always leave if he doesn't."

Flavius agreed, and once again the two men found themselves wandering through stalls and small stores set back off the plaza.

The two were coming out of a store where Flavius had purchased a small vial of oil that the proprietor assured him would cure almost anything if he cooked with it or rubbed it on an affected area. "It is the oil of the Argan tree, sir. It is difficult to collect, but its properties are wondrous," the merchant told Flavius. The oil did have a pleasant, nutty flavor and smell, and it came in a lovely blue bottle.

Demaratus was doubtful of magic potions, but he said nothing. It wasn't his money. He wondered what Flavius would think of the oil when he found out how it was gathered.

"So, Demaratus, do you know about this stuff?" he asked holding up the bottle as the two wandered.

"A little. It is gathered in an unusual way," the Greek answered, suppressing a smile.

"How's that?" asked Flavius with a hint of suspicion in his voice.

"The Mauri gather it from their goats," answered Demaratus, stopping to admire some cloth.

"The man said it came from a tree," said Flavius.

"Oh, it does," said Demaratus. "You see, the Mauri goats climb into the Argan tree and eat its fruit. It is about the size of an olive."

"But then how do they get the oil if the goat eats it?" asked Flavius, suddenly peering closely at his purchase.

"They wait and gather the undigested seeds after they pass through the goats," replied Demaratus.

"You mean this is from goat shit?" asked Flavius.

"Well, not goat shit. It just passes through goat shit, and then the Mauri grind and press it to make the oil," answered Demaratus.

"Why didn't you tell me I was buying goat shit?" said Flavius.

"It is perfectly good oil, Flavius. It is just gathered in a somewhat different way than olive oil," replied Demaratus.

Flavius turned and stomped back into the shop, from which he emerged a short time later putting coins back into his pouch. Demaratus was careful not to smile.

Flavius looked like he was going to say something to Demaratus, but the Greek nodded toward a crowd. The two men drifted over to watch. A semi-circle of people—the group in front sitting, the people at the back standing—were listening to a short, thin man who stood, holding a shepherd's crook. While the man was diminutive, his voice carried to the whole crowd, reverberating off the plaza walls.

"Eternal life in paradise is what I offer you, brothers and sisters. Life filled with joy, fine foods and wines, and celestial music. There is no night, only endless days of soft breezes and warmth. You have no needs except to bathe in the glory of the Lord, Jesus Christ." When he delivered the last words, he looked skyward and clasped his hands together. The crowd's eyes followed his gaze.

Then the man suddenly dropped his voice and looked directly at the crowd. "But you who do not believe, you who doubt, you who scoff, you, too, will have an endless life, but it will be a life of pain and damnation. You who commit adultery or lie with your own sex, you will be thrown into pits of fire. You youth who fornicate—several young men and women giggled— you will be cast into pits filled with worms and shit!" The giggling stopped. "You who slander will be hung by your tongues! You who flaunt your bodies will be hung by your hair! You who do not give charity to the poor, you will hang for eternity by your hands!"

At each category of the damned, his voice rose an octave until the word "hands" seemed to ring out from the very stones of the forum.

The crowd had grown silent. The man swept his eyes around the semi-circle, finally pointing his crook at young boy who could not have been more than 12 years old. "How long is eternity?" he asked.

The boy leaned back into his friends and looked uncomfortable. Leaning forward, the man asked again. "How long is eternity!" The boy shook his head mutely.

Keeping his eyes on the boy, he raised his arms in a circle. "If the world were made of solid iron, and every thousand years a tiny sparrow brushed it with its wing, when the ball had been worn down to nothing, eternity...would...just...be...beginning!"

By this time the boy and his friends were sheet white. One of them whimpered.

"By the Gods," whispered Flavius to Demaratus. "Is that man a Christian?"

The Greek nodded.

"This is a religion about scaring children?" Flavius asked incredulously.

"It does rely a good deal on fear and guilt," agreed Demaratus, "but I have never heard a Christian say what this man says."

"Do you want to burn for an eternity?" The man looked straight at the boy. "Although the fires of hell are hotter than anything on earth, still hell has no light, so you burn alone in the dark. Do you want this?"

The boy shook his head, terrified.

"Then all you need to do is to accept that there is but one God, and that he sent Jesus, his only son, among us to save us all from sin. That he chose to die by crucifixion to cleanse our sins, and that he was resurrected into heaven and became one with God! If you believe that, you will not go to hell, but ascend to Heaven for an eternity of joy! Wouldn't you like that, boy?"

The crowd automatically nodded in unison with the boy, who was bobbing his head up and down, tears streaming down his cheeks.

"Lies, all lies. Don't listen to him, good people," shouted a man from the edge of the crowd. A handsome man stepped forward dressed in a fashionable toga of good quality and wielding an ivory rod with a gold head. "He is a false Christian. He preaches Heaven and Hell to frighten you, and then says he can save you. But this is a lie! Your salvation lies within you, where God has placed a divine spark."

"Blasphemy!" screamed the small man, pointing his crook at the man in the toga as if it were a weapon.

"You dare accuse me of blasphemy, you dog!" shouted the man in the toga. Turning to the crowd he said, "This man would have you believe that the creator was perfect. If he was perfect, why is earth so flawed? If I had a God who made those mistakes, he wouldn't work for me very long."

The line drew a ripple of laughter.

Turning back to the man with the crook, the man in the toga said, "Why don't you tell these people what your false religion relies on? Faith, blind faith! If God did not mean for humanity to use logic, why did he give it to us? Are you saying logic and intelligence are not given by God?"

The small man took up the challenge. "There is no contradiction between faith and logic," he said, "Both are God given. But our Lord Jesus gave us rules to live by, rules that all can follow so that they can enter Heaven. Your rules are your own rules. Each person has different rules. How would a person know if Heaven was open to them? You Gnostics are nothing but philosophers in disguise, set upon the earth by the Devil to confuse good people."

The Gnostic stepped forward. "And now we come to it, citizens. Simple rules says the man. And who determines whether you follow these rules, nay, who designs them? God? No! Bishops. And who are these bishops? Flawed human beings like us all, but this man would have you believe that they speak for God. Bishops are dry canals that carry nothing but the tithes they demand. They are God's taxmen! And they live well."

"You are both doomed to spend an eternity in black fire!" a voice rang out. Pushing her way toward the two men was a middle-aged woman dressed in a rough smock and carrying a long, stout walking stick.

"Listen to them not," she beseeched the crowd. "They are vile and polluted. They fornicate! Only the pure can bring you to God, and those who stand before God must themselves be pure, as virgin as the day they were born."

The Gnostic smiled. "And if all are virgins, Marcionite, who will worship God when those are gone?"

"Look upon thyself in a mirror, false Christian," the woman replied. "Do you not think these good people see that you wear your real beliefs wrapped around you? How many poor would the cost of that fine toga feed? You Gnostics define your own rules only to defend your wealth. And you give no charity, because no Gnostic needs it."

Sensing an opening, the small man jumped in. Pointing to the Gnostic, he said, "His is a wealthy man's religion. In the true church, all stand equal before God."

"Even slaves?" called out a voice from the crowd.

"Slave or freeman. Rich man or beggar. All are the same in God's eyes," answered the small man. "Come to the true church and you will stand as equals."

"Unless you do not follow the dictates of the bishops," threw in the Gnostic. "If all are equal, why must you follow a bishop?"

Flavius looked over at Demaratus. "There is more than one type of Christian?"

The Greek nodded. "It has many sects, much like the Jews, but I have never heard of the variety this woman speaks of."

"But if there are many sects, who has the truth?" asked Flavius.

Demaratus cocked an eyebrow at the optio. "You think there is a truth?"

"Spare me Greek philosophy," mumbled Flavius, turning back to the three-way argument which, as the three protagonists pushed closer to one another, was getting louder and more heated by the moment.

The effort by the small man to ally himself with the Marcion woman came to naught when she turned on him and railed against "fornicating bishops."

"Well, one can see why you need have no fear of fornication," the Gnostic put in, addressing the woman. "Unless it was with a man who had lost his sight."

The barb drew a gale of laughter.

The woman turned and swung her walking stick at his head, but the Gnostic deftly avoided it. The small man was not so lucky, and the staff caught him across the ear and sent him sprawling backwards.

"Mad woman! Blasphemies!" he shouted, jumping to his feet and flailing her with his crook. The two were soon pounding away on one another in abandon, with many in the crowd making bets on who would win. The man was quick, but the woman's stick was stouter than his crook, and she was just getting the upper hand when four vigiles pushed into the crowd and broke up the melee. The people watching swore at the police and some even threw bits of food, but the crowd was in a good mood and let the vigiles drag the two offenders away. The Gnostic had disappeared.

A confu blast rang through the plaza, the horn announcing

the opening of the magistrate's court, in this case presided over by the governor himself. The crowd migrated toward the forum.

Flavius started toward the taverna again, but Demaratus argued they should wait. "I think we should see this Domitius Antonius in action, Flavius. Know thy enemy? And look at the first case." A group of about a dozen men and women were gathered together, praying.

"More Christians?" said the optio. "Well, it is still early." However, he took the precaution of positioning himself so he could watch the trial and the taverna at the same time.

The vigiles prodded the group of praying Christians forward toward the magistrate's chair, and a small, colorless clerk read from a list of charges. Amid "disturbing the peace" and "disorderly conduct," there was only one serious one: "These people did conspire to challenge the august power of the Emperor by refusing to pay their yearly script to divine Augusta, and further, to inciting others to flaunt the laws of the Empire."

"Isn't that what the centurion of the Second Century did?" whispered Flavius.

Demaratus nodded, "Although I do not think he incited others to follow him. This is a more serious charge."

"How do you plead?" asked the secretary.

One man—clearly a leader of some sort—stepped forward. "We do not accept the authority of this court. Only our Lord Jesus Christ can sit in judgment on us."

Sitting in a throne-like chair, the governor said, "Do you resist the laws of Rome?"

The man hesitated for a moment. "No, sire, only those that conflict with the laws of God. Our Lord told us that we can have no other gods but our Lord. We would sunder God's laws if we were to give a tithe to the cult of Augusta," he answered, putting a slight stress on the word "cult."

"I do not care if you believe that God dwells in the bowels of a pig," said the governor, a remark that drew a few gasps, but mostly laughs, from the crowd. "I care that you do not undermine the authority of the Emperor." Leaning to one side, he beckoned a somewhat uncomfortable looking Bishop Nicias to come forward.

"Is this your bishop?" continued Domitius.

The group glanced at one another, and the leader nodded.

"And do not you Christians believe that a bishop speaks the word of God?" asked the governor.

The group of Christians stirred, some nodding yes, others making ambiguous motions with their heads and hands.

Domitius addressed Nicias. "Did you order these people not to pay their scrip?"

"No, sire," answered Nicias.

"And should they pay their script?" asked Domitius.

Nicias looked more uncomfortable, but finally said, "We should render up to Caesar that which is Caesar's."

"Answer my question," said the governor.

"The question is complex," replied the bishop.

"The question is one that any child could answer," said Domitius, leaning forward and lowering his voice to almost a whisper. "Do you stand with these people, Nicias?"

The bishop took a deep breath. "No, governor."

Turning back to prisoners, Domitius said, "Your bishop

orders you to pay your script. Do you deny the order of your religious leader?"

"The blood of the martyrs waters the church and rears up many times as champions of piety," the leader said in a singsong voice.

The governor leaned back and looked at Nicias. "Well?" he asked.

The bishop turned back to the prisoners. "You must obey me in this matter, my children. My episcopal authority comes from our Lord Jesus Christ."

The prisoners whispered among themselves. Finally, the leader turned to Nicias. "Did not Matthew tell us that our Lord said 'you will be hated by everyone because of my name, and he that stands fast until the end shall be saved'?"

"Yes, and in the name of the Christ I order you to obey the representatives of Caesar. If you do not, I will excommunicate you, and you will burn in the fires of Hell for eternity," answered the bishop sternly.

The group once again conferred, whispering fiercely among themselves. Finally, the leader turned again and addressed the governor. "Bishop Nicias is bishop of Tingis. We are not of Tingis, and our bishop has told us that to martyr ourselves in the name of Christ is to sit at his side in Heaven. So I say unto you, representative of Caesar, let us be meat for wild beasts. We are God's wheat and the beasts will grind us into flour to make a loaf for Christ."

As the speech ended, the other prisoners began to sway, chanting, "We come unto our Lord. We ascend to the high throne. We bathe in God's grace."

"You will suffer in eternal damnation," said Nicias briskly, then turned to Dominitus: "They are no longer my charges. I render them up to Casear."

The governor had been following the whole exchange with the ghost of a smile on his face, as if something amused him. His secretary Salvius watched him. He was impressed that Dominitus had dragged the bishop along, allowing the governor to shift the onus to Nicias. Sometimes Dominitus surprised him. However, the governor would now have to devise a punishment, and because that is what the Christians wanted, Salvius could see no way that it wouldn't backfire on him.

The governor motioned the vigiles squad forward. "Aulus," he said, addressing the commander. "You will take these prisoners to the great cliff that overlooks the ocean above the harbor. You know it?"

"Yes, sir," Aulus replied.

"You will take them to the edge of that cliff"—the prisoners had continued to sway and pray— "and then return here," said the governor.

The vigiles looked confused. "Sir, am I to hurl them into the sea?"

"Did I say you should hurl them into the sea, Aulus?" asked the governor.

"No, sir," answered the still obviously befuddled commander.

"You will leave them there. If they wish to visit their Heaven, they have only to hurl themselves into the sea," continued the governor.

"Stop! You cannot do this!" shouted the leader. "That would be suicide, and suicide is a mortal sin and we would go to Hell!"

By this time the crowd was laughing. Even Salvius had a smile on his face. The bishop, however, was looking grim. The governor's sentence had held up his church to ridicule and undermined his authority.

Domitius theatrically rubbed his temples. "Theology gives me a headache. Take them away Aulus," he said. Then turning to the secretary, he said, "Next."

"Clever man," chuckled Flavius.

"Indeed," answered Demaratus, "and clever men are dangerous."

Flavius nudged him. Demaratus turned and saw a group of men break off from the crowd and head for the taverna. Quintus and Macro were among them.

The former optio and his tesserarus were just getting settled at a table when Flavius and Demaratus came through the door. Quintus waved them over.

"Found your man for you," said Quintus, and pointed to a small man sitting by himself at a corner table. Macro got up and went over to the table, said something to the man, and pointed back at Flavius and Demaratus. The man stood and followed Macro back to the table. He had an odd-looking cape on that hid most of his body. He was a Cretian.

"Gentleman, this is Xanthippus, a former archer in the service of the Mauri, Juba. Cretian, these are Flavius and Demaratus of the VII Legion Hispania. I believe you have a common enemy," said Quintus

The Cretian's face was controlled, expressionless, but at the sound of "Juba" his lips twitched.

Flavius signaled the proprietor for wine and then leaned

toward the archer. "Quintus tells me you know where Juba's camp is."

"I do," said the man shortly.

"Well?" prompted Flavius.

"There is a price," said Xanthippus.

"Always is," said Flavius cynically. "What is this going to cost us?"

"Juba" answered the man, and a look of almost animal hate flitted across his face, only to be quickly mastered.

Flavius frowned. "If we take Juba, we aren't likely to march him back here and turn him over to you. We couldn't do that anyhow."

Xanthippus shook his head. "I want to be with you when you find Juba. I will settle with Juba myself."

Flavius and Demaratus glanced at each other. "Look, we can make this worth your while, but we don't take civilians along with us," said Flavius.

"Then you can find Juba on your own," said the archer.

"Now look here," started Flavius, but Demaratus broke in. "Why do you want Juba?"

Xanthippus shrugged the cape off of his shoulders and put his right hand on the table. Flavius noticed the index finger was just a stump. "Juba took something of mine," he said, his eyes glittering.

XIV

Just as the sun was casting long shadows and the mountains to the east began a shift from dun-colored to purple, the long procession of Mauri and slaves reached what Aelia assumed to be Juba's camp. Women, making an odd yodeling sound, surrounded the main gate, a tall impressive structure of heavy wood studded with bolts. Two small towers flanked the entrance.

Aelia's heart sank when she looked at the thick, 10-foot-high walls. The "camp" was more like a fort, one capable of withstanding a siege at that; nothing less than an army could breach this place.

Men stepped aside and embraced women, while packs of small children tugged at the soldiers' skirts and swords. The slaves were herded toward large, covered pens, although a group —Aelia and Rachel among them—were pushed to one side. Rachel had started to protest when she was separated with a group of women and children she had been helping, but Aelia silenced her with a hand. "Wait. Let us see how things are before we protest. They do not look upon us with favor," she said. Rachel reluctantly pulled back, and the two women stood holding hands.

Most of the slaves were locked into the pens with guards posted at each gate. Two guards motioned the group of slaves that Aelia and Rachel were with toward a large tent near the western wall. Aelia saw that, while the walls were substantial, there were few permanent structures within the fort. Tents—scattered around haphazardly—filled most of the inner space, suggesting that the fort was not permanently inhabited. There were no stables for horses.

The group of women stood for about an hour in the hot sun, loosely guarded by a few youths with swords who studied them closely and commented back and forth in a language Aelia did not understand. Almost everyone had conversed in Greek and Latin during the voyage. Here, however, people were speaking the language of the Mauri.

The young men spent most their time looking at Aelia.

"They admire you, Roman," said Rachel quietly.

"If I had one of those swords they would admire me less," replied Aelia, who was staring back at the men.

"Calm yourself, Aelia. Your temper has already gotten us into trouble."

"No more than your mouth, Rachel," Aelia retorted.

"True. We Jews do that," said Rachel with a shrug. "But that is because language is all we have. We have no land, no army, nothing but our wits and our tongues. It is our only shield."

Aelia sighed, and looked away from the men. "So, between my anger and your mouth we are not likely to last long, are we?"

Rachel was silent for a time. "Yes, we will," she finally said.

"You have value as a source of ransom, and I have value because they think I am yours. They will use me to pressure you, but if they kill me, they have no leverage over you and by now they know you are truly a Roman."

"What does that mean?" asked Aelia.

"They know that you were willing to risk your life for me. That gives them an edge. They can always threaten me to get you to do what they want," replied Rachel.

"No, not that," said Aelia, "I mean your comment on my being 'truly a Roman.'"

"That you would rather die than be dishonored. Those who live by a code of honor cannot be threatened or pressured except through others."

"Wouldn't you die for your honor?" asked Aelia.

Rachel laughed softly. "Slaves with honor have short lives. My only honor is to survive. As I said before, I would sleep with a mule if it would get me out of my present circumstances."

"But to live without honor is to be merely alive. One might as well be a donkey," said Aelia.

"Better a live donkey than a dead woman. One day your master may grow careless and turn his back, and you can kick his head off and maybe get away. If you are alive, you can always hope that things will turn your way. If you are dead...," she shrugged.

"But honor..." started Aelia.

"Is a luxury for the rich and the powerful, Aelia," broke in Rachel. "I mean no disrespect to you, but honor in our current state counts only in that it may prove useful to us."

Aelia said nothing, not wishing to quarrel, but also because she was not so sure of her ground. Was honor really just a privilege?

The tent was large, but with 20 adult women and seven children it felt chaotic. Carpets covered the tent floor. There were pillows and blankets, but little else. A few small tables for the twice-daily meals the guards brought in were scattered about. What was most difficult were the children. Like all children, they surged with energy, but no matter how much Rachel and Aelia argued with the guards, the children were not permitted to leave the tent to play. The result was bored children who squabbled endlessly.

Most of the women in the tent were free citizens, although there was one other slave besides Rachel. The women had little experience raising their own children; they were no use when the little creatures fell to fighting or whining. It was left to Rachel to break up the arguments, organize games, and keep the children as occupied as possible in a tent with little in the way of diversions.

Aelia had never paid much attention to children, and it was obvious that most of the other women in the tent hadn't either, even though many were mothers. She tried to help Rachel, but she was awkward and the children did not warm to her. She was amazed how calm—and clever—Rachel was, and how she could get them to sit and play word games. Sometimes she told them stories that Aelia found herself listening to. Indeed, the more time she spent around Rachel, the more she felt worthless and pampered. It put her in a foul mood, because she was used to thinking of herself as intelligent and competent, and of slaves as inferiors.

At one point she even snapped at Rachel over some minor thing, and then realized that she could alienate the only real friend she had in this horrible place, as well as the most level-headed person in the tent. She quickly apologized. "I am sorry, Rachel, it is just that I am going mad in this tent with nothing to do."

"Then we must find something for you to do," said Rachel, then she smiled, "something that does not involve children."

Aelia reacted defensively for a moment, and then laughed. "No, I am not very good with them, am I?"

"No one is naturally good with children, Aelia. It takes time and practice, and most of these women only see their children when they are in the mood to see them. We slaves raise the children," she said.

"Do you hate us for that?" asked Aelia quietly.

"Hate? No, not for that. There are many things slaves hate, but not raising children. It is hard to see them grow up. For many years you are their playmates, you feed and dress them, tend to their scrapes, and introduce them to the world. Then one day they grow up and you are just a slave to them." Rachel shrugged. "But that is our life."

"I am sorry, I never thought of these things," said Aelia.

Rachel looked her directly at her. "That is what we hate, Aelia" she said softly, "that you never notice."

Aelia froze, not knowing how to react. But Rachel leaned forward and touched her cheek. "I do not hate you, Aelia

Dasumi, just my condition. And we stray from the point: giving you something to do. I have an idea about that."

"You seem to have ideas about everything and I seem to have ideas about nothing," Aelia said bitterly.

Rachel ignored her comment. "If there is a key to our freedom, Aelia, you hold it," said Rachel.

Aelia frowned. "How? Do you mean Himilco? He never comes here, so how will Himilco do us any good?"

"If Himilco does not come here, then you must go to him," answered Rachel.

Aelia shook her head. "Rachel, they will not allow even the children out."

"We will become water carriers, Aelia. I am sure the Mauri find carrying water to the tent and to the slaves in the pens to be a burden. We will relieve them of that burden, which will also take you outside of the tent," said Rachel.

"Carry water?" said Aelia. "I have never carried water."

"You have never been a slave either."

Aelia did not mind physical work, but carrying water? "I am not sure" she began, but Rachel took her by the shoulders. "Aelia, there are many things we may have to do to get ourselves out of this. Some of them will be a lot worse than carrying water."

Aelia was silent for a bit, then nodded. "Of course. If you think that is the best way to get me out of this tent, I will carry water. I have held conversations with dull men, and that is certainly more painful."

Rachel laughed. "What would men do if they knew how we talked about them?"

Aelia smiled back. "Thank the Gods they are too full of

themselves to notice." Then she sat back and narrowed her eyes at Rachel. "How do slaves talk about us behind our backs?

Rachel arched an eyebrow and smiled. "Since you are now a slave, Aelia, how do you think?"

The Roman decided not to pursue that line, afraid it might end up in an uncomfortable place.

Aelia was not convinced that the Mauri would allow her and Rachel out of the tent, but the guards had readily agreed. When Aelia asked Rachel why she thought they had been so willing to let the two women out, and not the children, Rachel smiled. "We are more attractive than the children, Aelia, and they like your long legs."

"I will do my best to show them nothing," retorted Aelia.

"On the contrary, you will show them as much as you can without satisfying their appetite. In fact," Rachel said leaning back and cocking her head to one side, "we might add some padding" she said, looking at Aelia's modest breasts.

"How dare you," started Aelia, and then stopped herself, and began to giggle. Both women fell into each other's arms shaking with laughter. Finally, Aelia pushed herself away. "Oh, you are a dangerous woman, Rachel Levi."

"And you are our weapon, Aelia Dasumi. Let us sharpen it for this Himilco," said Rachel.

And so Aelia found herself pushing aside the tent flap and stepping into the sunlight outside the tent. She had shortened her shift to better show off her long legs and extra fabric had been packed around her breasts. The two guards gave her an admiring look as she hoisted an empty bucket on her head.

Juba, Himilco, and a group of men sat on carpets around a small table filled with tea and fruit.

"Naravas, how long before our friends from the south arrive?" Juba asked a burly, bearded man eating a melon.

The man wiped his mouth with his sleeve. "A month at the earliest, Juba."

The Mauri leader considered this. "We will up the price of the slaves to pay for their care and feeding," he said. "And we need to send out a feeler concerning a ransom for this Roman woman and her slave."

Naravas nodded. "I will send a rider out at first light. Do we know what the Romans are doing about this?"

"Send out more than one rider, Naravas," interjected Himilco. "Let's find out what they are up to." Turning to Juba he said, "We should see what we can learn from our people in Tingis. I do not think the Romans will let this pass without a response."

The burly man chuckled. "Let them come. We taught those Hispania legionnaires a lesson last year, we will teach this lot a lesson as well."

"The problem with teaching Romans lessons is that they learn from them," said Himilco. "We should never take them lightly. They gave us a good fight in the town we raided."

"If the Romans march south my cavalry will crush them, Himilco," replied Naravas, tapping his thigh for emphasis. "The Romans are like turtles, and we are like a storm. Turtles cannot fight a storm."

"Enough," put in Juba. "Himilco has a good idea. Send out riders to watch and probe, and send one into Tingis costumed as a merchant. Have him contact our 'friend' the governor."

Aelia pushed aside the flap on the tent and stepped into the open compound of the fort. The two guards discreetly eyed her as she hoisted an empty bucket to her head. Rachel had shown her how to carry water on her head—she was still not very good at it—and Aelia had taken her turn carrying a bucket from the well in the center of the fort to the tent where the more valuable slaves were lodged.

She walked slowly, looking at the pens where most the slaves were kept, but she was too far away to recognize any. Several children were waving at her from behind the slats, and she waved back. Making her way to the well, she cast down the bucket and, painfully, hauled it up. Her whole body ached from the combination of the march from the sea, carrying water, and sleeping on hard mats. The food was awful, but Aelia was not a heavy eater, and she subsisted largely on fruit and a little flat bread.

Carefully pouring the well bucket into her carrying bucket, she hoisted it to the edge of the well and then steeled herself to lift it to her head.

"Learning new ways, are we?" said a voice.

Aelia turned to glare at the speaker, but quickly mastered herself.

"Greetings, Himilco," she said with a sentiment that was not entirely contrived. Himilco had taken her as a slave, but he had also defended her, and he was, in any case, an interesting man. And a shield against Bogud.

The Mauri nodded without smiling or grinning, for which she was thankful. She could not take someone drawing amusement from her efforts to act like a slave.

"We have sent a rider to Tingis to find out if someone wants you back," said Himilco.

Aelia felt a surge of relief but did her best to master it. She must not show weakness in front of this man.

"Why don't you give us all back?" said Aelia.

Himilco laughed. "My cousin and my uncle were taken as slaves by Roman slave traders. Can I have them back?" he replied.

Aelia said nothing.

Himilco pointed to the ground. "Sit, Aelia Dasumi."

"I am supposed to bring this water to our tent," she replied.

"If I say you sit, you sit. That is the way of slave and master. You know that,"

Aelia dutifully sat and stared down at the dusty ground.

"You know, Roman, slavery is dying out," said the Mauri.

Aelia looked up and frowned.

"Truly," said Himilco. "We do not have much use for slaves here in Mauretania Tingitana, and less so in Mauretania Caesariensis."

Aelia drew up her knees and replied, "Then there is no reason not to send us back."

Himilco grinned. "I do not think you will make much of a slave, Roman. You have far too many opinions."

Aelia sat up and put her arms around her knees. "What did you mean when you said that slavery was dying?"

"It is. Do you not see it, Roman?"

Aelia narrowed her eyes, thinking that Himilco was teasing her. But Himilco was not the teasing type and he looked like he was asking for an answer.

"Our agriculture is done with slaves," said Aelia slowly, "and most of the heavy work is done by slaves. It seems to me that slavery is how things get done."

Himilco swept his arm to cover the camp. "You see no slaves here except those we sell to others."

"But you," she hesitated "are not a modern civilization like Rome. You are like tribes here. You don't need slaves."

"Mauretania Caesariensis sends more olive oil to Rome than your province of Hispania, and it may soon surpass it in grain. And virtually none of it is produced by slaves," replied Himilco.

"How do you know this, you are just...," and then Aelia bit off her words.

"A barbarian?" said Himilco with a smile.

Aelia said nothing at first, and then replied, "Yes."

Himilco stared straight into her eyes. "Long before there was a Carthage, when you Romans were living in mud huts, our people built a civilization. Our armies were eventually defeated but not the Mauri. We will send all of you invaders home one day and rebuild what we once had."

"With slaves?" said Aelia.

Himilco shook he head. "We are discovering a different way, Aelia."

Aelia frowned. "What do you mean, who is 'we'?"

"To you, we are just Mauri. But to us, we are Nasamones, Musulamii, Gaetuli, and even some Pharisi. All of the major tribes of the Mauri are within these walls. They have not stood together for beyond most of our memories. Juba has united them. They were brought here with the lure of plunder, but victory is a greater recruiter than gold and slaves," said Himilco.

"And if we stay united, the Romans will find that it is time to go home."

"Many have come against Rome, Himilco. Their armies are dust," replied Aelia.

"Dust, Aelia? Are the Goths and the Franks that assail your northern borders dust? Are the Parthians that hammer on your eastern walls dust? How long will the legions hold back the tide, Roman?" he said, his hands balled into fists.

Aelia was quiet for a long moment. "Will all the beauty be swept away? All the great cities? All the culture and the philosophy? Is that what you want?" she finally said.

"All empires are built on the bones of the conquered, Aelia," said Himilco. "All those cities were paid for by the plunder of your legions. The stones were cut by slaves you gathered from the corners of the Empire, and your art and philosophy is paid for by the taxes you extract with the sword. Beauty for whom, Roman?"

Aelia wanted to strike back, but she heard the voice of Rachel in her mind: Himilco was a possible way out. She could not quarrel. But if she did not argue, he would be suspicious. She thought that Himilco might be attracted to her not for her looks, but her intelligence.

She dropped her head for a moment, and then looked up. "There is truth in what you say, Himilco, a truth I did not see until you seized and brought me here. But how will your empire be any different? Won't those who are not Mauri see you the same way as you see us?"

Himilco nodded slowly. "That is possible, which is why some of us want a different way."

"The different way you speak of is an empire without slaves? How is that possible?" she asked.

"Will you answer me some questions, Aelia?" he said.

She gave him a wan smile. "Do I have a choice?"

"With me, yes," he answered. "I can order a slave to do whatever pleases me, but I cannot order one to think. I need you to think."

She silently nodded assent.

"Are slaves expensive?" he asked.

"Very."

"Why?" he asked.

She hesitated. "It is hard to get them. When something is in short supply and there is a demand, prices go up."

He grinned at her. "My, we are the merchant's sister, aren't we?"

"I have forgotten more about commerce than my brother will ever know," she said hotly.

Himilco arched an eyebrow. "Do I detect a certain family tension here?"

Aelia composed herself. "Was my answer correct?"

"Indeed, but why are slaves in short supply?"

"Because more people want them?" she said tentatively.

Himilco shook his head. "Think of your cities, Aelia. Are there not more poor than there were a generation ago?"

"I don't know. I feel stupid that I cannot answer that question," she said.

"You are wealthy, Aelia, why should you know? But I am a well- traveled barbarian. I have been to Alexandria. I have been to Gedes. I have never been to Rome, but I know those who have been. Your wealthy grow wealthier, your poor, poorer." He reached into his cloak and withdrew a denarius and tossed it to her. "What is this coin made of?"

She caught it, already knowing the answer. "Silver and lead."

"Silver?" he asked. "How many of those coins do you think you would need to make a silver necklace, Aelia? A simple ring?"

"But the value is in the coin, not the silver, Himilco," she said. "The value is that it can be exchanged for anything you want in the Empire."

"Really, Aelia? Do the merchants of Corduba take it instead of real silver?" he asked.

"Only if we have to," she said quietly.

"But the merchants have a choice. Do everyday people?"

She shook her head mutely.

"There are fewer slaves not because the poor are buying them, but because the Empire is too busy defending itself to conquer new people," said Himilco. "You used to seize slaves with your legions. Now you rely on slave merchants, and they only provide a trickle of what you need."

"What does this have to do with your new empire? If you don't have slaves, everyone will run to the cities to make money. No one volunteers to work the land. But without labor to work your land, you have nothing," she said.

"I will answer that in a moment, but first another question," said Himilco, whose increasingly pedantic tone was getting on her nerves. She suppressed a desire to respond tartly, however, and, in truth, she found the conversation stimulating if for no other reason than that she had never had one like it before.

Himilco was not exactly the person he appeared to be, and he was probably as well traveled as she was.

"Tell me, Aelia, why does a slave work?" he asked.

"Because a slave has to work, a slave has no choice," she answered.

"What happens if a slave will not work?"

"The slave is beaten until he or she works," she replied, puzzled about where this was going.

"So, the only incentive for a slave to is avoid punishment, correct?" asked Himilco.

"Well, many slaves are loyal and many of us love our slaves," answered Aelia.

Himilco waved away her remark. "Those are household slaves, and I think you have found that they are not as loyal as you thought them. But you said you needed slaves to work in the fields. Do you expect love and loyalty from them? If you did, why are they guarded by legionnaires?"

Aelia was increasingly fascinated by the conversation. "Yes, I concede your point about punishment. But what else is there?"

"Suppose a slave were given part of what he or she produces?" asked Himilco quietly.

"What?" said Aelia, genuinely puzzled.

"Suppose a slave could keep part of what they produced? Would you have to punish them to get them to work?" asked Himilco.

Aelia shook her head, bewildered. "How would the latifundia make a profit if he gave it all to the slaves?"

"Because the slaves would produce more, Aelia. They know if they produce more, they get to keep some of it; it doesn't just all go to the landowner. Profit, not punishment, is their incentive," said Himilco.

"Is this a day dream of yours, Himilco?" Aelia said with a little laugh.

"No dream. It is already being done both here in Tingitana and Mauretania Caesariensis. It is also used in Numidia," answered Himilco. "And rather than slaves fleeing to the cities, they remain on the land and profit from it."

"They are free to go whenever they wish?" asked Aelia.

Himilco shook his head. "No, they cannot leave the land. They are bound to it, in that sense, like a slave. But they also profit from this relationship."

Now it was Aelia who shook her head. "You make my head spin, Himilco," reaching for the water bucket and hoisting it to her head. Carefully balancing the bucket on her head, she turned to face him. "Can we speak of this again, Himilco? You have turned my world upside down and I need to think about what you have said."

Himilco gave her a nod and a smile. "I look forward to it, Aelia Dasumi." He even gave a little bow.

Aelia tried her best to curtsy holding the bucket, but the best she could manage was to duck her head and bend one knee. But when she turned toward the tent, she suppressed a desire to break into a smile. Talk again, indeed. Maybe there was a chink in the armor.

XV

A man watched the garden gate. For two hours he had sat just off a small plaza with its fountain and water tap, as the dusk had turned to darkness. The gate opened at last, and a slave put his head out, glancing up and down the street in front of the house. He held up an oil lamp, the signal, and then vanished, leaving the gate slightly ajar.

Wrapped in a cloak and hood, the man quickly made his way across the plaza and slipped through the gate. There was no sign of the slave, and deep shadows ruled most of the garden. He hesitated, unwilling to step into the pool of light cast by the house lamps.

"What news do you bring?" said a quiet voice from one of the deeper wells of shadow.

The man peered into the darkness and then moved toward it.

"Stay where you are," the voice said sharply.

"How do I know I can trust you?" countered the man.

"You don't. But if I were your enemy, I would have seized you the moment you walked through that gate, and I guarantee you,

I have ways of extracting whatever information I want," said the voice.

The man shuddered. He was a warrior and not much given to fear, but there was a coldness about the Romans that he found alien. "We have taken a slave that we hear you Romans want back. She is a Dasumi, and made of gold. We want her weight in gold. If we do not get this, we will sell her to the highest bidder from the south and you will never see her again."

There was a long silence from the shadows. "The woman is not a concern for us. Do with her as you please. Tell Juba we have a more interesting proposal."

"We are more interested in gold than your proposals," retorted the man.

"Juba's raid is his own business. What profit or losses he draws from it is no business of ours," said the voice. "Your raid has stirred up a hornet's nest and brought the VII Legion back to Tingis. So far it is just a cohort, but it could be more. Do you want an entire legion about your ears?"

"We are not afraid of Roman legions," said the man evenly.

"Then you are bigger fools than I thought. We Romans have ways of persuading people that picking a fight with us is a bad idea. A single cohort cannot do much, but a legion could sear this land to its roots. Juba's great alliance of Mauri tribes would break up as each left to protect its people. I thought you had more sense than this," said the shadow voice.

The man was silent, digesting what he had heard. It was not a decision he would be making, but he saw its logic. "What did you have in mind?"

"Neither Juba nor we want the VII Legion here in Tingitana.

If this cohort were to be destroyed or badly wounded, the VII Legion would be forced to go back to Hispania. That is in both our interests. After they have left, we could come to an agreement with Juba about...," the voice stopped to consider, then continued, "'sharing' Tingitana."

"Destroying a cohort will bring your Roman hornets around our ears far quicker than anything else we could do," argued the man.

"We think not," said the shadow voice. "The VII Legion is already engaged with tribes in Hispania's west, and Rome has little use for this province, certainly not enough to send a legion to avenge a single cohort. The Goths, the Franks and the Parthians are far more a concern for them than a skirmish gone wrong in a province that gives Rome little more than a headache."

"You don't know that," argued the man.

"Life is risk, Mauri. If we are right, then there is great profit to be made," answered the shadow.

"How would we destroy this cohort?" asked the man.

"You do not have to destroy the cohort, just a piece of it. And we will arrange for it to be alone. I assume you Mauri can handle a century on your own?"

"Why would destroying a century make these Romans go away?" said the man.

"Because they will lose their leader in this fight, and they will have little choice. We will not send our auxiliaries out to support them because we will need the auxiliaries to protect the cities from a Mauri uprising. We will provide boats to take the VII Legion's survivors back to Hispania, and then things can go back to the way they were and Juba can sell his slaves," answered the shadow.

"You would send your own people to be butchered?" said the man with a sneer.

"Spare me your sentiments on ethics, Mauri. Your tribes have been killing one another for hundreds of years. Why do you think it was so easy to crush you?" the shadow said with a humorless laugh.

"How will this happen?" said the man.

"We will arrange it. We will send a man to Juba's camp with the details. Now go," said the shadow voice sharply.

"Juba will not be happy about the ransom," grumbled the man.

"Juba's happiness is not our concern," said the voice.

XVI

Aelia watched Rachel as she told a story to the children bunched around her. It was about people being carried into slavery in Babylon—Aelia had been distracted so she missed the beginning, but it seemed to be about the Jews—and how the Persians had come and set them free to return home. Rachel told it like it was history, but it was filled with all sorts of things which could never have happened, so it was just a fable. It was sometimes hard to separate fact from fiction when Rachel was telling a story, but the children didn't mind.

When it was over, and the children had been bedded down for the night, Aelia teased Rachel a little. "Do you ever tell any stories that are not about the Jews?"

Rachel shrugged. "These are the stories I was raised with, so I know them best. But what makes you think they are just about the Jews?"

"Well, there always seem to be Jews in them," replied Aelia.

"They are stories about war and bondage, Aelia, and about

people's desire to be free and live in their own land. They are stories about faith. Do you think that only applies to us Jews?"

Aelia flushed. As much as she tried to forget what Rachel was, she was not used to being talked back to by a slave. "You Jews seem obsessed by it," she replied, trying to keep the anger out of her voice.

Rachel looked at her solemnly. "If you are sold into slavery, Aelia, it will obsess you as well."

"I will never accept slavery," said Aelia fiercely.

Rachel said nothing for a moment, hugging her knees with her arms and glancing around the tent. Finally, she looked directly at Aelia. "Sometimes there are only two choices, Aelia, life or death. If my people chose death over life, then I would never have existed. To be a slave does not mean you have to accept enslavement, you just have to act as if you do. We are only slaves if our hearts and minds are enslaved. As long as we do not think of ourselves as slaves, then one day we will be free. But if we reject life and choose death, we will never be free. Death does more than destroy those who choose to walk its path. It destroys the future. And that is a sin."

"I do not mean to quarrel," said Aelia.

"Why not? We Jews love to quarrel. We argue with one another and sometimes we even argue with ourselves. The Torah asks us to question everything, and when you question, you disagree. So to be Jewish is to quarrel," said Rachel.

"What is the Torah?" asked Aelia.

"It is the book given to us by God. It tells us how the world began and instructs us on how we are to behave."

"There are many such books," replied Aelia. "Why do you think yours is the truth?"

Rachel was quiet for a time. "It is our truth, Aelia, not the truth for all. We do not insist that others believe what we believe. We are not like Romans and Christians."

"We Romans do not care what people believe, and are not Christians just a sect of your religion?"

"Romans do not care what people believe, but they insist that everyone pay dues to the cult of Augustus. To challenge that is to court death," replied Rachel. "As for Christians, they are no more Jews than you are Greeks for adopting their pantheon of gods."

"The cult of divine Augustus is not about religion, Rachel, it is about the power of the Empire. People may pay their scrip to Augustus, but they can believe what they like," said Aelia. "And our gods are different than the Greek gods."

"Yes," laughed Rachel, "the Greek gods are more like us Jews. They quarrel and fight and disagree. But both Greek and Roman gods live on Olympus, even though the Roman ones have changed their names. Oh, and the Roman ones seem to bribe more easily."

"I do not mock your god," said Aelia, her voice tight with anger.

Rachel reached out and touched her. "No, you do not. Accept my apology. It is easy to tap the anger we slaves feel for our masters. But you are not my master, you are my friend. And you saved my life."

Both women sat back and looked at each other, and then started to laugh quietly. "A fine pair we are," said Aelia. "Here we are plotting to subvert a Mauri commander, and we fall to fighting over gods."

"You said that someone would come to save us," said Rachel, changing the subject. "Who?"

Aelia sighed. "I don't know that he will."

"But who is he?" asked Rachel.

"He is a centurion," replied Rachel.

"A friend? More than a friend? Why this particular person?"

Aelia thought this over. "He is someone who...." She stopped. "I know him only slightly, but I feel...." She paused, "I don't know what I feel, but somehow I am certain he will come for us."

"Is he handsome?" asked Rachel.

"No. He has nice eyes, but he is a plain looking man. He does know poetry," she said.

"Ah. He is charming," said Rachel.

Aelia shook her head. "No, he just knows some poetry, and he is nice and different. I think most of all he is different. And when he relaxes, he is funny. I think he is a sweet man, which is hardly what one expects from the officer of a legion. And brave. He defeated the Lusitanians who had destroyed part of the VII Legion.

"Oh, that centurion," said Rachel.

"You know of him?"

"Aelia, slaves know everything their masters know, and when it comes to news, generally much more. Everyone knows about the battle with the Lusitanians. And you think this is the man who will come for you?"

"I don't know, Rachel. Maybe it is just a hope," sighed Aelia.

"There is nothing the matter with hope," replied Rachel. "It is all that keeps many of us alive."

By now the two women were lying on the carpets facing one another. They talked softy for a time. and then Rachel slipped off into sleep. Aelia stayed awake for a time, her mind jumping from one thought to another, until she, too, fell asleep.

XVII

The entire cohort was lined up for review, the five centuries in blocks behind their signifers and centurions. Marcus made himself see the whole picture rather than focusing on individuals. The lines were crisp, the men looked sharp. There was none of the slack that indicated a troubled unit. As head centurion, Marcus's job was to inspect each century, and he did it carefully and thoroughly. A cursory inspection undermined the authority of the optios and the tesserarii.

As he moved slowly from unit to unit, he discreetly examined his centurions. Aulus and Junius looked nervous and stiff. Publius, who had brought his century all the way from Terraco, looked bored, but his century looked competent. Manlius, the former optio, looked like an old man next to the other centurions, but Marcus was coming to rely on his steady, commonsense voice in the meetings of the Primi Ordines.

On the far left of the cohort were Cassius and his Lusitanians. The young commander had done an excellent job of purchasing horses and mounting his men, and while they were only 120 strong, they looked like a formidable cavalry force. Marcus had long disliked mounted units—he still distrusted horses of any kind—but Cassius had changed his mind about their usefulness in war.

When the inspection was finished, he dismissed the men for the rest of the day. A number had passes and headed into Tingis. Others went back to their tents to gamble or sleep. Marcus had doubled the guard at the gates and walls of the marching camp, so that a fair number went from the parade ground to take up their duties.

Marcus had called a meeting of the Primi Ordines but first he met with Flavius and Demaratus. They had developed a habit of informally discussing what the main topics were, a habit that reflected the closeness of the three. Marcus had recently added his tesserarius, Sextus, to the informal group, because he wanted to avoid creating a division among his officers. Sextus generally remained silent, however, which Marcus suspected reflected that the Hispanian was still feeling himself an outsider.

When the four had gathered in the command tent, Marcus gave a short report on what the governor had learned about Juba, virtually nothing.

"A couple of officers from the old III Augusta say he is near some city in the south called Sala. They say there's a beach there for his ships," said Flavius.

"That is more than we've gotten from the governor," said Marcus.

"It is possible that the governor knows more than he is telling us," suggested Demaratus.

"But why would he hide where Juba is from us?" asked Sextus. "What would his motive be?"

The rare comment by the tesserarius was met with silence.

Finally Marcus said, "We can't assume that anyone is hiding anything, but I do think we need to proceed to find out whatever we can on our own."

Flavius and Demaratus looked at one another, and then Flavius spoke up. "Well, sir, we met someone who might be able to help."

Marcus frowned. "Why haven't you said something before?"

"We were going to tell you, but it is kind of complex," answered Flavius.

"The man is a Cretian who holds a grudge against Juba," said Demaratus.

"How much does he want for his information?" asked Marcus.

"That's just it, sir. He doesn't want any money," answered Flavius.

"What does he want?" asked the centurion.

"He wants Juba, sir," said Demaratus. "He wants to go with us and he wants to kill him himself."

"Do you believe him?" put in Sextus.

Flavius shrugged. "The man said that Juba cut off his finger. He says he was with Juba on the raid into Hispania. He gave a description of Aelia Dasumi but none of us have ever seen her, so I can't be sure it's accurate."

"Give it to me," said Marcus shortly.

"He described her as tall and slender, with blond hair. Said she looked like a queen," answered Flavius.

Marcus nodded. "Go on."

"That's about it, sir," said Flavius.

"How did you make contact with this man?" put in Sextus.

"The officers from the Third Legion put us on to him," said Flavius.

"I need to talk with this man," said Marcus.

"Yes, sir. But the fellows from the Third said that if we try to march on Juba, he will just take off into the mountains and we will never catch him," said Flavius.

"We cross that river when we come to it. First, we need to find out exactly where he is, and then we figure out how to take him," said Marcus. The centurion rose, ending the meeting, but indicating to Demaratus he should stay.

When Sextus and Flavius had left, Marcus turned to Demaratus. "You are of the opinion that the ransom that Julius Dasumi gave you to free his sister is inadequate?"

"Yes, sir. Indeed, it might be seen as an insult."

Marcus paced silently for a bit. "Whom have you told?" he finally said.

"Only you and the doctor, sir. I only told the doctor because I needed to know what her brother's motivation might be, and I knew that Timotheus was close with Aelia Dasumi," he said. "The doctor thinks that Aelia's brother would rather not see his sister return to Hispania, thus leaving him in sole possession of his family's wealth."

Marcus stiffened when he heard the inclusion of the doctor. "How do you know the doctor won't talk to others? I wanted to keep this among the three of us."

"I realize I took a chance, sir," Demaratus replied, "but is close to Aelia, and besides..." he trailed off.

"Besides?" said Marcus.

"He is a fellow Greek, sir. We know how to keep secrets. He is very fond of her and would never say or do anything that might harm her," answered Demaratus.

"For the time being, signifer, let us keep it between the three of us," said Marcus.

"What shall I do with the chest of denari?" asked Demaratus

"Keep it close, signifer. It may yet serve us," replied Marcus.

The Primi Ordines was routine and perfunctory: drill, supplies, and plans for training marches. Marcus would take his First Century out for a march to the south in two days, and he wanted the Second ready to do the same as soon as he returned. Drilling on the parade ground was important, but marches did a better job of building stamina. He was impatient to get about the business for which they had come here, but a precipitous action by the cohort could alarm Juba and end any possibility of getting back the slaves. He would have to be patient until he had an opportunity to talk with this Cretian and devise a plan.

Marcus thought about the description of Aelia. It fit, but then he realized that he had only seen Aelia for about 12 hours. She felt more familiar than that because of the letters the two had exchanged, but he had to admit that the woman was as much fantasy as reality to him. He fell into a daydream about saving her. He loved daydreams. The actors in his dreams said what he wished them to, and he always gave himself the best lines. He worked out complete scenarios. He realized that this was not healthy, since his dreams were always more interesting and successful than his real life, but he couldn't help himself.

Sometimes he absentmindedly spoke the lines out loud, drawing curious stares from those around him.

But daydreams were not all fantasy. They were the way that Marcus thought about things, the way he devised his plans. When he finally settled on what he would do, he would daydream about it for hours and hours, working out logistics, maneuvers, and outcomes until he had a vivid image in his head. When Marcus had time to daydream, he could be a dangerous man.

His current fantasy involved Aelia throwing herself into his arms after he had finished dispatching Juba in single combat. The sentry at the entrance to the command tent broke the daydream.

"Sir, there is an auxiliary commander here to see you," the sentry said.

Marcus suppressed a flash of annoyance. It wasn't the commander's fault that he had disturbed Marcus's reverie. Remembering the admonition from his Legate, Titus Valens, to make alliances with the local auxiliaries, he told the sentry to send the man in.

For the next hour, Marcus did his best not to show his impatience, which meant he drank too much wine. The man—Macro Junius—went on and on about his concern over some small units garrisoning the road south to Frigidex, which Marcus listened to politely.

"Will you be moving the cohort south, sir?" asked the man. "I would like some of my units to march with you. Nothing like seeing a real legion on the march, is there, sir? I think they would learn a lot."

Marcus inwardly groaned. The last thing he wanted was to

march with a bunch of ill-trained locals, but the man did have a point. "I will be taking the First Century south in two days. If you would like, I would be more than happy to have some of your men accompany us."

"Thank you, sir, my men would be honored to do so. I will have a century here at dawn two days hence," said Macro, lifting his goblet in a salute, which of course forced another round of wine. By the time Marcus had gotten rid of the man, he had a slight headache and had quite lost the train of his mental idyll. In any case, he had much to do.

A rider leading two horses trotted through the streets of Tingis, breaking into a lope once he had cleared the gates. He had worn out all three horses by the time he reached Sala and headed into the hills east of the coast.

XVIII

Aelia had fallen into daydreaming in the hour before dawn. She had awakened into a shadow land where she slipped in and out of sleep. She began thinking about Marcus because she had fantasies about him coming to rescue her. But gradually she began to think more about this man whom she had met only once, and with whom she had exchanged maybe half a dozen letters. Usually, she quickly grew bored with men, particularly when they were at a distance, but for some reason she had kept up the correspondence and looked forward to his letters.

She did not know what attracted her to him. He was not very handsome (though she thought that an overrated quality in men) and not a social equal. Yet there was something about him that appealed to her. Maybe it was his awkwardness in her presence. She was used to smooth, well-versed suitors, and Marcus was exactly the opposite of the men who flocked around her.

As her daydreams grew more detailed—she liked to go back and embellish them— he began to take on heroic proportions, although she was having difficulty remembering exactly what he looked like. She knew this was silly—possibly even destructive, given that she needed to marshal all her intelligence and discipline if she was to get out of this situation—but she hugged the daydreams to herself. They were tiny moments of pleasure in a world that had turned painful and terrifying.

When dawn arrived, the guards brought in several trays of bread, cheese, and yogurt. Most of the women and children in the tent were wealthy citizens of Ambis. Rachel had taken charge of keeping the children in order, and Aelia had taken charge of distributing food. Rachel and she also fetched water for those in the tent and for the slaves held in pens on the other side of the compound.

Aelia found the tent, packed with whining children and their equally whining parents, stifling. She looked forward to her trips to the well.

She fell into a routine of meeting Himilco when she was drawing water. She always went at the same time to make it easy for him to just happen to be near the well. While she started off making herself as charming as she could be, the content of the conversations themselves began to draw her in. Himilco was an interesting man, and Aelia found herself attracted by both his passion and his intelligence. Himilco, in turn, learned that when he began to lecture, she grew impatient.

What started out as humoring Himilco in order to get information and curry favor became a serious intellectual engagement, one of the few with a man she had ever had in her life. Men listened to Aelia, but only because she was wealthy and powerful, or because she was beautiful. Himilco listened because she challenged him to be clearer, to examine the pitfalls in his ideas. And he, in turn, forced her to re-examine the way she looked at the world, to see that there might be a different way of doing things.

The talks also made her forget her situation, at least for the moment.

But Himilco did not show up at the well today. She dawdled, taking as long as she could, but he was not coming and she eventually headed back to the tent.

Usually, Rachel awaited her return, and the two women would dissect the conversations to see what advantage they might wring from them.

"He was not there?" asked Rachel.

Aelia silently shook her head.

Rachel worriedly rubbed her cheek. "I do not like it."

"Why? We have never agreed to meet. He may be busy," said Aelia.

Rachel shook her head. "Maybe, but there has been lots of comings and goings over the last few days. Something is going to happen, and that can't be good for us. Maybe he didn't come because he knows something bad is going to happen."

Aelia smiled. "You worry too much."

"You don't worry enough," snapped Rachel, and then immediately apologized. "When you are a slave, Aelia, anything that is not routine is a danger. I hope you are right."

"I expect it is nothing," said Aelia, patting Rachel's shoulder, but a shiver of fear went down her spine.

The next day she was nervous before she left for the well and took extra care to look attractive, even though this was more for herself than for Himilco. She was convinced that Himilco was largely immune to her physical charms. Taking a deep breath, she stepped out of the tent, praying he would be there. He was not. Depressed, she crossed the fort and cast down the bucket at the well. She was just beginning to pull it up when Himilco touched her elbow.

She started, and then smiled. "Himilco. I missed you yesterday. I was thinking...."

But the Mauri cut her off with a curt, "Listen to me."

A little miffed and a little hurt, Aelia said, "I always listen to you, Himilco."

"There is a problem, Aelia. No one is offering a ransom for you," he said.

Aelia physically staggered.

"I don't understand, my brother will pay whatever you ask, although he will probably take it out of my inheritance," she said, gasping out the words.

"The Romans in Tingis say they have no interest in you and that Juba can do with you as he pleases," said Himilco.

Tears sprang into her eyes even though she did not want to show emotion before her captors. "Let me write a letter to the governor, or a letter to Hispania. I promise you will be paid well."

Himilco shook his head. "There is not time for a letter to Hispania, and the refusal comes from the governor. In any case, there is another matter that will take our time."

Aelia felt herself on the verge of breaking down, of dropping to her knees to plead with Himilco, but her instincts told her it would have the opposite effect. Instead, she composed herself, ignored her tears, and pulled up the bucket.

It was Himilco's turn to look distressed. "There is a chance you will not be sold south, Aelia."

She carefully poured the bucket into the vase, hoisted it to the well wall and then lifted it to her head. "As you know, Himilco, slaves have no say in such matters. I am tasked to bring water to our tent. Do you have anything you wish me to do?" she said, putting as much coldness as she could into her tone.

He said nothing.

"Then you will excuse me, master," she said softly.

The walk across the fort was the hardest thing she had ever done. When she slipped inside the tent, Rachel was waiting for her. Aelia put down the water vase and fell to her knees, burying her head in her arms, and silently sobbing.

"What is it, Aelia?" cried Rachel, dropping to her knees as well.

Aelia choked out her story, fighting to keep her dignity, but failing.

Rachel listened for a moment and then enfolded her in her arms, making soothing noises. "It is a setback, Aelia, not the end of the game. The game is not done until we are dead, and there is always hope."

Rachel let Aelia sob for a while before gently shaking her shoulders. A number of other women had gathered around her asking why she was crying. "A man," said Rachel, which was not exactly a lie. "Leave us," she asked.

Putting her mouth close to Aelia's ear she whispered, "It is time to do something different."

The statement quieted Aelia for a moment. "What do you mean?" she said.

Rachel slowly took Aelia's hand and pulled it down to her stomach, sliding it over a hard object. When Aelia looked up, her eyes still clouded with tears, she whispered, "A weapon. We need another."

A tiny spurt of hope sprang up in Aelia.

XIX

Marcus rose before the first light of dawn. He had slept badly. The meeting with the Cretian archer, Xanthippus, had been disturbing. Marcus believed the man could lead him to Juba, but he saw no way to come to grips with the Mauri. He was confident that the cohort could defeat Juba's forces, even the Mauri light cavalry. He had a large supply of javelins with him, and their effectiveness against the Lusitanians in the fight at the meadow had convinced him that the light spears were effective at holding off cavalry.

Even more important, the meadow battle had won over his grudging officers, steeped as they were in the conservatism of the Roman Army.

He would also have his own cavalry, although it would likely be greatly outnumbered. Cassius assured him that his four turmaes would be enough to defend the cohort's flanks, and that as good as Mauri cavalry was, his men were a match. Marcus was not as convinced on this latter point as Cassius, but he was not about to say so. In spite of his doubts, however, he had confidence in the young cavalry commander.

But the problem was that Juba was unlikely to fight. Faced with a superior force, the Mauri leader would abandon his base and retreat into the mountains. Pursuing the Mauri into their heartland was a recipe for disaster.

He had pored over maps with the local auxiliaries, but there was no way he could surprise Juba. Once he began marching south, the Mauri would know he was coming. Even if they gave battle, they would almost certainly abandon their base before-hand, and Aelia and the other citizens would vanish forever. He cursed Aelia's brother for sending an inadquate ransom. He cursed the governor for his lack of cooperation. He cursed the useless auxiliaries who always had an excuse for not pitching in. And he cursed himself for not finding a way to get the job done.

Marcus harbored all sorts of secret doubts about himself. He was nervous before a fight, but everyone was, though few would admit to it. Nervousness was just being smart: a good com-mander should be nervous, because battles never come out the way you anticipate they will, and the best planning in the world tends to come apart once contact is made with the enemy. But this was different because this was a failure of his imagination. And no matter how many times he looked at the map he could not see a way past his dilemma.

A sentry brought him a bowl of olive oil and some stale bread for breakfast. For all the governor's promises about fresh food the men were eating week-old bread. He was beginning to chew on the bread when Flavius came in, fully dressed and ready to go. Marcus had yet to don his armor.

"Good morning, sir," said the optio, saluting.

Marcus grunted, then immediately felt guilty. He was being grumpy because of his problem, and here he was taking it out on Flavius who could not say anything in return. What Marcus did not know was that Flavius had figured out all of this several days before and hence did not take it personally. Bad-tempered commanders were part of being in the army, like bad food, long marches, and uncomfortable bivouacs.

"Shall I get the men set to go, sir?" Flavius said.

At that moment Demaratus came into the tent, saluted, and asked about the auxiliaries.

"They aren't here yet?" asked Marcus.

"No, sir. Shall I send a horseman out to see if they are coming?"

"Good idea, signifer. See to it," said Marcus, shrugging his way into harness and beginning to buckle on his gladis sword and pugio.

"The plan, sir?" prompted Flavius.

"We leave in half an hour, auxiliaries or not. If they are late, they can catch up. If they don't show, the Gods favor us," said Marcus.

Flavius grinned. "I'll see to the men." He saluted and left.

Marcus sat on a campstool and doggedly chewed at his bread made only slightly more edible by the olive oil. Not that it was great olive oil, mind you, and the water was stale. But he joined the army of his own free will, so he put it out of his mind. A mule brayed, setting off several others. To the accompaniment of this chorus, he slipped on his helmet, picked up his shield and pilum and went out into the cool, gray morning.

The First Century was drawn up in the intervallum, with Sextus and Flavius fussing to make the lines straight. Cassius was talking with Demaratus, although the cavalry commander was not accompanying them that day. Marcus wanted Cassius to send some horsemen out to the east to see if there might be a way to cut off Juba before he could get to the mountains, and the young commander was sending out small squads to scout the terrain.

"You sure you don't want us along, sir?" asked Cassius.

"No need, commander. We are just going out for two days. Twenty miles out, a camp, twenty miles back. It would bore your horses to death. I am more interested in what you can find out about an eastern approach to Sala," said Marcus.

"Yes, sir. I am sending out a turmae today. They will split into two 15-men squads to cover more ground," replied Cassius.

"Shall we wait for the auxiliaries, sir?" asked Flavius.

"No. They can catch up. A forced march will do them good," replied Marcus.

"Shall we march, sir?" asked Flavius.

Marcus nodded. "Three abreast. We will halt at noon." The officers scattered, Flavius to the rear, Sextus to the middle of the century, and Demaratus to the head, where Marcus joined him. He signaled and the cornus blew a long note. The century stepped out, past the ramparts and into the growing morning light.

The century rolled through gently rolling hills spotted with trees and bushes. The day was mild, and even in full armor it was, all in all, a pleasant outing. Marcus's mind was on his problem with Juba, so he paid the terrain little notice, and Demaratus was more than happy to remain with his own thoughts.

The century halted at noon and broke to rest. No fires were allowed, so the men ate bread, small, hard sausages they had purchased from merchants near Tingis, and fruit. Sextus, as was proper for a tesserarius, set out sentries, and Flavius wandered through the ranks keeping an eye on things. Marcus paced and worried. Demaratus found some shade and read from a scroll on the history of Mauretania Tingitana that he had picked up in town.

Marcus was so involved in his problem that he hardly noticed that Flavius and Sextus had gotten the century back in line and ready to go. By mid-afternoon they reached a small stream with a flat meadow on the other side. Marcus halted the column and waited for Flavius and Sextus to come forward. Everyone agreed that it was a good spot for a marching camp, and the century set about digging a ditch, building ramparts, and tapping down the long, sharpened stakes that topped off the earthen wall.

The men had made camp so many times that everything happened without orders or instructions. Within three hours the camp was complete and laid out, contubernium tents in neat rows, with a mule tied at each tent. Sentries were set, and the men were setting fires to cook their dinners. Marcus found marching camps comforting. They were always much the same. They even smelled the same, because the Roman Army pretty much ate the same thing no matter where it was: onions, garlic, lentils, and beans.

Men talked, gambled, repaired equipment, sharpened weapons, or just sat and watched their fires. There was an enormous gulf between men and the officers, but when the army was in the field, the gulf was not as great. At the end of a long march, buttoned up in a marching camp, they were comrades in arms.

Marcus lay in his tent, certain that he would not sleep, but Morpheus ambushed him.

The camp was struck, the century waiting the order to march. Marcus and the officers had decided to do a short march south, then make a long day of it back to the cohort base camp south of Tingis. Marcus had called for a brief meeting before the century started off, but Sextus was late. An annoyed Marcus was about to tell Flavius to go find him when the tesserarius appeared.

"Sorry, sir, but a couple of sentries saw some horsemen. I wanted to be sure what it was they saw," said Sextus, saluting.

Marcus liked Sextus. He was steady and he took his job very seriously. He was also never late, so the fact he was meant that something concerned him. Marcus had long ago found out that a good commander relied on his officers.

"Go on," prompted the centurion.

"Three men on the east rampart saw a group of five horse-men at first light, sir," answered Sextus. "One of the men is certain that he saw shields, although the two others are not as sure. They came up over a hill, stayed just a moment, and then disappeared."

No one said anything for a moment. "I don't like it, sir," said Sextus. "I think they were scouting the camp."

"They could just be merchants headed toward Lixus," said Flavius.

"Why the shields?" replied Sextus.

"We don't know that they had shields, tesserarius," said Flavius.

"Quintus is a steady man, sir. If he is certain he saw shields, I think they had shields," answered Sextus.

Flavius nodded, turning to Marcus. "Quintus is a steady man, sir, and he has seen combat. He is not the type to imagine things."

Marcus looked over the century. It was almost at full strength. One hundred and fifty-five legionnaires made up a powerful unit. Marcus now regretted not taking Cassius, but there was nothing to be done about it. "Put the mules in a string with a minimum number of men to watch them. I want to keep as many men as possible in the line." Normally, each contubernium would assign one man to escort their mule in the rear, which in the case of the First Century would take 19 men out of the line. By putting the mules on a common string, that could be reduced to one man forward and one man bringing up the rear.

"Take the javelins off the mules. I want each man to have two pila and two javelins. Put the men's extra gear on the mules. I want this unit ready to fight if it has to," Marcus went on.

Flavius and Sextus left to take care of it, leaving Demaratus and Marcus alone. "Do you think we might be attacked, sir?" the signifer asked.

"I don't think it is likely. Even if those horsemen had shields, it doesn't mean they are Mauri looking for trouble. What we are doing is just a precaution," Marcus answered. But there was something tugging at the edge of his mind, something that he couldn't put his finger on, but that tightened his stomach. He concluded that it was probably just his current state of turmoil.

It didn't take long for the century to reorganize itself and to set off. Instead of a short march south, however, the century headed north, back toward the cohort's fort.

XX

Cassius rode at an easy lope. He was pleased with the horse under him; indeed, he was pleased with the cavalry's mounts in general. These Tingitana horses took some getting used to. They were built smaller and lighter than Hispania horses, and they had odd, narrow faces and delicate hooves. But for all that, they were strong enough for light cavalry, and they could run circles around the horses at home.

Flavius had asked him to send out a rider to find where the auxiliaries were and he had returned saying there was no sign of them. That puzzled Cassius because Marcus had said they were coming, and he couldn't imagine a provincial auxiliary officer standing up the senior centurion of the First Century. He, Cassius, would cut his own throat before he would do that.

The rider had gone out only a short distance since it was assumed the auxiliaries were just dawdling. Cassius would ride until he found them. But he was already a long way north of camp and there was still no sign of the auxiliaries. The auxiliary cohort—well, it was really not more than 200 men, less than half the size of a full-strength cohort—was based at a small fort just where the road from Volubilis to the east met the road between Sala and Tingis. He expected to encounter the unit somewhere south of where the roads crossed.

He rode all the way to the crossroads, however, before encountering anyone but early morning merchants and a few ox carts. The small camp was just beyond where the roads met, and he trotted up to the two sentries slouching outside what he took to be the cohort's headquarters. They eyed his uniform and came to a semblance of attention.

"Would one of you announce me to your commander," said Cassius, dismounting and handing his reins to a young slave who had just appeared.

The man shook his head. "Can't do that, sir. Commander isn't here, sir. He has been gone since day before yesterday, sir. Our tesserarius is our senior officer, sir, because our optio went with him. He is right in there, sir," said the man, pointing at a door with his spear.

Cassius frowned, pushed by the sentries and went in. A man even younger than Cassius was seated at a small desk putting seals on some documents. He looked up, did a double take, stood, and saluted.

"Sir. Sergius Matius, tesserarius, Third Mauretania Auxiliary, First Cohort, First Century," said the man.

Cassius suppressed a grin. It was a lot of titles for a scruffy little command in the middle of nowhere, but then again, Cassius had been a tesserarius once himself, and he remembered being proud of his title at the time.

"The sentries tell me that your commander and optio are not here, is this true?" asked Cassius.

"Yes, sir. They left two days ago for Tingis, sir," answered the man. "I expect them back tomorrow."

Cassius digested this for a moment. "Why didn't your cohort meet our First Century this morning?"

"Sir?" said the tesserarius looking puzzled.

"Yes," said Cassius. "Your commander made an arrangement to have this cohort accompany our First Century south. They were to meet us early this morning."

The man shook his head. "This is the first I have heard of it, sir. Our commander returned from your camp and left immediately for Tingis. I received no order concerning joint maneuvers."

Cassius stared at the man for almost a minute, which made the tesserarius fidget. "Something is wrong," Cassius said out loud, more to himself than the officer.

"Sir?" said the tesserarius.

Without a word, Cassius spun and sprinted out the door, looking for his horse. He snatched the reins from the slave, leapt into the saddle, and put his heels into the mare's flanks. With a surge of speed Cassius headed off toward the VII Legion's camp.

"Really, Cassius, you must rein in your imagination," said Publius Fulvius, chuckling at his own wordplay.

The four centurions—Publius of the Third Century, Aulus Junius of the Fourth, Cerficius Nonius of the Fifth, and Manlius Valeranus of the Second—were gathered in the command tent at Cassius's request.

"Sir, something is very wrong," said Cassius, trying to keep his temper in check. He disliked the pompous Publius.

"No provincial auxiliary commander would stand up one of you, let alone our Primus Pilus," continued Cassius.

"I will grant you the man is rude, but what does one expect from these colonials," said Publius, picking through a bowl of grapes to find the most succulent ones. "But why is his rudeness a concern for us?"

Cerficius and Aulus—the "pups," Flavius had named them—looked uncomfortable and neither said anything.

"What do you suspect?" said Manlius.

"I am not sure, sir, but I am suspicious of this auxiliary commander. What if he knew something about what our First Century is headed into?" asked Cassius.

Publius shook his head. "The only evidence you have is the auxiliary commander's absence. That is not enough to put this cohort on the road, Cassius."

"Would a long march disturb your rest?" flared Cassius.

"Shut your mouth," roared Publius, surging to his feet. "You are addressing a superior officer. I could have you whipped for this."

"Gentlemen, gentlemen, calm yourselves. We are at war with the Mauri, not one another," said Manlius.

Publius was still standing, his face flushed. Cassius stood almost nose-to-nose with him, his fists clenched.

"Publius and Cassius, sit down!" said Aulus, which produced frozen silence and incredulous looks from Publius, Cassius, and Manlius. "Yes," he continued, "the pups can bark and they can also bite."

Cassius and the two older centurions immediately looked guilty.

"We know you call us the pups," said Cerficius quietly. "We know you will continue to do that until we prove ourselves. But we are all equals here." Publius started to protest but Aulus waved him into silence, "Even Cassius. He commands almost as many men as we do, even if he does not rank as a centurion."

Turning to Cassius, Cerficius said, "You must have more than this man's absence to be so alarmed. Talk freely."

Cassius took a deep breath as Publius, grumbling to himself, slowly sat down,

"You're right, it isn't just the man's absence that makes me suspicious, although I rate that important," he said. "Look at the pattern. The governor says he will supply us with fresh food and what do we get? Week-old bread and sour olive oil, if we get it at all. Everyone says they want to help us get our citizens back, but they don't know where Juba is, they don't have enough mounts, the roads need garrisoning. It's like we're stuck in glue, and from what I heard about the Legion's experience here last year, it was the same. Lots of smiles, lots of promises, nothing happens, and the Mauri always seemed to know exactly where the Legion was."

"It is their land, they know it," put in Publius.

"Yes, and maybe I am imagining things, but what if I am not? That is our commander out there with one century," said Cassius.

"I thought Marcus was an expert at fighting cavalry," said Publius.

"The Lusitanians made a mistake. They charged head-on. That is not how the Mauri fight. They stay at a distance and chop away at you. Maybe a cohort could keep them at bay, but a single century can only fight off that kind of attack for so long. What happens when they run out of javelins? What happens when their pila go? Short swords and shields are no match for good cavalry. Remember, it was this same cavalry that destroyed two legions under Scipio," said Cassius.

Publius looked doubtful, Manlius neutral, the pups had gone quiet. "Look, I know my job," said Cassius, "and I know what cavalry can and can't do. I know that if the First Century encounters a large enough Mauri force, it won't stand a chance. We have to move, and we have to move now! If I am wrong, you can blame me."

"A superior officer cannot take refuge in a junior officer," put in Publius dryly.

"This is our decision, Cassius," said Manlius. "And if we move, we all have to move together. We do not have enough forces to divide them. I, for one, think we must mobilize. Even if nothing comes of it, it is good training."

Aulus and Cerficius looked at one another, and Aulus said, "We concur."

Everyone looked at Publius who glowered back at them. "All right, all right, but you are all going to feel stupid when we meet Marcus coming back."

"Gentlemen, I will lead the cavalry out first if that is all right. I have some preparations to make before we leave. May I be excused?" said Cassius, visibly antsy about getting underway.

"Don't wet your saddle," grumbled Publius. "I say we let him go. It will be a good deal quieter around here."

Cassius gave a perfunctory salute and dashed out of the tent.

XXI

The First Century left their marching camp just as the sun lifted above the mountains to the east. The men were tense—Marcus had gathered them around him and told them to be alert—but the pace was the normal gait of infantry. There was no sense tiring the men. Fighting was exhausting, and if it came to a fight, it was likely to be a long one. He also did not want to give the men the impression of panic. Routine was the best antidote for fear.

Marcus considered putting out skirmishers, but cavalry would make quick work of them and he needed every man. Again, he rebuked himself for not taking Cassius along.

The road ran due north without bend or break, giving the century a clear view before and behind. If danger came, it would come from the flanks. So far, however, he had seen nothing. He noticed the men beginning to relax a little, which was fine. Tension was tiring.

The century had come to a place with hills on either side of the road, and Marcus's nerves began to prickle. It was one of the few places where the road went over a ridge rather than simply slicing through it Roman-style. Whatever was on the other side, the ridge obscured it. Just to the left of the road was a rocky prominence that jutted up from the flat ground around it.

"Signal a halt," he said to Demaratus, who dutifully lifted his signum and raised his left hand. The column came to a stop. Marcus swept the hills on either side of them, while Flavius trotted up to the head of the column. For a moment none of the officers said anything.

"See anything, sir?" asked Flavius.

Almost as he spoke two horsemen topped the ridge and stopped. Both wore helmets and carried spears and shields. They made no move, just sat and stared.

"Arrogant bastards, aren't they?" said Flavius.

"Confident," said Demaratus quietly.

"Deploy, optio. Be ready to form a testudo," said Marcus.

"Four abreast! Tighten up!" shouted Flavius, and headed for the rear.

The men moved four abreast and tightened the distance between them. If a testudo was ordered, the two men on the outside of the column would turn their shields outward while the two men in the middle would balance their shields on their heads, forming a roof. The effect would be not unlike the animal the formation took its name from, the tortoise. It would protect against spears, but it was hard to maneuver and slow. Marcus would wait to see what he was facing before forming it.

As soon as the men were in position he ordered the century forward, edging it toward the rocky hill. If it came to a fight with cavalry he wanted the high ground, and he wanted broken terrain that would make footing for the horses difficult.

Apparently the two horsemen came to the same conclusion, and one of them lifted his spear and pointed. Marcus could feel the ground tremble and moments later the hills on either side of the road were filled with cavalry. They came at a leisurely trot. And there were lots of them.

The hill was still a good 200 yards away, but Marcus could not afford to hurry. If the century got out of formation the cavalry would make quick work of them.

Demaratus shifted the signum to his left hand to keep his sword arm free. If there were an attack, he would drop the signum and take up his shield. Unlike the religious veneration in which the legions held their eagles, the signum was just a rallying point and a signaling device. No one wanted to lose one, but no one wanted a hole in the testudo either. The Roman Army was superstitious, but not stupid.

Marcus heard Sextus calling out instructions: "Hold your javelins until the bastards are close enough to piss on. Wait until you get the order before using them. Save your pila."

The javelins and the big infantry phylum would keep the cavalry at a distance, but there were only so many javelins and pila to go around. If he formed the testudo, the men in the center of the formation could pass their javelins and pila to the troops on the flanks, but that might leave the century with no spears by the time they reached the hill.

If they reached the hill.

The riders were now beginning to close with the century, some of them preparing to toss their light spears.

"Testudo," shouted Marcus. The flanks immediately faced their shields outwards, while those in the middle raised their shields just in time. A storm of lances arched in from the Mauri cavalry, but fell harmlessly on the sides and the roof of the formation.

The Mauri cavalry were growing bolder and sweeping closer and closer to the century. They would have to be taught a lesson. But unlike the Lusitanians, they kept their distance, charging in, tossing their spears and then wheeling out of range. Marcus would need to be patient, let the Mauri get overconfident. They apparently had no experience with Roman legionnaires and javelins. They would learn soon enough.

More and more cavalry were arriving. It was hard to judge their numbers, but it was certainly many hundred. Marcus felt as if his century were a small island increasingly surrounded by a sea of Mauri, a sea that was growing angrier by the moment. He would have to counter the growing arrogance of the riders, some of whom had taken to striking the shields of the legionnaires with their spears as if they were involved in a game.

One large group of cavalry had positioned itself between the century and the rocky hill and appeared to be working itself up to attack. Several other small groups were now ranging up and down the testudo, trying to hurl their spears into whatever small openings they could find. Several were successful. Marcus saw one legionnaire stagger back with a spear in his throat. The testudo closed up quickly, but the soldier would not be the last. Several men were glancing his way, their faces tense with fear. He would have to act.

The group defending the hill suddenly attacked. Marcus called out: "Left flank, Javelins."

The men had practiced throwing javelins and pila from the testudo formation. It was a tricky maneuver. The "roof" had to tip their shields up so the spear throwers could pull their arms back, aim and throw. As soon as the spears were thrown, the "roof" had to reclose. The men had done well on the parade ground, but intricate maneuvers under battle conditions were a different matter.

But the counterattack worked like a machine. The javelins caught the horsemen when they were 100 feet away, knocking riders off their horses, panicking their mounts and disrupting the attack. At least several dozen Mauri pressed on, however.

"Pila!" roared Marcus.

A wave of the heavy spears fell on the horsemen who had continued the attack, inflicting distressing damage on the front line and killing more than a dozen men. The losses caused the Mauri to wheel away out of range and let the century close on the hill. It was still a good 100 yards away, and more horsemen had replaced the ones killed, wounded, or just frightened by the century's counterattack.

"A lot of those bastards won't be pissing tomorrow," he heard Sextus cry out. A chorus of cheers greeted the remark.

The century's counterattack had dampened some of the horsemen's enthusiasm and they were being more cautious. They were attacking almost continuously, and as tight as the testudo was, there were inevitably gaps. Mauri spears began taking a steady toll on the century, although most of the men were wounded rather than killed. Flavius beat off an attack on the rear, and Sextus handled one on the century's right flank.

The Mauri were losing men, but there were so many of them —Marcus thought there might be as many as 1,000—that they could shrug off the damage the century was inflicting. Several horsemen rode right up to the right flank and tried to stab through the wall of shields. The testudo suddenly advanced on them, the men stabbing the horses through the gaps in their shields. Most of the horses bolted, but three went down with their riders. When the testudo flank retreated back into line three Mauri lay dead near their horses.

The legionnaires were tiring. They had beaten off several attacks, but the hill was still a good 200 feet away and the way was blocked by a dense pack of horsemen.

Two riders swept in from Marcus's right and attacked him. He threw a phylum, which brought one man down, but the other slipped inside and yanked his shield away. Marcus snatched at his sword, but without a shield he was not only defenseless, he had opened a hole in the testudo. The rider wheeled his horse, leaned forward and prepared to throw his spear. To Marcus it seemed to happen in slow motion, almost as if he were watching someone else. There was nothing he could do except die with as much dignity as he could muster.

But the man never completed the throw. Instead, he arched his back, and rolled off the back of his horse.

Marcus was suddenly aware that many of the Mauri cavalry had broken off their attack and were turning in circles as if they were confused. A horse, not 50 feet from him, screamed and pitched forward into the dirt, throwing its rider.

A Mauri horseman had picked out Marcus, who was still shieldless and separated from the testudo. Marcus watched the man put his heels into his mount and charge, his spear held out in front of him, his body covered by a round shield. Marcus crouched, his sword in his hand. It appeared that he had dodged one death only to be embraced by another.

But someone thundered by armed with an enormously long and ungainly looking spear. The Mauri turned toward the horseman, but long before he could close with the newcomer, the spear struck his shield, piercing it and bodily lifted the man off his horse.

The new rider turned, and flashed Marcus an enormous grin.

"Cassius," said Marcus.

"Yes, sir. Now, if you will take the century over the ridge, sir, you have some friends waiting for you. My cavalry and the Cretians will hold this lot off until you can reach the cohort." He swung the huge spear around—really more a lance than a spear—and dashed off into the thick of the Mauri.

"First Century! Column! Route trot! Carry the wounded," Marcus yelled. Now he could see the Roman cavalry wheeling and spinning their mounts, charging, retreating, and generally disrupting the Mauri, who still looked confused, riders scattering everywhere. He could also see two Mauri attempting to rally the riders. The two looked very much like the men Marcus has seen just before the attack.

The Cretian archers, strung out along the ridgeline, kept up a steady fire. With the Mauri so packed together, almost every shaft unhorsed a man or sent his mount kicking and bucking.

The century was already in motion, a number of men dragging

their comrades along with them. There were many wounded. The century would have been destroyed had Cassius not arrived.

Having picked up the century's signum, Demaratus joined him. "Our young Lusitanian has impeccable timing, does he not sir?"

"That he does, comrade. Are you injured?" asked Marcus.

"A small wound, sir, I am fine."

"Lead the century, signifer, I will join you later." Marcus, still holding his sword, strode toward the rear. Seeing Sextus, he ordered him to keep the men moving. Sextus had a bloody left shoulder, but looked fit. Flavius had pulled together a rear guard, which was backing up, shields to the rear and armed with the last of the javelins and pila.

"If we get out of this sir, I am buying the cavalry and those Cretians as much drink as they can down," said Flavius, backing up with his men and keeping a weather eye on a group of Mauri who were rallying.

"Did you see that great long thing Cassius was carrying?" said Marcus, which was a silly thing to say when they were still under attack and fighting a rear-guard action. But he was feeling light-headed. A close call with death does that to you, he thought.

"I did. A bunch of our cavalry had them. It's called a contus, but I've never seen it used in battle before. Trust Cassius to come up with something new," replied Flavius, who did not think Marcus's comment was odd.

The horsemen were edging back toward them, but a steady rain of arrows kept disrupting their formations. Then the arrows stopped.

"Cretians must have pulled back, sir, as should you," said Flavius.

The rear guard had reached the crest of the ridge and Marcus turned to see what happened to the archers. A hundred yards away was the cohort, its four centuries lined up in blocks four men deep. On each flank was a small group of cavalry. The Cretians were riding horses, and the first of his century's men had reached the cohort's front line.

"Look at that, Flavius. He put the Cretians on horses," said Marcus.

Flavius, who was still watching the Mauri, glanced over his shoulder. "Mobile artillery. Smart boy. He'll run the empire one of these days if we don't get him killed first."

Marcus could see that Cassius's men were rapidly getting themselves in trouble. There were not enough of them to defend their flanks, so they kept charging, then backing off and retreating toward the rear guard.

"Flavius. We need to go," said Marcus. "Or we are going to get young Cassius killed right here and now."

"Right, sir. All right, men. Let's go tell the lads some war stories," bellowed Flavius.

The men turned and dashed toward the rest of the cohort, which waited for them in silence.

"Cassius," yelled Marcus. "Break off and guard our flanks."

Cassius, who had lost his long lance, waved an acknowledgement, and beckoned to his cavalry. Marcus turned and ran after his men toward the deployed cohort.

Juba and Himilco sat on their horses and examined the

Romans drawn up on the broad plain. Behind the main line were the archers, and two small blocs of cavalry on either side.

"What do you think, my friend?" said Juba.

"I think I will cut a certain governor's throat if I get the opportunity," replied Himilco.

"The governor will indeed pay for this, but that was not my question." Shall we fight them?" said Juba.

"Only if we can defeat them. Their cavalry is not of much consequence, though it is the best we have encountered," said Himilco.

"Not the first time we have met them," said Juba.

Himilco shot a puzzled look at the Mauri commander.

"Don't you recognize that commander down there? It was he who fooled us in Hispania and very nearly brought on disaster," said Juba, pointing out Cassius with his spear.

"Are you sure?" asked Himilco.

Juba nodded. "I got a good look at him on the beach. For the second time he has showed himself to be a worthy opponent."

"We could sweep that cavalry away," said Himilco.

"The cavalry would just slip in behind those cursed archers and legionnaires with their javelins. It is one thing to overrun 150 men, quite another to take on a big body of soldiers like that. If I had my Libyans and some archers I would try it, but with the forces we have I do not think we would be successful," said Juba.

"So, what do we do?" said Himilco.

"We harass them, exhaust them, send them back to their camp, beaten," replied Juba. "We have hurt them, and almost killed their commander. They will not be back. And if they do return in force, we will join our friends, the mountains."

Juba wheeled his horse and galloped down to a milling body of Mauri cavalry standing off two hundred yards from the cohort. Himilco followed at a lope.

XXII

It had been a difficult withdrawal, an endless series of lunge and parry. The running battle unfolded pretty much as Juba had predicted. The Roman cavalry hid behind the legionnaires and archers, charging only when they had a momentary advantage. Himilco had tried to lure them away by having his cavalry feign panic, but the Roman cavalry was too smart to take the bait.

The horsemen had hovered around the soldiers, but the legionnaires were numerous and aggressive, and bloodied the Mauri on a number of occasions. When the horsemen tried to get close enough to throw their javelins, the Cretians picked them off. One of the Mauri was pitched from his horse when an arrow struck the animal. He was quickly seized by two legionnaires, and dragged back into their formation. Moments later the man's head had come sailing out of the ranks to bounce and roll over the ground. The Romans cheered.

The archers finally ran out of arrows, but by that time the cohort was close enough to their camp that the Mauri were becoming wary.

The Mauri began jeering at the cohort when the camp came

into view. "Roman dogs, fight!" "You shame your fathers, those of you who have them!" But the Mauri retreated when the Balearic slingers moved out from behind the ramparts and showered them with their pointed lead projectiles.

Marcus was the last man through the rampart gate, now defended by the quarter century left to guard the camp. He watched a Mauri ride forward and fling a Roman shield onto the road—it might have been the one Marcus lost before Cassius showed up—and spit. The man drove a spear into the shield, shouted something Marcus could not hear, and rode back. The Mauri cavalry followed.

Marcus rarely felt shame. He felt it now, shame and rage, a cold anger that allowed him to clear his mind despite exhaustion. A germ of an idea began to form as he stalked into camp and called the men to gather around. Except for the guards on the ramparts and gates, they silently surrounded him. Some were so badly wounded they sat or lay on the ground. The doctor had already started to treat some.

"Comrades," said Marcus. "You fought well. There is no shame in what happened this day. They would not dismount and fight like men." He paused here for a moment, and added, "And as you know, I will not get on a horse."

The remark raised a ripple of laughter.

"You stayed together. You demonstrated the discipline of the Roman Army. And you brought your comrades safely back home. Be proud. There will be another day, that I promise you," said Marcus. A ragged cheer went up, but without much enthusiasm. The men knew they hadn't won a victory, and that it was they, not the Mauri, who had retreated.

"Officers," said Marcus, "see to your men," effectively dismissing the cohort. He signaled Flavius, who strode to his side. "Tell the other centurions there will be a meeting of the primi ordines when the men have eaten. I want you, Demaratus and Cassius there."

Flavius saluted and moved off to tell the centurions. As exhausted and drained as he felt, Marcus made himself find Sextus. He took him to one side. "Your performance today gives you honor, tesserarius."

"Thank you, sir," said Sextus, looking exhausted too, but pleased.

"I will be calling on you to take more responsibility in the near future, Sextus. I am certain you can handle it," continued Marcus.

"Yes, sir," replied Sextus, looking puzzled.

Marcus put his hand on Sextus's shoulder. "When it happens, you will understand."

"Of course, sir," said Sextus, but he still looked confused.

Marcus returned the salute and headed for his command tent.

"It was betrayal, sir," said Cassius, leaning down and striking the table for emphasis.

Marcus and the four centurions sat around a table on which wine, bread, olive oil, and some rather sad looking fruit was scattered. Flavius and Demaratus sat on stools at the back of the tent.

"We don't know that, Cassius," said Marcus. "There may be an explanation for why the auxiliaries never showed up."

Marcus looked exhausted, as did the other men. Aulus nursed

a wounded arm, and all of them were cut up or nicked in some way.

The Primi Ordines was listening to Cassius rage at the auxiliaries, the governor, and anyone else in Tingitana he could think of. Marcus let him run on for a bit, waiting for an opening. The man had saved them all today; he certainly deserved the right to talk himself out.

"That's the way I see it, sir," he said finally, slumping onto a stool.

The silence that followed had as much to do with general exhaustion as agreement with Cassius.

"You may be right, Cassius, but that presents us with a dilemma," said Marcus.

"The only dilemma I can see is whether we crucify that bastard auxiliary commander or chop him up and feed him to the dogs," said Cassius.

"I suspect the problem goes higher than a lowly auxiliary commander, whom I assume will be on extended assignment deep in the mountains by the time we get back to Tingis," said Marcus.

"But sir, we have to do something!" cried Cassius, "We lost close to 20 men today, and twice that wounded."

"I am aware of the casualty figures, tesserarius," said Marcus quietly.

His tone pulled Cassius up. "Of course, sir. I spoke out of turn," he said stiffly.

"Our dilemma, gentlemen, is that we must find a way to come to grips with our enemy. But it appears we have two enemies, the Mauri and the governor. We are caught between two forces. The only way out is surrender," he said.

"What! By the gods, what are you talking about?" cried Publius, stirring himself from his chair. "We are not defeated, how dare you...." All the other centurions began to speak as well, and even Flavius looked shocked. Only Demaratus remained calm, smiling slightly. Flavius looked at him oddly.

"Quiet, gentlemen. I have no intention of handing my sword to the Mauri," said Marcus. "Our surrender will be to the governor, but it will not turn out quite the way he imagines."

"Why don't we march on Tingis and seize the governor," said Cerficius. Everyone looked at him, as much because one of the pups had spoken out in a meeting with Marcus as at the nature of his idea.

"We can't arrest governors and mix it up with the civilian authorities, Cerficius. We have pretty explicit orders about that," put in Manlius. The older centurion frowned, "What did you have in mind, sir?"

"Let me first talk about the tactical situation as I see it," said Marcus. "We cannot come to grips with the Mauri with our present force. We saw that today. Unless we do something stupid, I don't think they can defeat us, but neither can we defeat them. Maybe if we had a lot more cavalry we could do it, but we don't, and our other enemy, the governor, is not likely to provide it."

"If he did, it would be useless in any case," grumbled Cassius.

"I agree with Cassius," said Marcus. "As for infantry, does anyone here think the local auxiliaries are up to the task, even if we could trust them not to join with the Mauri?"

Everyone was silent.

"Further, even if we were to assemble sufficient amounts of competent cavalry and infantry, the Mauri would simply refuse battle and take to the mountains, along with our citizens," continued Marcus. "Does anyone disagree with that analysis?"

The silence continued.

"The only way to accomplish anything, then, is to fool both our enemies, correct?" asked Marcus.

Manlius shook his head. "I still don't see where this is going."

"We have a man who says he can take us to Juba's camp," said Marcus. "I spoke with him and I believe him. In any case, we have little choice but to trust him."

"But even if we know where this Juba's camp is," said Publius, "so what? As you yourself pointed out, marching south will only force the Mauri into the mountains."

"If we march by land, true," replied Marcus.

By this time Demaratus was smiling. It was not the first time that the Greek's thinking had paralleled his own, although in this case it was that as a former sailor, Demaratus was the one person in the tent whose thinking was not chained to the land.

"There's another way to march?" said Aulus quizzically.

"Juba's beach," said Flavius, finally putting the pieces together.

"Exactly," said Marcus, hauling himself to his feet and fetching a map. He spread it out and the others gathered around. "This is the town of Sala, and the beach Flavius is talking about is about five miles south of it. According to our informant, Juba's fort is about six miles in from the beach. We will land at dusk, make a short march, and attack Juba at dawn."

Publius shook his head. "How will we get there? If we take

ships from Tingis, the governor will alert the Mauri, and we can't very well get ships anywhere else without the governor or his spies knowing about it."

"The governor will supply us with the ships, Publius, because we will surrender to him. We will march back to Tingis, defeated, and the governor will be more than glad to send us back to Hispania. Only we won't be going to Hispania, at least not right away," replied Marcus. "We will take those ships south and land near Sala."

Marcus had only a vague outline of the plan when the meeting started, but as he talked, it fell into place.

"If we land at this beach, won't it be full of Juba's men? Isn't this where he keeps his fleet?" asked Manlius.

"He doesn't have a fleet," interjected Flavius. "It seems he hires ships when he needs them. He used Greeks in his last raid. The beach is mostly deserted."

The mention of "Greek" caused everyone to glance at Demaratus.

"Yes, it is shame he used Greeks," said Demaratus. "If he had used Romans we wouldn't be in this difficulty.

"And why is that?" asked Flavius.

"Because if the Mauri had used Romans none of them would have made it alive to Hispania," he observed mildly.

The line brought a laugh. Flavius shook his head. "I should have seen that one coming."

"But isn't it risky? It will only work if no one sees us," said Publius.

Marcus bit back the urge to remind him that war is inherently risky. Publius would be insulted, and in any case, it was a valid point, and one he didn't have a clear answer to.

"I think the cavalry could handle that part, sir," put in Cassius, "There is no way we can take enough horses with us on board the ships, so I was thinking that we would stay behind. Not everyone. I would select 60 men. We would head east to stay off the main road, and then meet you south of Sala. We could secure the area around the beach."

"Do you think maybe the locals wouldn't notice that Roman cavalry was suddenly in their midst?" said Publius dryly. He was nursing a grudge against Cassius, but Marcus had no idea what it was, nor any interest in finding out.

"We won't look like Roman cavalry, we will look like Mauri. I watched their tactics as well as their dress today, and I think I can turn us into Mauri. All we have to do is avoid talking with anyone, but that's not a problem for cavalry," said Cassius, ignoring Publius.

"And what if you encounter real Mauri cavalry?" persisted Publius.

"We kill them," said Cassius.

Publius looked like he was going to continue to pick at Cassius, but Marcus shut him off. "I approve, Cassius. See to it." Then turning to the rest, he said, "Speak to no one about this plan. No one, do you understand? Not even your officers." Turning back to Cassius he said, "Commander, you will need to separate off the men you choose from the rest of the cavalry without letting them know what is afoot. Can you do that?"

"Yes, sir. I have already thought it through," answered Cassius. Once again Marcus thanked the gods that the young horseman had survived the destruction of the old First Century last year and was now part of his command.

"Gentlemen, we have much to do. Flavius and Demaratus, please remain." The centurions and Cassius got to their feet, saluted, and left.

Marcus turned to Flavius first. "Optio, we are going to need some of the men from the III Augusta. Do you think we can persuade some of them to join us without telling them about our plan?"

Flavius nodded. "I think we can, but we may have to take two of their officers into our confidence."

"Can they be trusted?" asked Marcus.

"I am certain of it, sir," replied Flavius. "They have no love for the governor and aiding us may help Rome decide to reconstitute the Legion. They want their III Augusta back. I can't guarantee how many would join us, but some will."

Turning to Demaratus, Marcus said, "Signifer, we can seize the ships, but we can't navigate them."

"I have been thinking about that problem, plus a few others, sir," said Demaratus. "We will need to take the ships out of sight of land before we head south, sir. We will need to know the currents and, most of all, calculate when we are off our landing site without using the coastline."

"Can you do that?" asked Flavius.

"It can be done, but I will need to spend time with the local sailors and fishermen," said Demaratus.

"But how can you figure where you are without seeing the land?" persisted Flavius.

"It is not as complex as it sounds. I need to know the

distance, our speed, and the speed of any currents in our path. You calculate the time involved and hope to end up where you want to be," answered Demaratus. "We will take precautions, of course. I may take a ship in toward shore to get our bearings, but so long as it is not the whole fleet, it should not give us away to observers on the land."

"All right," said Marcus. "I am releasing both of you for two days. Sextus and I will organize the century."

Flavius looked uncomfortable.

"Yes, optio?" Marcus prompted.

"The men are not going to like this, sir. They know we didn't win today, but they know they didn't lose either. It will look like we are retreating like whipped dogs," he said.

"Which is exactly what I want them to look like, Flavius," said Marcus. "The governor and the Mauri must believe we are a defeated cohort retreating to Hispania."

"But that will damage your honor, and hurt your standing, sir," persisted Flavius.

"I understand that, Flavius, but there is no other choice if this ruse is going to work. My honor is not so fragile that it can't take a dent or two," Marcus replied. "I want you to leave at first morning."

Both saluted and left, and Marcus slumped in a chair, hungry but too tired to chew. He knew he was taking a terrible gamble. A thousand things could go wrong. The cohort could get lost at sea. Cassius could be destroyed or miss the landing beach. A spy might ferret out the plan. Juba might defeat him. He sighed and made himself eat and drink. He fell asleep on the table. His dreams were troubled.

XXIII

The longer the captives were held, the laxer their guards became. Aelia and Rachel had volunteered to haul water and food for the slaves in the pens, and they were just completing their second trip when the gates flew open and hundreds of Mauri riders came pouring through.

The two women had heard them leave two days ago, but the guards, sullen and bad-tempered because they had been left behind, would not tell them anything. When Aelia asked one of the guards when he thought the riders might return, he snapped, "When they finish killing all the Romans."

The remark gave her a spurt of hope: Were they coming? Would she be saved? She immediately suppressed the thought. She'd had enough dashed hopes in the past several weeks. The one hope she clung to lay with Rachel's knife. It had been left by accident and was hardly a real knife, more like a cheese cutter. But it had a blade and a point, and Rachel had slipped a rock into the tent and used it to hone an edge on the blade. Small and ineffectual looking, it would kill, if necessary, either a guard or herself. She would not leave this place alive, of that she was certain.

When the horsemen returned, they seemed subdued, nor were they carrying any booty. The guard had either been lying or there had not been a fight. But then women started wailing and keening and Aelia could see that a number of the riders were wounded. There had been a fight, and it appeared that the Mauri had not won it. Unbidden, hope surged again.

"We had best get back to the tent," whispered Rachel. "Some of the women may decide to take out their anger and sadness on us."

As much as she wanted to stay and watch, Aelia recognized that Rachel was correct, though she doubted the men would let the two of them be killed. They still had value in the slave market.

She saw Himilco and Juba dismounting and handing their mounts to grooms. She wanted desperately to speak to Himilco. "Let me try to talk with Himilco," Aelia said to Rachel, only to be shushed.

"We are slaves. We do not initiate conversations, particularly with powerful men. We must act our place," whispered Rachel fiercely. "Avert your eyes and get back to the tent!"

Aelia did not think of herself as a slave unless she was trying to score rhetorical points with Himilco, and even then, it was an act. Rachel, however, had been born a slave and knew how one was supposed to act. Aelia was certain she would never learn it, which is why she clung to the straw of Rachel's knife.

The two women hurried past the men and horses and ducked into the tent.

Himilco and Juba sat on a rug sipping water and dipping bread into a mixture of olive oil and peas. They were alone in the tent—the other commanders and officers having gone off to find their families or feed and water their horses.

"What have we won here, my friend?" asked Juba leaning back on a bolster.

"We have forced the VII Legion to retreat, and we have bloodied them. I do not think they will be back," answered Himilco.

"But we did not destroy them and we should have," said Juba.

"Forcing them to retreat is a victory, and it will be said that Juba made the Romans run back to their camp. It will be easier to recruit among the tribes," said Himilco.

"We cannot defeat them with cavalry, Himilco. We might have today if the other soldiers and cavalry and those cursed archers had not showed up. But the Romans pay attention, in particular this group. If they come, they will come with lots of cavalry."

"Their cavalry is no match for ours, Juba," argued Himilco.

"Maybe not, but that was good cavalry we fought today. I would like to have their commander with the long lance riding with us," said Juba, dipping bread into the yellow-green mixture.

"It was the archers that saved them, not their horsemen," argued Himilco.

Juba shook his head. "Horse archers I understand. But archers who ride horses, that is new."

"But we drove them away, and we humiliated them. That is what our people will see," said Himilco.

Juba laughed. "Do you ever see the bad side of things, Himilco? If we had been defeated today you would be telling me that we were successful because the enemy used up all his spears and arrows and went to bed tired."

"And you see every flaw, every tiny crack," said Himilco.

"I do that because it is the flaws that can kill you. We need archers, or at least slingers. Cavalry is fine, but is not enough. And if we are really to drive these Romans out, we will need infantry," said Juba.

"We have our Libyans," pointed out Himilco.

"They are mercenaries, my friend. They fight for loot. We are fighting to take back our land," said Juba. "In any case, there are not enough Libyans, and even these are getting restless."

"Juba, our people are horsemen, not Roman legionnaires. We can't ask them to be something they are not," said Himilco.

"If we do not become something different, Himilco, we will always be a small people whose only friends are the mountains." Juba shook his head. "Fighting Romans is complex."

"I will grant you that," smiled Himilco.

"What of the slave merchants from the south?" said the Mauri leader, changing the subject.

"They should have crossed the Asama River today. I think they will be here in a week."

"Good. I am sick of these slaves, and we need to pay off the Libyans and give our people some money. We should divide up the loot tomorrow. It will keep everyone happy until the slave merchants arrive," said Juba.

"I will see to it," said Himilco.

Aelia and Rachel strained to lift the heavy bucket, finally slipping it onto the well's edge.

"What do you think happened?" whispered Rachel.

"I think the Mauri didn't win," answered Aelia. "But it would appear our side didn't either."

"Then we may have lost," replied Rachel grimly.

"I think not," said Aelia. "If we had lost there would have been a celebration."

"Let's get this water to the pens, then we can talk about it in the tent," replied Aelia, hefting two of the buckets. As she did, a gleam caught her eye. It was a knife, like the kind a butcher uses to cut meat from a bone. Animals were sometimes butchered near the well where the blood could be washed off. Someone must have lost the knife in the mud and blood. It had a wooden handle and a wicked looking blade. Rachel's little knife would do if they decided to commit suicide. This knife was a killer, and Aelia desperately wanted it.

Rachel followed her eyes. "If they catch us it is death."

"It is death anyhow," replied Aelia.

"On the way back," whispered Rachel.

Aelia hesitated. She wanted that knife because it seemed a gateway out of this place, although her rational mind told her she was just grasping. She wanted to grasp. She wanted to drop her buckets, snatch it up, and stab the first man she could find, to die in a flash of honor and glory, taking her tormentors with her. But Rachel would die as well. She steeled herself not to look at it, nodded, and set out to the pens.

The guards opened the pens, and the other slaves crowded around, passing the buckets around and drinking directly from them. The whole time Aelia could not get her mind off the knife, which she began to imagine was her key to freedom. She steeled herself to look exhausted, and patiently waited until the slaves had drunk. Then she and Rachel took back the buckets and pounded on the gate to be let out.

As the guards stood aside, Aelia said, "We need water for the tent," in what she hoped was a normal, conversational voice.

Rachel did not look at her but fell in beside her.

As Aelia got nearer the knife, she searched for ways that she could pick it up without drawing attention, but Rachel was already ahead of her. As they neared the knife, Rachel stumbled, sprawling forward over the knife. She pushed herself up, dusted herself off and picked up the buckets, stealthily slipping the blade into one of the empty buckets.

Aelia made a sympathetic comment and kept walking toward the well and then froze. Bogud leaned against the well rim, watching the two of them. If the man looked in Rachel's bucket, the woman was dead. She had to do something.

Taking a deep breath, she marched up to the well, put down her buckets, placed her hands on her hips, and smiled at the huge Mauri. "So, Bogud. Did you bring back a trophy from your great victory over the Romans?"

The man's face flushed with anger. Stepping away from the well, he slapped Aelia full in the face. "How's this for a trophy, Roman whore."

Aelia reeled back, tasting the blood in her mouth, her head spinning. Out of the corner of her eye she saw Rachel slipping by him, a move that caught his attention. "And where are...," Bogud started to say.

Desperate, Aelia mastered her dizziness. "It must be nice for you to have a Roman you can beat up, instead of ones that send you howling like a dog." She knew the word "dog" would get him.

With a roar of anger Bogud grabbed her by the throat and lifted her bodily from the ground. "There is only one dog here," he said, shaking her like a rag.

His massive hand had shut off her air and she struggled to pry his fingers off.

"Choke, bitch," said Bogud.

Aelia stopped fighting, rolled her eyes up and feigned unconsciousness, going limp in his grasp, her head flopping over to one side, although she was not entirely acting.

"Master, she is valuable," she heard Rachel say. Bogud sent her reeling with a backhand blow. But Aelia felt his grip on her throat relax, allowing her to gulp down some air. He pulled her close to his face. "You won't die this easily, whore." He dropped her where she fell into a heap at his feet.

Turning to Rachel, he said, "Water, slave of a whore."

"Master," said Rachel, bowing slightly and quickly pulling the bucket from the well and offering it to him. He grabbed it, took a long drink then flung the half empty bucket back at her, knocking her back into the wall of the well. Turning, he casually kicked Aelia, sending her sprawling on her back, and strode off.

Rachel dropped to her knees at Aelia side. "Are you alright?"

Aelia nodded, and looked a question at her.

"Come, we need to bring water back to the tent," she said, pulling Aelia to her feet and helping her to the well. She pitched the bucket back down the shaft, where it made a soft splashing noise. They pulled the well bucket up after giving it a few moments to fill, and poured it out into their carrying buckets. As she reached down to carry the bucket, Rachel slipped the knife into the water. The two lifted their buckets and trudged back to the tent. Rachel mastered her panic as they approached the two guards, but both were deep in conversation and waved them through.

As the flap dropped behind them, Rachel reached into the water and slipped the knife inside her shift. Aelia felt a jolt of pure joy: now they had real teeth if they needed them, and a way out if they wanted it.

XXIV

Flavius and Demaratus rode through a river bottom filled with early morning mist, climbed a gentle slope, and pulled their horses to a stop. Tingis lay sprawled out just ahead.

"We must be discreet, comrade," said Demaratus. Both had cast off their uniforms and wrapped themselves in the coarse hooded woolen covers of the locals.

"Easier for you than me," replied Flavius. "I am going to be dealing with men who know me. No sailors will know you."

"True, but if they do discover who I am they will also know what we are about. Someone returning to Hispania is not going to be interested in southbound currents. I will have to keep with Greeks. I am not sure I can trust anyone else," Demaratus said.

Flavius grinned. "I thought you said you didn't trust Greeks."

"In Greece I don't, but away from home is different," replied Demaratus.

Flavius shook his head. "Marcus is smart and the best commander I ever fought with, but what we are trying to pull off here has a thousand things that can go wrong."

Demaratus nodded agreement, leaning forward to pat his horse that had become restless with the smell of the city ahead. "We can do our part," he said. "I will leave you here, sir. It is best we do not enter the city together. I will go around and enter the city from the east where the docks are."

Flavius felt a surge of resentment at a junior officer telling him, a superior, what to do, but he dampened down the sentiment. The Greek knew far more about this kind of thing than he did, and the one indispensable part of this whole scheme was Demaratus's part in it. The moment he reached this conclusion his irritation vanished. Leaning forward, he grasped the signifer's hand. "May Fortuna ride with you, brother. I will see you at the boats."

Marcus had decided that it made no sense for the two men to return to the camp, which in any case would be breaking up and getting ready to march back to Tingis. Indeed, if anything would draw attention to their presence in the city it would be two men riding back south. They would slip into the cohort when it reached the city. Both of them were carrying their uniforms wrapped up in a blanket behind their saddles. They would each have to find a place to stay and to stash their uniforms until needed.

"And you, comrade," replied Demaratus returning the sentiment. He wheeled his horse and trotted off to the east. Flavius dismounted and sat for a bit so that he would approach the city alone. Eventually mounting, he walked the horse toward the main gate, pulling the hood over his head and tucking his face behind its folds. It was a good thing they had not stayed in the city when they arrived three weeks ago. Few in Tingis could recognize him, and, dressed as he was, he hoped no one.

He dismounted before reaching the gate and walked through, surrounded by traffic coming and going. Some merchants were headed out of the city to points south, while others were bringing in ox carts loaded with goods. Herders were shepherding goats and sheep toward the market, while farmers brought in baskets of onions, cucumbers, and vegetables he didn't recognize.

Two bored looking auxiliaries presided over the gate. Neither of them gave him a glance. So much for the governor's talk about the city's fear of the Mauri, and hence the need of the cohort to stay in the city. He turned off the main decumanis and into a side street, where he found a taverna.

Asking where he might find a place to sleep and where he could sell his horse, the patrons fell into arguing with one another over the best accommodations and who would steal him blind for his horse. He listened for a while until he got a general idea of where to find a place. The horse question settled itself when the proprietor offered to take the animal off his hands.

The price was low, but Flavius didn't care. It wasn't his horse. However, he made himself bargain over the price. A man who sold a horse without bargaining was probably selling you someone else's horse. They finally agreed on a price which was just high enough for Flavius to preserve his honor and low enough for the proprietor to be pleased enough not to question his good fortune.

Hoisting his bundle to his shoulder, Flavius went looking for a place to stow his uniform and take a bath. He would make contact with Quintus, the optio of the disbanded III Augusta, later. He needed a good soak first.

Demaratus sat tucked into a shadow near a warehouse, watching boat crews loading and unloading their crafts. The port was full of shipping, but it had a different feel than most. For one thing, there were fewer slaves. A lot of the work was being done by what were clearly local people, mixed in with the crews.

A ship nosing its way toward a quay caught his attention. It was a Liburna, a small, fast galley, a lovely little thing with Greek lines. But it wasn't what he wanted. He wanted fishermen. No one knew the sea like fishermen who memorized its currents and quirks, both as a way to find fish and to survive. They were also bolder than merchants, going further from shore, wherever their eternal search for a catch took them. The port had lots of fishermen, but so far, he had not seen any Greeks.

He pushed himself erect and wandered toward the nearest taverna. As much as he wanted to avoid being seen, it looked like he would have no choice.

Demaratus was getting ready to depart his fourth taverna when four men pushed their way through the door, all speaking Greek. There was no doubt as to their profession: the group trailed a strong odor of fish. And best of all, their Greek had a strong Attica accent, Demaratus's home province. As they commandeered a table and called for wine, olive oil, and bread, Demaratus took a seat near them. The men were boisterous—Demaratus worked out that they had just returned from Cartenna to the east, and the trip had been profitable—and he let them drink some wine before turning to whom he took to be their captain.

"It is a while since I have heard properly spoken Greek," he said. "Where do you hail from?"

The table went quiet for a moment. "Piraeus," the captain finally said.

"Does that thief Theomester still run the port?" asked Demaratus.

"What would you know of Theomester?" said the captain, a note of suspicion in his voice. In a strange port it was only sensible to be careful.

"Aristeus," answered Demaratus, "cargo master out of Piraeus. I have been running wine and marble to Britiannia. And you?"

"What are you doing in Tingis?" said one of the other men, ignoring his question.

Demaratus shrugged. "We made a profit, but just. I have a new venture in mind."

"And what would that be?" asked the captain.

"Something to the south," he replied vaguely.

The captain relaxed. If Demaratus had given him a host of details, it would have raised suspicions. No merchant voluntarily gave out any information.

Demaratus signaled the proprietor for more wine and after several cups the conversation grew animated. The four—the captain's name was Gelon—were mainly fishermen, but also carried some cargo. Demaratus also suspected they were not averse to an occasional bit of piracy.

Eventually the conversation worked itself back to Demaratus's "venture." The signifer feigned being drunker than he was and let slip that he and his men were looking for a ship and planning to sail a considerable distance to the south, though he gave no details and carefully deflected questions on what they might be after.

"Sailed in those parts?" asked Gelon.

Demaratus shook his head. "Never been south of Tingis. Have you?"

"We have fished south of Sala," answered one of them, taking a long pull from his cup. Demaratus signaled for more wine. The fishermen could drink.

Demaratus nodded. "What can we expect?"

Gelon poured his cup full and took a bite of olive oil and bread. "This time of year you want to stay away from close inshore."

"Why?"

"There is a current that comes up from the south. It's hard going inshore. Best to head out to sea. About 30 miles out there is a current that runs south. Pick that up and it will take you a long way," answered the captain.

"If I want to put into Sala, how do I find it?" asked Demaratus.

"There's a cape that juts out south of Frigidex. You can't miss it because it has a long arm of water landward of it that runs up to the north. It's like a long finger. A few hours south of the cape the coast dips in and Sala is right at the mouth of a river."

Demaratus wanted to ask about a beach south of the town, but he didn't want to give out too much information, particularly since it might raise suspicion about why he would want to put in at a beach as opposed to a port. Instead, he changed the subject to home, and the four fishermen brought him up to date on their view of current politics. By the time he managed to extract himself, it was dark and his head was spinning, but all in all he was rather satisfied with himself. He had even managed to extract an estimate of the distance and the time it would take to sail from Tingis to Sala.

By the time Flavius got to the tavern off the forum, the crowd from the III Augusta was already filling many of the tables and singing marching songs. The music suggested that the men had either been at the tavern all day, or had visited several others before ending up at their favorite gathering spot.

There was no way that Flavius could walk in without being recognized and that would be a very bad idea. He caught the eye of a young boy who was hanging around a vegetable stand, motioning him over with a lift of his chin. The boy approached Flavius tentatively. He was, after all, a stranger.

"How would you like to earn a coin, lad?" said Flavius.

The boy stepped back, unsure of what Flavius wanted.

"All you have to do is to go into that tavern over there and ask for Quintus Sextus. Tell him an old friend of his will be waiting right over there by those steps," said Flavius, indicating a temple at the forum's southwest corner. He held up a copper between his thumb and forefinger.

The boy still looked a little doubtful. "Who will I ask?"

"You ask the man with the apron behind the bar," said Flavius.

"Can I have the coin now?" said the boy.

Flavius gave him an exaggerated searching look. "Can you be trusted, lad?"

The boy grinned. "Yes, sir."

"Good boy," said Flavius, handing him the coin. The boy snatched it, trotted across the plaza and slipped into the tavern. A few moments later he re-emerged and ran back into the market.

It was several minutes before Quintus emerged from the tavern, accompanied by Macro, his tesserarius. Both had cast off their cloaks, and Macro was loosening his sword in his sheath as he came out the door. Careful lot, thought Flavius. Given the odd situation with the III Augusta, he didn't blame them.

The two men walked slowly across the plaza, scanning all corners, alert, slowing when they got to the temple steps. Flavius sat in the shadow of a pillar to make himself as invisible as he could, so much so that the two men did not notice him and passed right by.

Rising behind them he said quietly, "Comrades. It is Flavius of the VII Legion. Do not use my name."

Both had whirled at his words, reaching for their swords. Flavius made a quick survey of the plaza and the forum, but no one seemed to notice.

"What is this about, and why are you skulking about out here?" demanded Macro, still holding on to the pommel of his sword.

"Your comrades in the VII Legion need help, and I will thank you not to use that tone on a superior officer," growled Flavius.

"You're not my..." started Macro, but stopped when Quintus put his hand on his arm.

"What is afoot, brother?" said the optio.

"Can we find a place to talk and not be seen?" asked Flavius.

The two men looked at each other. "There is a temple to

Angerona near where we live. No one goes there anymore, and I have never seen a priest. I guess Angerona is one of those gods people have forgotten about," said Macro. "I don't think anyone would bother us there."

"If we both go with you now, it will get people talking," said Quintus. "We will meet you there in two hours."

Macro quickly gave him directions, and both men returned to the tavern. Following the directions, Flavius made his way across the city and, after casting about a bit, finally located the small, dark temple. It was a sad little affair, pretty much gone to wrack and ruin. The alter looked unused, and a small marble basin at its base was filled with dirty, stagnant water. A carving of the goddess above the door—her fingers pressed to her lips—had begun to wear away from rain and weather. "Goddess of secrecy, are you? Well, let's hope you can keep ours," whispered Flavius.

He pushed his way through the doors and looked around. Dried leaves lay scattered over the marble, and the place for the cult statue was dark. He made his way across the temple, looking to see if anyone was in residence. But there was no one, and if there had ever been a goddess here, she was long dead. He found it sad.

Flavius wrapped himself in his cloak and sat against one wall, his eyes on the door.

Slowly the afternoon darkened, and just at the point when he was becoming restless, Quintus and Macro pushed through the door. "Comrade?" Quintus called out.

"Here," said Flavius pushing himself up.

The three stood near the statue so they could watch the door, using the dying afternoon sun filtering through the door as light.

As quickly as possible Flavius laid out the scheme. There was no sense not giving the details of where the VII Legion planned to land, because both of them would figure it out anyway, on top of which the two men had to buy into the scheme. They would not go into something like this blind, particularly if they were leading their own men into it.

"How will you get the ships south?" asked Quintus.

"Remember that Greek I had with me, the signifer? He's a sailor. I saw him handle a ship through the biggest storm you ever saw just off Sardinia. We didn't lose a man and landed safe and fat," replied Flavius.

"Why would a sailor ever join the Roman Army?" asked Macro.

"I don't know," answered Flavius. "Greeks are odd."

All shook their heads at this obvious truism.

"Well, comrades, are you in?" asked Flavius after a short silence.

The men looked at each other and nodded. "We're in," said Quintus. "I think we can count on about 50 men to join us."

"You will have to tell them a tale, comrades," said Flavius. "If word gets out to what we are up to, the governor will send word south and Juba will fly the coop. Or worse, he will be waiting for us."

"I thought about that," said Quintus. "What I figured was that we could tell them that the III Augusta was going to be reformed, and that after the ships dropped off the VII Legion in Gedes, they would take us east to meet up with the rest of the III Augusta at Hippo Regius."

"How will they take it when they find out what is really up?" asked Flavius.

"A chance to stick our thumb in that bastard Domitius's eye? They'd follow your Marcus across the River Styx for that," put in Macro.

They settled on a schedule. The First Cohort would be in Tingis early the morning after next, and Quintus and Macro would meet them on the docks.

"Will there be enough ships?" asked Macro.

"Marcus sent a message to the governor yesterday night requesting ships," answered Flavius.

"Then they will be there," said Quintus. "The fat bastard would row them himself to get rid of your lot."

Flavius grinned. "We figured that."

The three arose, shook hands, and Quintus and Macro left. Flavius waited a half hour, and then left himself. He would lie up tomorrow in his room to keep out of sight. He wondered how Demaratus's mission had gone.

XXV

Marcus stood by the north gate, watching the cohort break camp. The men were packing up the tents and gear, while the officers bawled at them, joined occasionally by braying mules. The stakes that surrounded the camp were being piled for burning. There was no sense carrying stakes if they were headed to Tingis. He felt bad for the men, but their hangdog expressions and attitude of defeatism is exactly the way he wanted them to look.

Many of the men would not look at him, and even Sextus was strained and overly formal. He felt particularly bad about Sextus, but there was nothing he could do to take the man into his confidence. If he had, Sextus might have acted differently and that might have caused someone to guess that this was more than a simple retreat. The rigid hierarchy of the Roman Army meant that the men had to figure things out on their own, and they were masters at ferreting out their officers' state of mind. The fact that Sextus was so clearly unhappy would make them think that the cohort was really returning to Hispania.

At the same time, he knew that keeping Sextus in the dark would drive a wedge between Marcus, Flavius, and Demaratus on the one hand, and Sextus on the other. He would have to deal with it later, but there was nothing to be done about it now.

The job was finally finished, and it was still early morning. Even a foul-tempered cohort can get itself on the road in an hour. The cohort was lined up, four abreast under the signifers of their centuries. Sextus had pulled a man from the ranks to hold the First Century's signum, which caused no little comment. The absence of two out of his four officers had been a topic of discussion throughout the entire cohort. It was a weak spot in this plan: where were Marcus's signifer and his optio? Marcus told Sextus that both had gone into Tingis to help with the shipping. Sextus did his best not to look skeptical.

The four centurions converged on Marcus, and all five centurions stepped out of earshot.

"Any problems?" asked Marcus quietly.

"The men are feeling pretty down," remarked Publius.

Marcus bit back a tart comment that he could see how the men were feeling without Publius enlightening him. There was no sense in quarreling, but it annoyed him that Publius would point out the obvious.

"The governor sent word late last night that he was gathering the shipping. I have no doubt that it will be there," continued Marcus. "We will march straight to the docks."

"Any word on Flavius and Demaratus?" asked Manlius.

"No," replied Marcus.

He was about to order the cohort to march when there was a stir among the men up front. Sextus came trotting back. "Some

Mauri horsemen, sir. Say they want to talk with you. Say it's important."

"How many?" asked Marcus.

"Four, sir," answered Sextus.

"Should we deploy, sir? asked Publius.

"No. Sextus, you are in command of the century," he said and started forward.

"Sir! You can't just walk out there," protested Publius.

"Well, I could run, but it wouldn't be dignified," replied Marcus, drawing grins from the puppies. "Tell the archers to cover me."

The Mauri were drawn up in a little group about 100 feet to the right of the First Century. They were muffled in cloaks and hoods and unarmed as far as he could tell. Like all Mauri, they disdained saddles and guided their horses with a simple halter.

As he approached them, Marcus tried to think of why these horsemen would want to talk with him. Since they appeared unarmed, he kept his hand away from his sword, but he had taken his shield with him.

Drawing to within 20 feet of them, he stopped. "Well?" he asked.

The four horsemen did not reply, but one of them pushed back his hood and gave him a big grin. "Good morning, sir. Your Mauri ala greets you."

"Cassius? I would never have recognized you," said Marcus, relaxing.

"And we would like to keep it that way, sir. I have almost 60 men back in a small wash. The rest of the ala is already in Tingis telling everyone that the Mauri pretty much wiped us out. My second in command is solid; he will make sure there is no leak. Our 'casualties' will explain why so many of us are missing," said Cassius. "We have almost 70 extra mounts with us, so when we meet you at the beach, I can mount my men."

Marcus shook his head. "Well done, Cassius."

Marcus started to put his shield down, but decided against it. He would never lower his shield if the horsemen were really Mauri. "Let's talk a bit, Cassius, tell me your plan. This should look like a negotiation."

"Yes, sir," replied Cassius and went into the details of how he intended to swing his men to the east and then strike for the coast.

"How will you know where to head west?"

"The Sala will be the sixth river we come to, sir. We will cross it and follow it to the coast," answered Cassius.

"May the gods go with you, Cassius. We will see you at the beach," said Marcus.

"And you as well, sir," said Cassius, remembering not to salute at the last moment. The four horsemen wheeled their mounts and galloped off to the east.

When he got back, the four centurions were waiting for him.

"What was that all about?" asked Publius, with an edge in his voice. He was smarting over Marcus's remark about running.

"They said they could lead us to Juba if the price was right. I told them we had been too badly hurt in the last battle and had to return to Hispania to rest and reorganize. I think it is a trap, and in any case the last thing we want the Mauri to think is that we are ready for another fight," replied Marcus.

The four men nodded, although none of them looked happy.

No Roman liked to withdraw in the face of an enemy, even if it was a ruse. And there was no guarantee the ruse would work—in which case they were giving up their honor for nothing in return. Marcus sympathized with them, but at the same time he was growing sick of Roman honor. He was quietly elated, however, that none of them had seen through Cassius and his men's costumes.

The sun was beginning to climb over the mountains to the east when the cohort got underway.

Flavius and Demaratus had made their way to the docks separately, slipping through the largely deserted streets. They met where the ships were being readied and immediately made themselves officious and annoying, as if that was why they were there. Anyone who saw them would think they had been sent to help organize the cohort's departure.

Flavius filled in Demaratus on his mission, and the Greek seemed confident that he had the information he needed. By late morning the ships were lined up at the quays, and the First Century made its appearance. So did the governor, accompanied by his secretary, several local officials, and auxiliary officers. Flavius and Demaratus eyed them coldly.

"I'd like to cut that lot's throat," said Flavius.

"If we are successful, it will be the same thing," said Demaratus.

"How do you figure that?" asked Flavius.

"Juba will assume he has been betrayed. He will close off the south to our friend, the governor. This will make Rome unhappy," answered Demaratus, "Making Rome unhappy these days is not conducive to a long and happy life."

Flavius turned to stare at him. "How do Greeks learn to talk so pretty?"

Demaratus smiled at him. "It is possible your standard of comparison only makes it sound that way," adding "sir."

"Sir my ass," grumbled Flavius. "If I...."

Demaratus cut him off with a nudge. "Your people, I think."

A crowd of men, many of whom Flavius recognized from the tavern, were making their way to the docks, carrying sacks and chests. Quintus and Macro were in the van.

It was at this moment that Marcus appeared. The governor and his entourage made their way toward the centurion.

"Sir," said Demaratus to Flavius, "do you think it best that you greet our friends from the III Augusta? They came here because of you. I will let Marcus know you are with them."

Flavius resented Demaratus's prodding him, even though he had couched it as a suggestion. Except, of course, that like many of Demaratus's suggestions, it was sensible and Flavius considered himself a sensible man. He looked closely at Demaratus, but the man's demeanor was nothing if not respectful. Of course, the Greek could change personalities like a man could change his clothes, but he was right this time, which added an extra edge of annoyance.

"Don't give him any details," rumbled Flavius.

"No, sir," replied Demaratus looking like he swallowed the "of course not." Somehow watching Demaratus suppress a comment reestablished the balance, and Flavius went off to greet the men of the III Legion a more contented officer.

Demaratus edged over to where the governor and his men had surrounded Marcus, catching the centurion's eye. "Sir, a group of men from the old III Augusta is asking if they can come with us. They apparently miss the army, sir, and are willing to join up as legionnaires. I think we have enough ships because it is only a short sail across to Gedes. Is it all right if they join us? Flavius is speaking with them now."

"Take care of it, signifer. We lost a lot of men in the battle with Mauri; we can use the replacements. Tell Flavius to swear them in," said Marcus, looking harassed and exhausted.

"The man is good," thought Demaratus to himself as he returned to Flavius. Marcus looked for all the world like a beaten man, ready to go home. Glancing over his shoulder, he saw the governor looking properly sympathetic, his men all looking like they had attended the same school of acting. He longed to wipe away the smug, self-satisfied attitude that lay just under the surface. He felt a little tremor of nervousness: revenge would depend on him. If he failed to navigate the ships to the rendezvous, all would end in disastrous farce. Flavius and Marcus trusted him, which only showed how little they really knew about the sea.

The lead ship shouldered her way through the light Atlantic rollers streaming in from the west. By keeping his eye firmly on the horizon, Marcus managed to hold down the first warnings of seasickness. He could not afford to be ill at this critical time.

Behind his ship clustered a ragged fleet plowing through the gentle seas, the ships so packed with men they rode low in the water, some with no more than a few feet of running board. The land behind had begun to slip beneath the waves, and Hispania rose up as a growing blue mass to the north and east. Marcus shot a discreet look at Demaratus, who shook his head ever so slightly. They were still too close to Tingis.

Marcus wanted to pace, but there was little room for that, and in any case, it made him look nervous. He was not worried about the captain—what could he do in any case? —but it would make his officers nervous and that could be translated to the men. He steeled himself to wait, watching as the land on the horizon steadily grew larger. Seabirds, on the lookout for any scraps of garbage that might come their way, wheeled over the armada.

After what seemed like half a day but was probably no more than an hour, Demaratus pushed his way to Marcus. "We are far enough from Mauretania now, sir, and not close enough to Hispania for anyone to notice us."

Marcus nodded, caught Flavius's eye, and made his way aft to the captain and man at the tiller. "Sir," said Marcus politely, "Would you drop your sail and...." Marcus was trying to think of the words for stopping when Demaratus supplied them: "Heave to, captain."

The man looked at Marcus quizzically. "I can't do that sir. I have orders to take you to Gedes. The orders come from the Governor himself."

"Your orders have changed," said Marcus, "drop your sail."

"Now look here, sir, I have my orders and no centurion can override the orders of a governor appointed by the emperor," the man said hotly.

Flavius put his sword at the man's throat. "You would be surprised what a centurion can do," he said quietly.

The captain's eyes widened with fear. "You can't just take my ship, sir," he protested.

"We are not taking your ship or the others, just borrowing them for a few days," said Marcus. Turning to Demaratus he said, "Please see to the sail and signal the other ships to cluster around us."

Demaratus saluted, grabbed two confused looking crew members, and the three began unhitching ropes and lowering the sail. Some of the other ships were also lowering sails and a few were breaking out oars and beginning to row up to where the lead ship was now wallowing in seas. The other centurions had acted as soon as they had seen Marcus's ship drop its sails and heave to. Eventually, most of the ships were clustered together, although several remained outside the inner ring of vessels.

Marcus climbed on the stern railing and held onto the side of the tiller. He waited until he saw the faces of his men jamming the rails and straining to hear.

"Comrades of the First Cohort of the VII Legion Gemina Hispania Pia and our brothers from the III Augusta, we are going back into battle, only this time it will be on our terms. The Mauri think they have defeated us, which will only make our revenge all the sweeter when we strike them. Give a cheer, comrades. Honor and glory to our endeavor!"

A storm of cheers broke out. Men pounded one another on the back and some led a chant: "Marcus, Marcus, Marcus."

Demaratus was conferring with the man at the tiller and a glum-looking captain. The man nodded and turned the ship to the west, nosing directly into the rollers and heading out into the broad expanse of the Atlantic. The fleet—somewhat raggedly

—followed, spreading its sails but also dipping their oars into the sea.

To the east, Hispania slowly faded away.

XXVI

Aelia carefully surveyed the fortress compound, but she could see no sign of Bogud. Warily, she lifted the two buckets and stepped past the guards who barely gave her a glance. Rachel did not accompany her because one of the children was ill, and the Jewish slave had become the defacto nurse and doctor for the high-status prisoners.

She moved as quickly as she could, dropping the bucket into the well, drawing it up and filling her buckets. There was not much traffic coming in or out the main gate, which was flung open. She had a momentary vision of a column of Roman troops pouring through, cutting down the guards, a war horn sounding a blast. She quickly disciplined her mind to block it out. That path led to madness.

The weeks of hauling water to the slave pens had made her stronger, and she easily carried the two pails across the yard and helped dole out the water. The slaves in the pens asked for news, but she had nothing to give them. She smiled at them, however, patted the children through the pen bars, and chatted and gossiped. The guards frowned at her, but she disarmed them with a dazzling smile and a polite inquiry about how they were. They were very young men. A beautiful woman could make them awkward just by noticing them. They squirmed a little and pretended to ignore her, shooting her looks when they thought she wasn't looking.

She made several more trips to the pens and then finally headed back to the well to draw water for the tent. Himilco leaned against the wall, waiting for her. He looked grim and uncomfortable. A shiver of fear ran through her. She had a premonition of bad news.

"Greetings, Himilco" she said politely, stopping to push a forelock out of her eyes.

The man nodded, but didn't meet her eyes. The premonition grew, but she remained silent, waiting.

"You will be sold in two days' time, Aelia," the Mauri said with a rush, adding, "I am sorry."

"Sorry because your profit will not be what you imagined?" she said quietly, fighting to keep from crying. She would not give him the satisfaction.

"Of course not," he snapped. "If your friends had not been so cheap, we would not be having this conversation."

"If you had not come to my house and kidnapped me, we would not be having this conversation as well," she replied.

"Spare me your hypocrisy, Roman. How many Mauri have you taken from their houses and sold into slavery? How many millions from every corner of your empire have you dragged to Rome in chains?"

Aelia tilted her head back and smiled. "And so Himilco will

even the scales of justice, my captor who spins fine words about the evils of slavery and sells me into it. I have two days, sir, before my new masters arrive. Would you like to take me?"

She slowly dropped each bucket and then placing her hands beneath her breasts, lifted them up towards him.

Himilco flushed. The barb had struck home.

"Look who comes, master," she said. "Your comrade, Bogud."

Himilco turned and saw the huge Mauri, his face in its perpetual frown, striding toward the well.

Leaning closer to Himilco, Aelia whispered, "Tell me, master, if Bogud rapes me here, will that lower my value when I am sold? Should I resist so that you can profit? I am not clear on these things. Will you give me your guidance?"

"Shut your mouth," he said, his voice tight with anger.

"Of course, you are my master," replied Aelia, ducking her head and dropping to her knees.

Bogud had reached the well and suddenly looked unsure of himself. Aelia was on her knees, her head bowed, Himilco standing beside her, his hands on his hips.

"Ah, master Bogud," said Aelia looking up with a smile. "If you intend raping or beating me, I fear you must stand in line after my master Himilco. He has first claim."

The big Mauri looked confused, glancing at Himilco, who was looking equally uneasy.

"Here, masters," said Aelia. "Why don't both of you take me?" Dropping to her knees, she lowered her head.

"Shut up, woman," said Himilco. "Have you no shame? Get up."

"Shame is for those who are free, master. A slave has no shame," she said. She could see the blood rush to Bogud's face.

Maybe they will kill each other, she thought. Only the hope that she could humiliate these men kept her from giving in to despair.

Himilco reached down and yanked her to her feet. "You stand when I tell you to stand," he roared.

Aelia frowned. "It is so much harder to fuck when you are standing, but my master knows best."

"I'll fuck her," said Bogud reaching for her, only to have Himilco push him away.

"She is more valuable untouched, Bogud," said Himilco.

"Take your hands off me, Himilco. She is not yours. We all own her," bellowed the huge Mauri. "If I want her I can take her."

Himilco moved so swiftly that Aelia did not even see where the knife came from, but one moment he was standing to one side of Bogud and the next he had a blade at the man's throat. "Maybe you would prefer this, son of a goat," he said softly.

Bogud looked like he was going to bluster but stopped. Something in Himilco's eyes told him that what he did next would make the difference between life and death. He was silent a moment. "You have no special rights to this slave, Himilco. I intend to bid on her when she comes up for sale. I have the right to inspect my goods."

His tone was restrained, which probably saved his life.

"You were not going to inspect her, you were going to rape her," said Himilco.

"You cannot rape a slave, master Himilco," put in Aelia, so desperate was she to see these two men fall on one another.

"Shut your mouth," snarled Himilco, never taking his eyes off of Bogud and keeping the knife firmly pressed on the man's throat.

Bogud turned his eyes toward Aelia. "If you are my slave, do you know how long it will take for you to die?"

Aelia shrugged. "If you are to be my master, then my death will be by boredom, and boredom always seems to make things last forever."

Bogud smiled, although there was no humor in it. "Live your life fully, Roman whore, for you are mine day after tomorrow." He stepped back from Himilco's knife, adding, "and I will not forget this, Himilco of the Gaetuli".

"Your memory does not concern me, Bogud," said Himilco, keeping his blade in front of him.

Without another word, Bogud turned and strode off.

Himilco turned on Aelia, grabbing her by her arm. "Mad woman. Do you seek your death?"

"Seek it? I embrace it! Death holds no fear for me, Mauri, and because I do not fear death, I am afraid of nothing," said Aelia. "Not that pig Bogud, not you, not your fine Juba."

Himilco lashed out with his fist, sending her sprawling on the parade ground.

"Ah, yes," said Aelia, pulling herself up to her knees. "Tell me again, Himilco of the Gaetuli, about slavery. Beatings render your philosophy difficult to remember. Is it a good thing or a bad thing, I cannot recall." Struggling to her feet she swayed slightly, dizzy from the blow. "Strike me again. It may jog my memory, master."

Himilco reached out to steady her, but she pulled back her arm. "Touch me as your whore, touch me as your slave, but do not touch me as your friend."

Himilco took a deep breath. "I reached out to you because you are a person."

"A person? A slave is not a person. Will you think of me as a person as I die under Bogud's tortures?" she asked.

Himilco looked away, mumbling that Bogud would not have the money to purchase her.

"A promise, Himilco? I seem to remember other promises. This is as good as those," she said.

"I will talk to Juba," replied Himilco defensively.

Aelia laughed. She had long ago learned that the worst thing you could do to a man was to laugh at him. Himilco flushed, which only made Aelia laugh louder, although there was an edge of hysteria to it.

"Silence, woman," said Himilco.

Aelia immediately fell silent, but made a point of stifling her laughter. "Of course, master. May I go now? The tent is in need of water."

"Get out of my sight," he said.

Aelia bowed, picked up the two buckets and turned toward the tent.

She passed the two guards who stared at her. They could not have missed the drama at the well even though they were too far away to hear what had been said. She slipped the tent flap aside and stepped inside. She carefully put down the two buckets, then fell to her knees and began to shake.

Rachel was immediately at her side, drawing her into her arms. Aelia sobbed out the conversation with Himilco and Bogud. "We are doomed, Rachel. I cannot bear it. I will not give that man the satisfaction of my death."

Rachel held her, rocking back and forth. "I know, I know. But we must wait until the last moment. There is always the chance of rescue, and if that fails, our deaths on the eve of their auction will shame them. We must wait, trust me."

Aelia pushed away, holding Rachel at arm's length. "Do you speak truly? Or are you telling a child that the medicine will not hurt?"

Rachel put her hands in her lap and looked directly into Aelia's eyes. "I will send you beyond this world, sister. I pledge that on the memory of my people. But we will not pass through that door until the morning of the second day. Do you trust me?"

Rachel covered Aelia's hand with her own. "Maybe that will come to pass, but until it does, we will continue to live and help others around us."

XXVII

Marcus paced slowly back and forth near the ship's stern, willing himself not to look to the east where Demaratus's ship had gone in search of the landing beach. The trip south had been uneventful but disconcerting. Marcus had been out of sight of land on numerous occasions, but there was something about the vastness of the Oceanus Atlanticus that made him nervous. He had listened patiently to his signifer's explanations of currents and how ocean's rollers affected their course, but much of it went over his head. His seasickness did not help, although it was not particularly bad. He thanked the gods for that. He watched Demaratus heave a line overboard and somehow figure out their speed. But the sea was an alien place to him, and not just because it made him sick. On it he was powerless, at the mercy of forces that he did not understand.

The flotilla had moved south, flying before a steady wind and pulled by what Demaratus assured him was a powerful current. There were no markers to check their passage against, no capes, and no coastlines. They had to remain out of sight of land if they had any hope of surprising Juba. How could anyone find a specific point on a coast that was out of sight? As much faith as he had in his signifer, he glumly had to conclude this might be beyond anyone's capacity.

Flavius was trying to catch his eye, but he ignored the optio. He was too nervous to engage in conversation, so he ducked his head and paced.

"Ship," called out a voice from the bow.

Marcus went immediately to the side, quickly joined by Flavius. Sextus seemed to be keeping a distance, probably because he was hurt by being left out of the planning.

"Is it Demaratus's ship?" asked Flavius.

Marcus could not tell one ship from the other, but he answered "Yes," knowing that he was risking his reputation, but what other ship would be headed due west? Then the vessel dipped its sails twice, the prearranged signal that they had made a successful landfall.

Demaratus's ship had already begun to turn on its heels, using a combination of sails and oars. Marcus nodded to the captain. "Follow that ship," and the crew hoisted the sail and turned to the east. As Marcus's ship turned, so did the flotilla, thrusting its way through the quartering seas, and headed for the yet unseen coastline ahead. With the afternoon already drawing to a close, Marcus prayed they would be close enough to land when it was still light.

Within several minutes a blue bar appeared on the horizon and the coast grew swiftly. Demaratus's ship headed straight between two headlands, where Marcus could see surf reaching up a sickle-shaped beach, a small river flowing in on its north edge.

The beach was deserted except for a group of horsemen bunched where the sand gave way to a mixed terrain of scrub and trees. Marcus prayed the horsemen were Cassius's men. If they were locals or Mauri the enterprise was already a failure.

The sails came down as the ships approached the beach, and the crews backed water with their oars as sailors dropped off the bows holding ropes. Slowly they grounded the ships.

Marcus worked his way forward, vaulted the low railing, dropped into the waist-deep water, and waded ashore. A dismounted horseman—Marcus could now see it was Cassius—was waiting for him just above where the waves reached up the beach.

"Greetings, sir," said Cassius, saluting, still dressed in his Mauri costume.

"And to you, comrade," answered Marcus. "Report."

"Yes, sir," the Lusitanian answered. "We have located Juba's camp, although it is more a fort than a camp. It is no more than a two-hour march, but at night it will take longer. There are guards posted; however, so far we have seen no patrols. I think Juba believes he is safe."

"We will teach him that no one is safe from the VII Legion," said Marcus grimly. "How substantial is this fort?"

"I am not an expert in such matters, sir," said Cassius, "but the wall is twice as high as a man. There are two gates, with a tower at the main gate. The horses are kept outside in a series of pens south of the fort."

"Numbers?" asked Marcus.

"We were careful not to get too close, so I cannot be sure. There are certainly many more Mauri than we have. There are a number of camps near where the horses are kept. If I had to estimate, I would think 4,000 to 5,000 fighting men, and almost as many women and children," Cassius answered.

"Are you certain you were not seen?" asked Marcus.

"On the way here we encountered few people, and most barely gave us a glance. I think our costumes worked. I kept the bulk of the men far away from Juba's fort and scouted it with just two others. I am certain we were not observed."

The men were piling out of the boats and forming up around them. As the boats lightened, the sailors pulled them further up the beach. Flavius was in deep discussion with the two officers from the III Augusta. It looked as if they were arguing. Marcus would deal with it when he was finished with Cassius.

"Sir?" said Cassius, breaking into his thoughts.

Marcus pulled himself away from the argument. "Yes?"

"I have picked a route, and some of my men are cutting trees for ladders," said Cassius.

"What about the Mauri cavalry?" asked Marcus.

"The bulk of my men will attack the pens south of the fort. While some loop ropes over the corrals to pull them down, others will toss torches to frighten the horses," answered Cassius.

Marcus nodded. "Excellent, Cassius. Prepare your men to guide the cohort."

Cassius saluted and trotted back up the beach toward the other horsemen.

By the time Marcus got to Flavius and the III Augusta officers, the argument had cooled somewhat, although Flavius looked relieved to see the centurion. The optio quickly ran down the gist of it, which boiled down to the fact that the men from the III Augusta wanted in on the fight with Juba.

"Sitting around and guarding boats is not something Rome is going to pay a lot of attention to, Marcus," argued Macro. Marcus initially stiffened at the tesserarius addressing him by name rather than rank, but then remembered that both men—indeed everyone from the III Augusta—were only under the nominal control of the VII Legion. They were all essentially civilians. Giving them orders would only make things worse.

"We understand you want to be with us," said Marcus, "but if the boats aren't here when we get back, the only thing Rome will remember is that we all died in some harebrained scheme because we were too stupid to secure our ships. That wouldn't do the III Augusta any good, not that it would make all that much difference to any of us."

"We came to fight, not to nursemaid ships," replied Macro.

Marcus nodded sympathetically. "We all know that, but we are going up against five times our numbers, and it isn't all cavalry. Some of it is Libyan infantry. I think we outnumber the Libyans, but we don't know for certain. Their cavalry will have 10 times ours, and they know this ground. Unless we are lucky, or they panic, this means we get in, grab our citizens, and make a fighting retreat. Do you see it any differently?"

The two officers were silent. The fact that Marcus was talking to them as equals was making them think about the whole scheme, not just their own honor.

Finally, Quintus nodded. "That sounds right."

"Which means we have to have the ships here when we get back. Their captains and crews don't work for us, they work for the governor, and they would be out of here the moment we left. Sala is too far, and I am not sure that they wouldn't bar the gates against us," continued Marcus.

Quintus and Macro looked at one another. Finally the optio said, "We need to talk to the men."

"Of course," said Marcus. "If you need to, call on me."

Both men nodded and went to gather up the III Augusta.

"Think they will do it?" asked Flavius.

"Yes," said Marcus quietly. "They are good men."

Sextus appeared to report that the centuries were forming, and what the orders were concerning the slingers and archers.

"We need the archers, Sextus, with as many arrows as they can carry. We will leave the slingers with the ships so that the men from the III Augusta will have some cover fire," replied Marcus.

"The III Augusta will be staying with the ships?" asked Sextus.

Marcus indicated with his head where the III Augusta men had gathered around Macro and Quintus, and where a lively argument was going on. "If they don't, we might as well all climb back on the ships and go home, Sextus."

The argument among the men of the III Augusta had turned into a discussion with comments back and forth, pretty much paralleling the way the discussion had gone between Flavius and the III Legion's officers. Finally, Quintus broke off and walked over to Marcus. "I think you need to say a few words to them, sir." Marcus noted the use of "sir," indicating that at least Quintus was on board.

Marcus followed him back and the men from the III Augusta

gathered around him. The atmosphere was not hostile, but watchful.

"Men of the III Augusta," said Marcus. "Your comrades from the VII Hispania need your help. I know you would like to storm Juba's fort with us, and don't think we wouldn't want you by our sides. But we need a disciplined force to relieve us if we get back to the beach. We need someone to hold off the Mauri while we get our wounded and the citizens into the boats. Who else can we call on? I could leave a century here and take you, but you are legionnaires. You know a cohort fights as a unit. The VII Legion has trained together, fought together, we know each other. If our situations were reversed, what would you tell a century from the VII Hispania to do?"

The men were silent, but he saw many of then nodding their heads in agreement.

"I promise you this: if we all return to Hispania safely I will go to Rome in person to plead your case," continued Marcus. "I will take the citizens you have saved from slavery with me and present them to the Senate. In the meantime, I pledge that while we wait for the Senate to come to its senses," a comment which drew some grins, "you can serve with the VII Legion as your own century, with your own officers."

The men were openly nodding now. "We're with you, Marcus," someone called out from the back. Others chimed in with "Aye," and "We'll hold the ships safe and sound, sir."

Marcus raised his hands above his head. "Thank you, comrades. The VII Gemina Hispania will not forget this."

One crisis was solved, but there were many others waiting for him.

Cleomanes, the commander of the Cretians was insisting that Marcus discuss Xanthippus with him.

"Who commands him, sir?" the archer optio asked.

"You command, Cleomanes," replied Marcus.

"He says no one commands him, sir, because he is not a member of the Roman Army. He says he made an agreement to lead you to the Mauri camp and, in return, he seeks to avenge himself on this man, Juba," responded the Cretian.

"He is a Cretian like you, optio, can't you just settle this matter between you?" said Marcus.

"Like you Romans?" answered Cleomanes. It was a tart reply that bordered on insubordination but Marcus could see the archer commander was tense, his face tight with anger. Marcus made himself take a deep breath and not respond for a moment. It was clear that Cleomanes and Xanthippus had had words over the issue. Marcus needed to be careful. On one hand, he could not afford to alienate the man who made it possible for him to come to grips with Juba. On the other hand, he had to back Cleomanes. He could see Xanthippus hovering toward the back of the archers, watching the exchange between him and Cleomanes. Marcus beckoned to him.

Looking defiant, Xanthippus made his way through the archers and, after glancing at Cleomanes, faced Marcus.

Marcus leaned forward so that only the two men could hear him. "Xanthippus, Cleomanes is in command of the archers. While we are on the march to Juba's camp, you will follow his orders. After the attack begins, you are on your own and free to do as you wish. We do not need you to find the Mauri camp. My cavalry has already done that."

"They found it because I told them where it was," retorted Xanthippus. "Is this how the Roman Army repays its debts?"

"You will have your chance at Juba because of the Roman Army, archer. We cannot march unless we command those who march with us. Once we attack the camp, you command yourself. If that is not acceptable, you will remain here on the beach," replied Marcus.

There was a long silence between the three men. Finally Xanthippus said, "I agree." Marcus looked at Cleomanes, who nodded his acceptance.

Marcus signaled the Cretian optio to stay for a moment. When Xanthippus returned to the other archers Marcus said, "He is a man consumed with revenge."

Cleomanes nodded. "I would not be this man Juba," he replied. He saluted and went back to his men.

No sooner had Cleomanes left than the other centurions were asking about the march routine. What equipment? Two pila and two javelins, no food, but water. Where would the archers go? At the rear, which seemed to suit the Cretians. March routine? Two abreast to reduce collisions that might make noise, and not a sound until they were inside the fort. Each century hurriedly knocked together some scaling ladders and designated two men to carry each one. It was too far to carry a battering ram, and in any case it would take too long to find one. It would be over the walls with the ladders. If that failed—well, there was no need to plan for that. No one would make it back to the beach.

Darkness had set in by the time the cohort was off the beach and headed up a wide ravine. Cassius said the dry riverbed went almost to the fort and would offer the men at least some concealment on the march. On the other hand, the floor of the river was covered with rocks and patches of soft sand, which would have made marching difficult under any circumstances, but a nightmare in the dark.

Slowly, the cohort made its way eastward, paced by horsemen on each side. Every so often Cassius would appear and give a report on how close they were getting. Marcus initially worried about the time. The men had to be in place and ready to attack at first light, but there was little reason for concern. The cohort reached the jumping off point Cassius had elected two hours before dawn.

Removing their helmets, the centurions and Cassius silently crept up to a small ridge. Behind them on a flat pan of what must in winter have been a large pond, the centuries rested. Grouped into their eight-member contuberniums, they sat in circles passing water bottles among them and softly whispering. There was no need to tell the men not to make any noise. They were well aware of what would happen if they were discovered before the cohort could strike.

The fort lay in the middle of a broad plain. Marcus could see the wink of campfires beyond it to the south where Cassius said the horse pens lay. The wall they would assault was a good 200 feet long, with the main gate at its center. The gate was closed, and Marcus could see two sentries lounging in a small tower overlooking it. There was no other movement on the wall, which was made of roughly finished stone and covered with plaster. He assumed there was a platform running around the inside that would fill with soldiers once the fort was alerted to the attack.

To Marcus, the distance from the ridge to the wall looked to be about 400 feet, and he could see no moat or ditch surrounding it. Marcus supposed there could be some hidden "lilies" filled with sharpened stakes guarding the entrance, but he doubted it. This was not a fort that was built to withstand a siege and, given the Mauri were essentially horse people, that made sense.

"I want the First Century to take the right side of the wall, the Second the left. I want six ladders on each side. Third and Fourth centuries will follow them, and I want the Fifth in reserve but deployed on the fort side of the ridge. The archers will divide and follow the First and Second. I want them to keep those walls cleared. No noise until the gate is ours. Cassius will strike the horse pens first, making lots of noise, which should distract the guards on the tower. As soon as we hear the noise, we attack. Any questions?"

"Do we know where our citizens are?" whispered Manlius.

"We do not, but I assume they will be in pens, maybe tents. We don't know what we are going to find, so be ready for anything. Four blasts on the cornus is the retreat. Cassius, you will guard our flanks," said Marcus.

The rest of the questions were minor and technical. Marcus would not lead the First Century because he was acting as overall commander and would need to see the whole battlefield if he was to know when to commit the Fifth Century reserves.

When the commanders crept back to their units to pass on the orders, Marcus gathered his officers around him. "Flavius, you will lead the First Century. Your job will be to secure the gate. Sextus, you will be acting optio. Keep the men going up the ladders and over the wall. Demaratus, you will be with me.

There is no reason for a signifer in this action, and we won't get home without you. I will also need someone in authority to disseminate my commands. Questions?"

The officers looked at one another and shook their heads.

"All right. It should be light soon, so get the men ready," said Marcus. Flavius and Sextus saluted and left, leaving only Demaratus.

"Sir," said Demaratus quietly, "The captains are more than capable of getting their ships off the beach and out to sea."

"And would any of us know where they would take us?" asked Marcus. "If you were caught between us and the Governor, would you wager on the choice the captains would make as to what shore they would land us on?"

"No," said Demaratus, "at least not my life."

Marcus grinned at him. "Are you worried that you will miss out on the blood and glory by staying with me?"

"I am willing to make that supreme sacrifice, sir," said the Greek with a straight face.

"Well, I will certainly call your sacrifice to the attention of the VII Legion's legate," said Marcus.

"No need, sir. I would rather my deeds speak for themselves," said Demaratus, adding "exactly what is it you want me to do?"

"Just what I said. Stay by me and be prepared to fill in where I need you. We are going into this fight blind. I will need more than my eyes if we are to get out of it," replied Marcus.

The night sky began to lighten in the east, and the squads formed themselves into three lines with six ladders in the first row. The first row was handing their spears to the second. The men up front would need their hands free for the ladders and the fighting at the top of the wall. Everyone stashed their javelins, which would be used in the retreat. The archers deployed behind the third line, their quivers stuffed with arrows. More arrows were left with the javelins for the retreat.

Behind the First and Second centuries, the Third and Fourth were deployed in three lines as well. The Fifth was last, and they kept their extra spears and javelins. They would need them if the first four centuries were repulsed, or if they had to conduct a fighting retreat. The cornus blowers were carrying their horns with the mouthpieces to the rear so that they would remember not to blow them until ordered. The signifiers had put down their signums and taken up shields and spears. Everyone was needed for this attack.

The units had inched up so that they were hidden behind the ridgeline. To the east, the sky had gone from cobalt to dark gray, and some high clouds had caught the first red sparks of the sunrise. The lines were silent, the men as still as statues.

Suddenly there was the distant sound of men shouting and horses screaming. Cassius had struck the pens south of the fort. Marcus took a quick look down the line, drew his sword and pointed. The first two centuries swept up and over the ridge and across the plain. With the exception of the squeak of leather and armor, there was no noise. It was as if an army of ghosts was approaching the wall.

Both guards had been looking to the south and were still looking in that direction when they heard the sharp sound of the ladders striking the wall. Even before the two could sound the alarm, the first men were scrambling up the ladders. There was indeed a platform that ran around the inside of the wall, but no one was on it. One of the sentries called out, but his words were cut short by a well-aimed arrow. The second leapt from the tower and disappeared.

Legionaries were still climbing the ladders and disappearing over the wall when the gates swung open.

Marcus raised his sword and bellowed at the Third and Fourth centuries: "Drop your ladders. To the gate. Sweep the inside!" Turning to Demaratus he said, "Tell Cerficius I want him at the gate but not inside yet. We don't want to trip over one another."

Demaratus sprinted for the rear with the message.

Marcus ran forward to where the centuries were pouring through the gate. Flavius and Manlius had sent men along the platforms to secure the high spots of the fort, and the archers were already climbing the inside ladders to join them so that they could get clear shots at their targets.

Most of his men were in the fort before the Mauri began to tumble out of tents and barracks. He noticed heavily armed men who looked like infantry—most likely the Libyans—beginning to emerge from a group of several large tents. They would be his first targets, and he pointed them out to Flavius and Manlius.

He also began casting around for where the citizens might be. A group of pens lay on the left near a well. "Sextus," he called, "send two contubernium to free those slaves." The man nodded, called out some names and led the way himself.

At the far right of the compound was a large, ornate tent. That would be his second target.

XXVIII

Aelia planned to kill herself at first light and, her mind racing, had not a thought of sleeping. She and Rachel talked softly after the others had fallen asleep. Rachel slipped her the knife, but was evasive about what she would do in the morning. Aelia had already concluded that Rachel would not join her in death, but Aelia could bear it no longer. The two women had held each other, kissed, and Rachel had finally fallen asleep.

Aelia had no intention of falling asleep, but sleep ambushed her in the early morning hours, and she dreamed of walking a hillside outside Corduba. The ground was cool under her feet and a few scattered white clouds dappled the sky. She sensed she was with other people, but she could not see them, as if she had wandered off from a group of picnickers. There was a growing chorus of voices, but she could not see anyone. A wave of fear passed through her. Suddenly a great horn blasted, and she sat bolt upright, confused and disoriented.

"What was that?" asked Rachel, looking as if she, too, were still half asleep.

"A war horn, Rachel, a Roman war horn. I forget what it is called, but I have heard the soldiers blow it when they enter a town," Aelia answered, her excitement rising.

Then other noises began to filter into the tent, men shouting, and the sound of steel ringing on steel.

"Rachel, they have come for us," cried Aelia.

"We don't know that, Aelia. This could be a raid by other Mauri," answered Rachel.

"No, no, no. I know it is Marcus. I know it. He has come to save us. Quick, we have to be ready," said Aelia, scrambling to her feet and kicking some of the few people still sleeping with her foot.

"Ready for what?" a woman asked.

"They may decide to kill us rather than let us be rescued," said Aelia. "I have heard of this. We must defend ourselves."

One woman looked at her blankly. "Defend ourselves. With what?"

"Your nails, your teeth, whatever you have," cried Aelia. "We fight!"

Rachel dashed across the tent, snatching a small wooden table on her way toward the entrance. She wedged it so that anyone entering the tent would either trip over it or be forced to slow down before kicking it aside. Then she grabbed a round bronze dish, on which the guards brought them their food. Stepping back, she flattened herself against the tent wall.

Aelia followed her, but placed herself directly in front of the flap, behind the small table, so that anyone coming through it would focus on her. She whipped out the knife and held it with both hands in front of her. She had no illusion that she could stop an armed man from coming into the tent, but she would focus their attention on her, giving Rachel time to attack them from behind.

Aelia turned to the other women. "Take the children to the back of the tent. Some of you stay behind me as if you are supporting me. No one look at Rachel. We must keep their attention on us."

Some of the women were so terrified they could not even walk, and literally crawled to the back of the tent. The children, still sleepy, followed them or were swept up by other women and taken to the rear. Three women, pale and trembling, stood behind Aelia in a rough semi-circle. Rachel waited quietly near the tent entrance.

The noises grew louder, punctuated by shouts, terrifying screams, and relentless blasts from the horn. Aelia recognized orders shouted in Latin. This was no Mauri raid.

There was a stir near the door, and one of the young guards stepped through, spear in his hand. He saw the table and stopped, puzzled. Looking up, he saw Aelia, her knife outstretched and the circle of women behind her. He never saw Rachel, who slipped behind him, raised the heavy bronze dish over her head and brought it down with a crash on his helmetless head. The man staggered, dropping his spear, and Rachel slammed the dish against him and then beat him senseless as he lay on the tent floor.

Aelia knelt quickly, pulled the man's sword from its scabbard and handed it to a woman behind her. The woman looked at it dumbly until a younger woman pushed her aside, took the sword, and wielded it in front of her.

Rachel snatched the spear and slipped back to her post by the door, while Aelia tried to turn the man over to find his knife. But he was heavy and she was so excited and trembling that she couldn't manage it. A motion by the door caught her eye.

Stepping through the tent flap was Bogud.

He was wearing a helmet and breastplate and had his sword out of his scabbard. On seeing the man on the ground, he immediately stepped back. The move saved him from Rachel's spear thrust, which slid off his breastplate. He whirled, smashing her with his sword arm and sending her spinning to the tent floor. He stepped forward to finish her with his sword.

It was a fatal mistake.

All of the weeks of captivity, of shame, terror, and helplessness boiled over in Aelia to ignite her into an incendiary fury. Screaming like a vengeful Harpy, she ran straight at Bogud, who was distracted by Rachel. He raised his shield to keep her off, but Aelia slipped past it and drove her knife straight for his face.

Too late, Bogud realized his danger and tried to swing his sword back toward her, but Aelia would not be denied. The blade slid up the Mauri's cheek and into his right eye. He screamed and flailed at her, but she stabbed again, opening his cheek.

Dropping his sword he grabbed her, but not before Aelia drew the knife across his throat. A great spray of blood engulfed her, and Bogud's grip loosened, letting Aelia draw back the knife and strike again and again and again. Her fear and hate, coupled with weeks of hard labor, gave her the strength to break loose from Bogud's grip and to stab at him over and over. The huge Mauri staggered and fell back over the table. Aelia was on him in a flash, raising the knife over her head and plunging it into his neck.

As Bogud's struggles slowly subsided, Aelia saw another figure come through the flap, and she leaped up, stabbing at the figure. The knife slid off a shield and the man clamped her arm in an iron grip. She flailed at him with her other arm, trying to pull her knife arm free.

"Aelia, Aelia. It is Marcus," said a voice she dimly heard, as if from down a long corridor. She heard the words, but they did not register, and she continued to struggle. Finally, the man pulled her to him so she had no room to fight and pressed his face almost into hers.

"Stop, Aelia Dasumi. It is Centurion Marcus Favonius of the VII Legion. Look at me!"

Slowly the face under the helmet came into focus, the brown eyes and misshapen nose. She stopped struggling and looked at him. "Marcus? Is it really you, Marcus? I thought you would never come."

Marcus held her by her shoulders. She was drenched in blood, her hair awry and matted with gore, her eyes still wild. "I am sorry we came so late, Aelia, but we must quickly gather everyone up and leave. We are outnumbered," he said gently.

She nodded, "Yes, gather everyone up. Yes, Rachel will help," she answered in a dazed voice.

But Rachel had turned away from the scene at the entrance to a section of tent wall near her. The tent's fabric bulged inward slightly, until a sword tip appeared and sliced a long cut. A figure pushed through, stumbling on the lower edge of the tent. Rachel thrust the spear at the man, who deftly blocked it, but she spun the heel of the shaft around and smashed it into the side of his helmet. The man sprawled on his back, and Rachel aimed the spear at his exposed throat.

"Stop! Stop!" Marcus called out behind her. "He is one of us, a Roman."

Rachel had the tip of the spear at the man's throat. She halted her thrust but kept the blade under his chin. The man looked up at her, grinned, and winked. She almost stabbed him for his insolence. She pressed the tip of the spear a little deeper, which, to her great satisfaction, strained his grin a little.

"Flavius Priscus, optio of the First Century, First Cohort, VII Legion Hispania Gemina Pia, at your service, my lady," he said, eyeing the spear point. "If you take this spear out of my throat, we will see if we can't get you back home."

Rachel kept the blade point at his throat. "At home I am a slave, Roman."

Aelia pulled away from Marcus and went to her. "No, Rachel, you will never be a slave again. I promise you."

The woman slowly withdrew the spear point, allowing Flavius to scramble to his feet, picking up his sword in the process. Speaking to Marcus he said, "Hard fighting by the back gate, sir." Nodding toward Rachel, "Maybe we could get the Queen of the Amazons here to go over there and send those Mauri packing."

Rachel gave him a stony stare.

Marcus nodded, "As soon as we can gather up our people, sound a retreat." Turning back to Aelia he said, "Can you get everyone out and to the front gate? We have to go."

Aelia was calm now, though she was still trembling from the adrenalin coursing through her veins. "Yes, of course," and then, turning to the other women, told them to gather the children and nothing more. Rachel was already pulling women cowering at the back of the tent to their feet, prodding one with her spear. The woman who had taken the guard's sword had thrust it in her belt and then almost tripped over it. Soon a crowd of women and children were gathered at the tent flap.

"Rachel, take the rear and make sure no one wanders," Aelia said. Gripping her knife, she pushed herself through the tent flap and into the chaos of battle.

The fighting was concentrated by the back gate, and groups of men swirled around one another, smashing shields into shields, stabbing and slashing with swords. The line of Romans seemed thin to Aelia, while more Mauri kept trying to push through the back gate. As long as the Romans held the gate, however, the walls prevented the Mauri from using their superior numbers.

Aelia led the women and children across the compound and toward the front gate. The ground was littered with Mauri dead and an occasional legionaire. A number of the dead had been killed by arrows, which drew her attention to the platform surrounding the walls. She could see archers crouched down and firing shafts into the crowd of Mauri at the back gate.

An officer—a very good-looking Greek with an impeccable uniform—ran toward her. "Lady Dasumi?" he asked. She nodded acknowledgement. "Take your people outside the front gate. There is reserve century there."

"I must get the people in the pens," said Aelia.

"Already done, Lady Dasumi. Quickly now. We will be sounding a retreat any moment," said the officer.

She hesitated. "You're the Greek, aren't you? You are Demara-tus," she said.

He gave her a curious look. "Yes," he said simply.

She reached up, took his face in hers and kissed him fully on the mouth. "Thank you Demaratus, friend of Marcus," she said.

He laughed. "It pays to be a friend of Marcus, Lady Dasumi. But please...."

She laughed back at him, giddy with her freedom and the moment. She led the group through the gate and toward a line of men with shields, which she took to be what Demaratus called the "reserve century."

Himilco struggled to force his way through the back gate. He had thought to take a group of men around the wall and fall on the enemy rear, but the cursed Roman cavalry was blocking his attempts. The Mauri horses had been scattered in the first moments of the battle, and he had nothing but dismounted men. Every time he attacked Roman horsemen, they fell back, but then counterattacked, riding into his flanks and rear. His men were unused to fighting on the ground, so they were uncoordinated and got into each other's way. The Roman cavalry, on the other hand, was skillfully handled, constantly keeping Mauri off balance and intimidating them with charges.

After failing to work his men around the cavalry, Himilco began sending them to the back gate, where he hoped the weight of numbers would finally break through the Roman lines. But the gate kept the front small, so even though the Romans were outnumbered, Himilco could not get his superior numbers into the battle.

The main problem was that he was confronting the Romans at what they did best. The Libyans were inside the fort, but pinned to the sidewall, trying to avoid the archers. Himilco could not get to them or even see how the battle fared. He suspected the Libyans were busy defending themselves. They had not hired on to fight Roman legions.

Slowly, the Romans began backing up, letting more Mauri crowd into the gate to try to slip around their flanks. But the Romans were fighting well, and the Mauri were losing men. Most of the Mauri did not have full armor and carried small cavalry shields. The enormous Roman scuto not only gave the legionnaires protection, they were effective as battering rams. When the Mauri pressed too close, the lethal Roman short swords stabbed from between the wall of shields. The Mauri, pushing forward, were forced to drag the dead and wounded away before they could get at the Romans, on top of which the Roman archers were taking a steady toll on his men, particularly anyone who looked or acted like a commander.

The Roman war horn blasted again, but this time it had a different note. It quickly became apparent that the soldiers were retreating, albeit in good order. More and more Mauri pushed into the fort, but the Romans had secured their flanks with the inside walls, and Mauri were beginning to flinch from frontal attacks on the wall of shields.

Juba was suddenly at his side. His left arm was streaked with blood, but Himilco could see no wound.

"Are you all right, Juba?" asked Himilco.

Juba nodded, and then shook his head. "We should have expected this."

"We were betrayed by that worm of a governor," said Himilco hotly.

"Maybe. Maybe that Roman bastard over there is smarter than we thought he was," replied Juba.

"The men are gathering up horses. We will see how smart he is when we have our cavalry," said Himilco grimly.

The Romans were retreating across the parade ground, but keeping in good order. Himilco noticed the arrows had stopped. The archers had already cleared the walls. As he swept the walls with his eyes something caught his attention. One archer looked vaguely familiar. Then recognition came: Xanthippus! How was that possible?

"Juba, watch out...," he started, but the arrow struck the Mauri commander in his right eye, burying itself deeply into his skull. Juba dropped without a sound.

Himilco knelt and lifted Juba by his shoulders, but he could see the man was already dead. He clasped the Mauri to his breast and held him, rocking back and forth for a moment before laying him down. A number of other Mauri had begun to gather around. It was a dangerous moment. Juba's death could take the heart out of the Mauri attack. Himilco rose to his feet. "They have killed Juba. Revenge! Revenge! The Romans must die! Fall upon them, brothers!"

XXIX

Marcus watched the Mauri crowding through the back gate. Maneuvering his men would be tricky. He needed enough men to prevent the Mauri from slipping around his flanks, but not so many that there would be a crush of Romans as they retreated through the front gate. He thanked the Gods that the Mauri had no archers, so there was no need to form a testudo.

"Publius! Aulus!" he cried out, catching the centurions' attention. "Move your centuries out the gate. Tell Cerficius I want the Fifth ready to counterattack." Both men acknowledged him, passing orders on to their officers. Turning to Manlius on his right, he said, "The Second will stand with the First."

The Mauri had flung themselves with renewed fury at the Romans, but the legionnaires were backing up in good order. Glancing over his shoulder, Marcus could see the men of the Third and Fourth centuries stepping out of line as the men from the First and Second filled in. The gate was no more than 40 feet behind them, and their front was now narrow enough to make it difficult for the Mauri to flank them.

Still and all, it was hard fighting. What the Mauri lacked in armor and infantry tactics, they did their best to make up with fearlessness. But fearlessness against Roman infantry was expensive, and the Mauri were paying a fearful cost for their courage. Marcus worried most about the Libyans, but they were nowhere to be seen. They had been hurt in the fighting by the far wall, and it was possible that they had had enough.

"Manlius," Marcus called across to his left. "Get ready to take the Second out the gate. The First will cover you."

The man nodded and signaled his optio. Marcus saw Flavius and Sextus instructing the men on covering the retreat of the Second. There was a sudden lull in the attack as the Mauri fell back, exhausted for the moment. The respite allowed Marcus and his officers to align the First to defend the gate, while the Second slipped out behind them.

Now the front was only about 25 men wide, and Flavius was rotating the troops so that the front line stayed as fresh as it could be after almost an hour of fighting. There were several spirited attacks on his line, and then the Mauri fell back once again, many of them dragging their dead and wounded.

"Optio," shouted Marcus. "Tell the Fifth to be ready. Sextus, the century will fall back to my right. Clear a path to the gate for the Fifth."

The First's front line backed out of the gate and swung to one side of the wall. The Mauri hesitated for a moment, then poured into the vacuum, directly into the teeth of the Fifth Century. A wave of spears, quickly followed by another, caught the Mauri packed at the gate. The small shields were no defense against the heavy pila spears, and even those wearing armor fell before the onslaught. The attack collapsed, with most of the Mauri falling back into the fortress, leaving a wall of dead and dying jammed into the gate.

The drop off in the attack allowed the cohort to reform. Cassius came dashing up on a horse flecked with foam and wounded in the flank. "Sir, the Mauri are remounting. There are not a lot yet, but they outnumber us. We should begin to fall back. We will try to keep them off your flanks."

Marcus nodded an acknowledgement and looked for Demaratus. The Greek slipped through a picket line of cavalry and strode toward him. "Sir, I have started the citizens toward the coast. A contubernium from the Fourth is leading them. I gathered the archers and told them to await your orders."

Not for the first time did Marcus think that Demaratus was probably the second-best officer in the VII Legion.

"Demaratus, tell the archers our main problem will be the Mauri cavalry. We can handle any infantry or dismounted horsemen they throw at us. Their instructions are to spread themselves out along the line of retreat and kill horses. I don't care about Mauri. I want dead horses."

"Yes sir," said Demaratus, and vanished back into the lines of infantry that were already beginning to form.

Marcus called a quick meeting of the four other centurions. "Keep a wall of shields on our flanks, comrades. I want those Mauri to think twice about charging our lines. The archers will be inside our lines with an order to kill horses. Route march. Don't let the men think we are in flight. This is a fighting retreat. Questions?"

"What order, sir?" asked Publius.

"Your Third will lead, Publius. Aulus, you follow with the Fourth. Manlius, put your Second behind Aulus. The Fifth will hold the rear guard. We will be right behind you, Cerficius."

The officers scattered to move their centuries into place. Only Cerficius remained. "The rear line will have to face the enemy and also retreat at the same time," said Marcus to the young centurion. "It is tiring to walk backward. Rotate them often."

"Yes, sir," said Cerficius, "and thank your for this honor. I hope your trust is well placed."

"You did a fine job at the gate, Cerficius. You will do a fine job on this," replied Marcus.

"Even if I am just a pup, sir?" said the Fifth's commander with a grin.

Marcus grinned back at him. "Show the Mauri that Roman pups have sharp teeth."

"Yes, sir," replied Cerficius, saluting, turning to organize the rear guard.

Flavius and Sextus had already gotten the First Century in line. The men would march two abreast, the lines spread about 10 feet apart. In essence it would be a wall of shields on both sides with archers and officers ranging in the middle. Cassius's cavalry was swirling around the edges, a hundred or so feet from the lines of men. A group of Mauri horsemen came charging out of some brush, but the Lusitanians drove them back.

The single line of shields on both sides was a risky formation. If the Mauri eventually mounted enough horsemen, the Roman lines would be vulnerable. The Mauri could cast their javelins across the line of shields they faced, so that they fell on the undefended backs of the men on the opposite line. If that became a problem, Marcus would have to pull men from the front lines and form a modified version of the testudo. That, however, would weaken his front lines and slow down the retreat. For the time being, however, it was not a problem.

It had taken the cohort a little more than two hours to reach the fort, but that was at night, and the march was mostly uphill, gradual though it was. In full daylight, headed downhill, the cohort moved swiftly. Marcus had expected hard fighting all the way to the beach, but the Mauri attacks were disorganized and it was hard for the horsemen to get at the legionnaires. The wide gully down which the cohort marched made it difficult for the Mauri cavalry to maneuver, particularly when they were under fire from the archers and had to deal with constant counter attacks by the Roman cavalry. Marcus drifted back toward the rearguard, but the rearguard was quieter than the flanks.

A few of the Mauri had spotted the formation's vulnerability, however, and had begun throwing their javelins and spears over the heads of the front line to fall on the men facing away from them. Marcus pulled out every fourth man and set them among the archers with orders to stop the javelins and spears with their shields. Still, some got through, but the inner line of shields stopped most of them. And while it did slow down the retreat, the cohort was making good time.

As they approached the coast—Marcus caught a whiff of salt air that told him they were close—the attacks increased. Cleomanes appeared to report that the archers were low on arrows. Marcus was starting to worry when a runner came back from the leading century with news that the beach was in sight, and that the III Augusta had dug a ditch and built a barricade of sharpened stakes.

"I want the slingers to move up to the barrier, and tell Centurion Publius Fulvius to get the citizens on board the ships," said Marcus. The man saluted and dashed back down the trail toward the beach. "Cleomanes, pull your men out and get them to the ships and the reserve arrows. Hold your fire until the First Century makes a dash for the boats. We will defend the barrier until everyone is on board." The Cretian commander saluted and started calling out the names of the archers as he headed for the beach as well. Soon a group of them followed him.

Marcus found Cerficius at the rear of the column where the Fifth had just beaten off a Mauri charge. Marcus noticed the Roman cavalry was getting thin. Cassius had been taking casualties, and the weight of the Mauri numbers was beginning to tell. Out of the corner of his eye he saw a Roman cavalryman supporting a wounded comrade, while a third rode behind him. But he could not see Cassius anywhere.

"Cerficius," Marcus said to the commander of the Fifth, "The First will hold the barrier the III Augusta built for us at the beach. Slip your men through the stakes and go straight for the ships."

"Good men, that III Augusta," said Cerficius, who was looking a good deal older than he had yesterday. Marcus was certain that the Fifth's commander had lost his "puppy" nickname. The rearguard century had seen hard fighting the whole way to the beach, and the men were looking exhausted, although Marcus noted they perked up considerably as Cerficius's officers passed on his orders: the end of this fight was near.

Next, Marcus found Sextus and Flavius—he hoped that Demaratus was already loading the civilians on board and would get the first ships out to sea—and told them his plan.

"Yes, sir," said Flavius. "As soon as we see the ditch, we will get the men over it and through the barrier. What about the III Augusta?"

Marcus was distracted for a moment. A Mauri charge had driven in a flank of the First Century, but the horsemen were at a disadvantage in the rocky gully bottom, and the legionnaires inside the front lines quickly surrounded them, hamstringing the horses and stabbing at the animals' flanks and faces. Most of the horsemen pulled back, but the riders whose horses were disabled were pulled off and killed. One managed to roll away and make a successful dash for the gully's rim.

"Let them stay with us. We need the support and they should have the honor of fighting," replied Marcus, bringing his mind back to Flavius's question.

Another runner had appeared, saying the Third was through the barrier and the Fourth and Second centuries wanted orders. "Tell Centurions Aulus Junius and Publius Fulvius to leave whatever pila or javelins they have left with the III Augusta and board the ships. My tesserarius will be in charge of loading them on." The man vanished.

Flavius tapped him on the shoulder. "Ditch in sight, sir."

Marcus glanced over his shoulder. It was not a major barrier—Quintus knew that the First Cohort would need to cross it rapidly—but it was enough to keep the horses at bay for a bit. The sharpened stakes were set about five feet apart. They were not meant to be a full defense barrier, just something to slow down a cavalry charge and keep the Mauri at a distance. Marcus could see the men from the III Augusta manning the barrier with thickets of javelins and pila beside them. The first men from the Fourth Century were already crossing the ditch and climbing the dirt wall. Men from the III Legion were helping them up.

The Mauri must have seen the same thing, and the attacks were now almost continuous. The men from the First Century were dropping down into the ditch, their shields to the rear since the ditch prevented any flank attack by the horsemen. He looked around for Cassius, suddenly worried that the men at the barrier would not be able to distinguish his men from the Mauri. But the Roman cavalry seemed to have vanished. He hoped they had not been overrun. He was very fond of Cassius.

A Mauri cavalryman some distance from the Fifth Century's line was suddenly unhorsed. Marcus caught the whistle of the slingers' projectiles. Against any unarmored Mauri, sling projectiles would be almost as deadly as arrows, and they would play havoc with the horses.

Marcus jumped into the ditch and walked at a sedate pace toward the stakes. He wanted no whiff of panic to affect the troops. Reaching the berm, he sheathed his sword and scrambled up. A few hands helped pull him over at the top.

Quintus Sextus and Macro Lusilius—looking pleased with themselves—were both there to greet him.

"Welcome, back, sir," said Quintus. "Orders?"

"The First will fall into line with you, Quintus, while the Fifth retires to the boats. Can the III Augusta cover our final retreat?"

"Aye," grinned Quintus, "that we can."

Marcus glanced toward the boats and saw that two were already off the beach and turning their bows toward the open ocean. Soldiers were wading out and climbing aboard other ships, while others waited their turn on the beach. Demaratus moved among the troops and pointed out ships to the officers. Several archers had already climbed to the bows and were ready to cover the III Augusta's last dash.

To Marcus' relief, he saw Cassius wheeling a group of cavalry to the south. A stream and swamp covered the northern flank of the beach, so the only danger of a Mauri flank attack would come from the south.

The Fifth was now streaming across the ditch while the slingers pelted the bolder of the horsemen who tried to follow them. Marcus glanced up and down the stake barrier. He had about 130 men, but those from the First Century were exhausted. The 60 soldiers of the III Augusta would have to bear the brunt of the fighting if things turned desperate.

The Mauri were gathering on the far side of the ditch, and Marcus saw a leader moving among them, urging them on, and getting some of the men to dismount. Marcus wished he had some archers. He would have dearly loved to bring the man down. He pointed him out to slingers, but the man was outside effective range.

A surge of horses poured into the ditch, and the riders tried to get close enough to throw their spears at his men, but the area was small and crowded and it was hard to maneuver the horses. On top of which, soldiers rained pila and javelins down on them. The horses were so packed it was almost impossible to miss them, and the attack collapsed.

Several hundred dismounted Mauri followed, leaping into the ditch and scrambling for the barrier. Again, the pila and javelins took a heavy toll, and the slingers systematically picked off anyone who came close to the stakes. A few groups managed to make it up the barrier, where they were met by a wall of shields and armored infantry. That attack, too, fell back, although the Roman troops were running low on spears and javelins. While the slingers continued to pummel the men in the ditch, the soldiers hoarded their last pila.

More ships were pushing off, and the beach was slowly clearing. Marcus signaled Sextus and Flavius to start moving squads of the First toward the boats. The line began to thin, although the Mauri seemed to have lost some of their appetite for close-in fighting.

Marcus caught Quintus's eye, and the optio strode over to where he was standing behind the stakes. "Quintus, your men are going to have to make a sprint for the boats at the end. Archers will cover us, but no rearguard fighting. Have the men drop their shields and go for the boats."

"Right. We won't be sorry to see the last of this place, sir," said Quintus, who headed back to where he had left Macro, his tesserarius, to pass on the orders.

A commotion on the right turned out to be the Roman cavalry dismounting. Cassius put his sword to his horse's neck and sliced the huge artery running up its center. The horse screamed, and Cassius whacked it with his sword, sending it toward a line of Mauri working their horses down a steep slope to the beach. His men quickly followed his example, until a stream of horses gushing blood and mad with panic thundered through the Mauri line, scattering and disorganizing it.

Cassius saw Marcus and trotted down the beach, arriving breathless. His Mauri garb was bloodied, but it was hard to tell if the blood was his, an opponent's, or his horse's.

"Sir," Cassius gasped, then remembered and saluted. Marcus grinned at him. "No need, commander, just report," he said.

"We will keep the Mauri off our flank, sir. The soft sand will make it difficult for them to use their horses. But we can't hold long," gasped Cassius.

Marcus could see that the Mauri, who had recovered from the flood of panicked horses and had managed to get their own mounts down to the beach, found them floundering in the sand. The dismounted Roman cavalry made short work of them. But Cassius's line was thin, no more than 40 men, and as unarmored as the Mauri.

"Sextus," roared Marcus, "send two contuberniums to support the cavalry."

The tesserarius nodded and designated two squads of the First Century to back up Cassius's men. They were only 16 men, but they had armor, their huge infantry shields, and a phylum apiece. Plus, they were used to coordinating their attacks. They ran up the beach and threw themselves into the battle of the sand dunes.

Even with the infantry, however, the right flank could not hold for long. "Cassius, attack the horsemen, then make a dash for the boats."

"Sir, wouldn't it be better...," started the Lusitanian.

"Follow your orders, commander," snapped Marcus. The

centurion knew Cassius wanted to hold the flank to be sure the Mauri horsemen wouldn't get between the retreating III Augusta and the boats, but even if the enemy horsemen did, they would be under fire from the archers and quickly overrun and destroyed.

Cassius raced back up the beach, shouted some orders Marcus could not hear, and the surviving cavalry, with the two squads from the First Century, went on the offensive, smashing into the milling Mauri horsemen. The attack was a surprise, and Mauri did what any sensible cavalry would do— back off and regroup. The Roman cavalrymen made a dash for the boats, followed by the infantry squads.

Quintus had seen the maneuver and stretched his line to cover part of the flank, but the Mauri continued to mill around on the ridge above the beach. The dismounted Mauri were also holding back.

It was time to go.

"Quintus," called out Marcus, and pointed to the boats, which had cleared the beach and were gently rocking in the surf, rope lines cast down for the men to board. As the men started up the ropes, hands reached down and hauled them aboard. Demaratus was still on the beach.

"Men of the III Augusta," bellowed Quintus, "drop your shields and board the ships. Now!"

The men planted their shields in the ground—they might cause the Mauri to hesitate, being unsure if anyone was behind them—threw their final spears and javelins, and ran toward the boats. The cavalry was already clamoring aboard as the men from the III Augusta waded into the surf and grabbed hold of the boarding ropes.

There was a wild cry from the Mauri, who flooded over the stakes and down to the beach, while their cavalry struggled through the sand. But most of the boats were already headed out to sea, and archers cut down the Mauri who reached the surf line, trying to stop the last of the Romans from boarding the ships.

Demaratus was suddenly at his side. "Sir, now. Come with me," and he took Marcus's arms and pulled him toward a ship that was already fully loaded and rocking in the waves.

The two men waded into the surf. They were chest high before they made it to the hands reaching down for them. Almost as soon as they were pulled clear of the water, Demaratus called out, "Back oars," and the ship moved away from the beach into deeper water.

The last two ships near the beach were following them, while the Mauri poured down to the beach. But there was nothing the Mauri could do except throw a few javelins and rage.

Demaratus told the helmsmen to port his helm and the oarsmen "to dig." The ship slowly spun on its axis and headed out to where the rest of the fleet waited, bobbing in the waves. The last two ships trailed behind. A great cheer went up from the ships, with men waving their shields and pounding their swords.

Aelia and Rachel crowded by the railing, watching the last ships pull away from the beach. "Do you see him?" asked Rachel.

"I am not sure. I saw the Greek board with someone wearing

a centurion's helmet, but it was too far for me to see a face. I pray the gods he is safe," she replied.

Rachel patted her arm. "I am sure he is. He is a smart one, your Marcus."

"Yes," but Aelia wondered whether Marcus was hers, or even that he wanted her after the way she looked when she encountered him in the tent. Her hair was still matted with blood, her gown now pink where the sea had diluted it. She shuddered. Misinterpreting her tremble as cold, Rachel put her arm around her and drew her to her side.

"Rachel, you will always be my friend, won't you," whispered Aelia.

"Of course, mistress," started Rachel, but Aelia cut her off. "I am not your mistress. No one will ever be your mistress," said Aelia fiercely. "Aelia Dasumi calls you her sister. Will you be my sister, Rachel?"

Rachel looked into her face, "Aelia, I am still owned by another, and...."

"No! Do you think I would let them take you for a moment? You are free from this moment on. No one will dare say otherwise. This morning I was a slave. Now I am Aelia Dasumi. And you are my sister."

"Well, they wouldn't argue with you looking the way you do right now," said Rachel with a ghost of a smile.

"And they would be wise to avoid that encounter," replied Aelia, answering her with a broader smile. The two women kissed and embraced.

Then Rachel pushed her away from her and looked her over

critically. "But we will have to do something about the way you look. What will your centurion think?"

"He will think that being polite to Aelia and Rachel Dasumi is good for his health," she said putting her hands on her hips and throwing back her head. Both women dissolved into laughter that drew some odd stares from both soldiers and former slaves packed into the ship.

Himilco sat on his horse overlooking the beach. The Roman ships had clustered offshore waiting for the final stragglers, but were now raising their sails and heading out to weather the cape north of the beach.

Anger, bitterness, sorrow welled up, threatening to overwhelm him, but he drew a deep breath. The battle was lost, the war had just begun. He must now play Juba. He knew the tribes would scatter, but he would be patient. The memory of the defeat would eventually dim, and Himilco would carefully stoke the anger and the desire for vengeance. "We did not lose, we were betrayed by the Romans we thought our allies," he would tell them. There would be no more slave raids to Hispania. He would set his sights on Volubulis. It would take time, but one day the land would be the Mauris' again.

A picture of Aelia came to his mind. He blushed. She had played him, the bitch. But for all that, she was an interesting woman. He would miss their talks. He wheeled his horse off the ridge and down to where most of the cavalry was milling around and towards where the men from the beach were making their way.

It would be a long war.

XXX

After the ships had put off from the beach, Marcus had them cluster a half-mile off shore to take stock of the condition of the cohort and the freed citizens. Timotheus—who had waited with the III Augustus at the boats—was trying to concentrate the badly wounded in one ship, but some were too injured to move. With the ships gathered, Timotheus could move from one to another, triaging the wounded and giving opium to those in pain.

Marcus had his ship close with Aelia's, and when the two bumped, he swung himself aboard. Aelia was waiting for him, still wearing the bloodstained dress, although she had poured water over her hair and washed out some of the matted gore.

"Marcus Favonius," she said with a wide smile. "You have delivered us. I never doubted that you would."

Marcus felt awkward and unsure of himself, so he bowed stiffly and replied, "My lady Dasumi, I am honored that I could serve you."

"By the Gods, Marcus," said Aelia, "you will have to do better than that." She grabbed him by his chain armor, pulled him down and kissed him full on the lips. Tilting her head back she grinned at him. "A lady wouldn't do what I just did, so you will have to stop using that silly title and call me Aelia."

He reddened at the ripple of laughter around him, but he also felt himself relax. "I am sorry, Aelia, I just wasn't sure, that is certain, that, uh...."

She laughed and took him by the arm. "Women have discovered there are two types of men: Those who always know exactly what to say, and those who are tongue tied. The former are amusing and useless. The latter are a trial, but they have potential. All they need is a good woman to properly instruct them. Now come and let yourself be a hero for a moment."

She pulled him along toward the bow where most of the freed Romans had congregated. They crowded around him, touching him, shaking his hand, some of them with tears in their eyes. He was embarrassed but touched, and he mumbled what he thought were the right things to say: how brave they had been, how they had helped in the fight, how much their loved ones missed them, how soon they would be home. They blessed him, cried, cheered, still drunk with their freedom.

Aelia finally extracted him and led him toward the side. "Rachel and I will return to your ship with you, Marcus. I don't intend letting you out of my sight again."

Marcus nodded. "Of course, gather your things."

Aelia laughed. "Slaves have no things, Marcus, just their clothes, and we are thin even in that."

The two ships were lashed together, and Marcus put out his hand for Aelia to transfer to the other ship. She ignored it, instead jumping lightly across the two railings, followed by Rachel.

For a moment, Marcus felt a little silly standing there holding out his hand, but he shrugged and followed them. Slavery must make one athletic, he thought.

The soldiers on the ship looked at the two women with open admiration. For the first time Marcus noticed that Rachel was an attractive woman, but in an entirely different way than Aelia. As Aelia was light-skinned and blond, Rachel was olive skinned with thick, blue-black hair. Aelia was thin— thinner than he remembered her—while Rachel was strongly muscled, with wide shoulders.

Aelia lifted her hands. "Men of the VII Legion Hispania, Aelia Dasumi thanks you," she said. The men stirred. Everyone in Hispania had heard the name "Dasumi," and word had it that one of the family had been taken in the slave raid. "We know what you did for us. We know the comrades you left in Mauretania because of us. We know the scars you bear. We will not forget this, soldiers of the VII Legion. You will reside in our hearts."

The emotion Aelia put into her words silenced the soldiers, who looked down or shuffled their feet, suddenly embarrassed.

"This is my sister, Rachel. There is no way we can thank you for what you have done," she said. After a short pause she added, "But a year's pay in gold might help."

The men roared a cheer. A year's pay in gold was worth three times a year's pay in silver denari, which were so adulterated with lead these days that the lead rubbed off on the men's fingers.

Aelia turned to Marcus. "Find us a space where we can talk. And I need that good-looking Greek of yours."

The boat was jammed, but a centurion was, after all, a centurion. Marcus cleared a small area in the bow and waved for

Demaratus, who was with the man at the tiller. As the Greek threaded his way toward the bow, Flavius joined him.

"Who is the stocky officer?" whispered Aelia. "Wasn't he in the Mauri tent?"

"Flavius, my second in command," answered Marcus. "Yes, he was in the tent. Rachel almost killed him."

"Maybe almost killing him is the way to his heart," said Aelia, arching an eyebrow at Rachel. Rachel said nothing but crossed her arms.

Both men saluted and bowed to the two women. Flavius looked uncomfortable. Marcus wondered why and then caught his optio glancing at Rachel and then looking away. Marcus kept his face expressionless, but he suspected Aelia's quip might not be far off the mark.

"Gentlemen, I will have an opportunity to thank you properly when we return to Hispania, but I need to ask a question now," said Aelia.

The three exchanged glances.

"Did my brother send a ransom with you?" she asked.

There was a long silence. Finally, Marcus answered, "Yes."

"Do you still have it?" she asked.

Marcus and Flavius looked at Demaratus. "Yes, Lady Dasumi. I still have it."

"Would you bring it to me, Demaratus?" she asked.

Demaratus looked at Marcus who nodded. The signifer turned and returned to the stern where he rooted around in some belongings and retrieved the wooden chest. He brought it forward.

"Open it," said Aelia.

Again Demaratus glanced at Marcus, who nodded. The signifer lifted the lid.

Aelia stared intently into it. "Was there more?" she finally said.

"Yes, Lady Dasumi. I used some to pay the soldiers from the III Augusta who guarded the boats for us. But only a small portion of it," replied Demaratus.

"Was it all in this," she paused, "coin that passes for silver?"

"Yes, Lady."

"There was no gold?" she asked.

Demaratus was silent.

Aelia nodded, her face white and stiff as ivory. "I will take this, Demaratus. I must return it to my brother," she said quietly.

"Of course, Lady," replied the signifer, handing the small chest to her.

"There is one other thing I must ask the three of you. I hesitate to do so after all you have done, but my sister and I have need of you. When we return to Corduba and my home, I wish you to be with us."

"Of course, Lady Dasumi," answered Flavius, which startled both Marcus and Demaratus.

"Oh, thank you. Flavius. Marcus has always spoken so well of you. I knew we could count on you," said Aelia, leaning over to kiss him on the cheek. Turning to Marcus, she said, "Again, I am in your debt."

Marcus bowed. "It will be an honor, Aelia," he said.

She grinned at him. "Now don't go all ladies and honor on me, Marcus," which only flustered him more. "You will excuse us. Rachel and I will visit the man at the tiller."

As the two left, Rachel whispered to Aelia. "Why are we visiting the man at the tiller?"

"Because Flavius spoke out of turn and we have to let the boys work this out," whispered Aelia.

"How did he speak out of turn?" Rachel asked.

"He isn't in command, Marcus is. But Flavius committed them to accompany us to Corduba. I think they would have anyhow, but if men don't do things in certain ways, they get confused. Our being there would only make things more difficult," replied Aelia.

"Why do you think Flavius did that?" asked Rachel.

Aelia smiled at her. "Why indeed?"

Rachel reddened.

As the two women left, Marcus turned on Flavius. "I was not aware you had taken command, optio," he said.

"Sir," protested Flavius, "they are going to confront that toad of a brother. He could kill them."

"And which one are you most concerned with, Flavius?" asked Demaratus with a grin.

"Keep a civil tongue in your head, signifer," growled Flavius.

"Quiet, both of you!" said Marcus. "Flavius, you spoke out of turn. It is not your place to commit the leadership of the First Cohort to any plan of action without agreement from me. Demaratus, you do not speak to a superior officer in such a manner. Do you both understand?"

The two men nodded. Demaratus still looked amused, Flavius just sheepish.

"Demaratus," said Marcus, changing the subject. "We need

to get underway. How long do you estimate before we get to Gedes?"

"If the fishermen are right about this current, sir, I think tomorrow morning," he answered. "If you don't mind, I should like to pass the word that we are getting underway to the other ships."

"See to it," said Marcus.

As Demaratus headed aft, Flavius shuffled his feet and looked embarrassed. "I am really sorry, sir, it just came out."

"Attractive women will do that to you, Flavius" answered Marcus.

"Sir, you don't think it was just about that woman Rachel, do you?" said Flavius.

Marcus smiled. "Not just, optio. Not just."

The cluster of ships began to break up. Sails were raised, and the ships put their shoulders into the Atlantic swell, sending spray over the bows and plunging Marcus into the depths of seasickness.

Aelia was making her way back to Marcus when Demaratus caught her eye. "Lady Dasumi, I would let the centurion be with himself for a while."

"Why?" she asked.

"The sea and our centurion do not agree with one another, Lady Dasumi," replied Demaratus.

"Then I will go to him and help him through this," she said.

"Umm. The centurion is somewhat sensitive about his condition, my Lady. He will attempt to ignore it in order to be polite, which will, of course, make the condition worse. And he will be unable to...," said Demaratus pausing for the right word.

"Vomit," supplied Aelia.

"Well put, Lady Dasumi," said Demaratus with a bow.

"Aelia shook her head. "Men and their dignity. How do you stand yourselves?"

"It takes years of practice and a certain slowness of wit, my Lady," answered Demaratus with a smile.

Aelia laughed. "A man who is aware of himself? You are a rare one, Demaratus. I will take your advice and keep my distance."

The signifer gave her a little bow and turned back to the tiller.

Instead, Aelia sought out the doctor, who was just finishing suturing a wound.

"Timotheus, may I bother you for a moment?" she asked.

"Of course, Aelia, although try to be brief. We have much work to do," he said, indicating the long line of men sitting or lying on the deck waiting for his ministrations.

"I just wanted to suggest you might have one of your assistants put a few drops from one of your poppies into a cup of wine and give it to the centurion. I believe the poppy has the effect of reducing the symptoms of seasickness," she said.

"I will see to it once the most seriously wounded are taken care of, Aelia, though I won't promise he will drink it," said the doctor.

"That is his choice, Timotheus, and forgive me for diverting you from your work," replied Aelia. He nodded and finished bandaging the wounded soldier.

Aelia rose and made her way back to where Rachel sat on the ship's deck.

The ships reduced sail with the coming of night, which made for a smoother ride. Marcus began to perk up—whether from the doctor's potion or the change in the sea was unclear—and Aelia finally got an opportunity to stand by the rail with him and talk.

At dawn, the ships hoisted their sails and Marcus and Aelia watched the coastline of Hispania loom up in the pink glow of a cloudless morning. Aelia kissed him on the cheek and excused herself.

In the combination of organization and chaos that grips every ship headed into a port, Marcus lost sight of Aelia.

A mile outside the harbor, a woman in a long, hooded cape drew up beside him. He glanced at her and looked away.

"Ah, men are so fickle," said Aelia's voice.

Startled, he looked at her again. "Aelia? Why are you dressed so?"

"My brother must not know, Marcus. He must think me dead or in the hands of the Mauri. Is not surprise an important asset in war?" she asked.

"Almost more important than anything, Aelia. What will I tell the people at Gedes?"

"That I was lost in the battle. No one will run a horse from Gedes to Corduba bearing that news, and if they do, well, all the better," she said.

Marcus shook his head and smiled. "You are a dangerous woman, Aelia Dasumi."

"You have no idea, Marcus Favonius, you have no idea," she replied quietly.

XXXI

Governor Domitius Antonius paced the floor of his atrium, feeling pleased with himself and irritated by the tardiness of his secretary. He had sent Salvius—under protest—to deliver a small chest of silver to Juba. The thought of the Mauri leader deflated some of his self-satisfaction. The man was becoming a nuisance. He would have to be dealt with. But for now, he had served a purpose.

Domitius had been delighted to be rid of the VII Legion, as well as those troublemakers from the old III Augusta, but he was left with a small problem. True, the Dasumi woman was still in the hands of the Mauri, so he could look forward to a healthy increase in his net wealth from her brother. The down payment was already locked away in his treasury. But that fool Juba had missed destroying the First Century, so it was possible that word of Julius Dasumi's paltry ransom would slip back to Hispania. That, in turn, might affect the size of the final payment.

Affect it for a while, that is. He still had the Dasumi letter in hand. If there were any problems about the final payment,

Domitius could always threaten to let the letter leak out. Of course, that might cause problems for him. It was complex, and exactly the kind of complexity the governor liked solving.

But Salvius was supposed to be back by last night, and here it was midday and where was he? The ships that had taken the VII Legion to Hispania were also late. Didn't anyone believe in doing things on time around here, he grumbled to himself.

The more he thought about things, the more his mood blackened. He flung himself into a chair and tried looking at documents, but his mind was not on them, and he resumed pacing.

He was in the middle of constructing a blistering speech to fling at his secretary when a slave entered and bowed.

"Yes?" asked the governor impatiently. "Is that worm Salvius back yet?"

The slave bowed again. "Not yet, my Lord, but he sent a chest to you."

"A chest?" mused Domitius. "Well, bring it in and put it on the table. Is there a letter with this?"

"No, my Lord. A man delivered it to the palace."

"Where is this man?" asked the governor.

"He left after saying that this chest was from your secretary and was valuable," replied the slave.

"Did you talk to this man?" asked the governor.

"No, my Lord. The men at the gate did."

Domitius nodded. "Have them whipped."

"Yes, sir," said the slave. He left, returning shortly with a wooden chest bound with brass. He placed it on the table. "Would you like me to open it, my Lord?"

"Get out," said the governor absently, staring at the chest.

The man left and Domitius examined the object. It was larger than the chest he sent to Juba, but what it might contain he had no idea. Domitius Antonius did not like being in the dark. He did not like surprises. And this chest was both.

It was actually a nice piece of work, though the Mauri decoration was a tad too ornate for the governor's taste. The chest had a hasp, through which a carved piece of ivory had been thrust to keep it closed. He slipped the ivory out and lifted the lid.

The head of Salvius Getha, late secretary of the governor of Mauretania Tingitana, stared up at him.

Epilogue

There was a gentle rap at the door.

"Yes?" called out Julius Dasumi. He was working through an enormous stack of receipts, which his secretary was carefully organizing into piles of "urgent," "important," and "can be put off."

The door to the study opened and his hall slave bowed.

"Yes? I was not to be disturbed. You flirt with the whip, slave," snapped Julius. He was a large, sleek man dressed in a rich toga, his fingers sporting several expensive but tasteful rings.

The slave had a strained look on his face. "Forgive me, sir, but your sister Aelia is at the front door."

Julius started to say something and then stopped. Without a word, the secretary vanished. Julius Dasumi saw himself as a man who was always in command. Projecting command made others accept it, and running the affairs of other men was a lucrative undertaking. The slave's words sent a chill through him. How was this possible? The last word from Mauretania was that Marcus was slinking home, and that he was finally free of his sister. He actually bore her no ill will. In a way, he liked her. But she was an impediment. Her 50 percent control meant that he could do nothing without her acquiescence, and the two were rarely of one mind. She had to go, and the fortuitous slave raid gave Julius an opportunity to be rid of her without complications. A note and discreet but generous bribe to Governor Domitius Antonius had made sure that Marcus and his soldiers would never find her, and that was the end of it.

And here she was at his door.

He took a deep breath. He would have to handle this with delicacy, but Julius was a subtle man and he could act any part.

"By the Gods, she is saved," he said, rising, throwing his toga over his shoulder and striding toward the front door. Throwing it wide he opened his arms, "Aelia, my sister, you have been delivered! The Gods have answered my prayers."

Aelia stood at the door. Alongside her was a dark young woman, taller and broader shouldered than Aelia. His sister was dressed in what could only be called a rag, stained an uneven pink. Her hair was loose and wild, and she wore no jewelry. In truth, she looked a little mad, but she smiled at him.

"Brother Julius. You are still here? I was worried that I might miss you," she said.

Julius looked confused. "My dear Aelia, I have waited here hoping against hope, praying each day, that you would be released. If the VII Legion is responsible for this, they can expect a generous reward. Why would I be anyplace but here, dear sister?"

"Why indeed, dear brother? Come and embrace me, Julius."

Julius hesitated a moment. The rag she was wearing was not only a rag, but dirty as well, but he stepped forward and threw his arms around her. As he did, he felt a sharp prick at his back.

"Dear Julius," she whispered. "What you feel at your back is a knife. A knife that I used to kill someone. You embrace his gore which has also colored my dress."

He started to pull away. "I don't understand, sister, is your mind...." but as he tried to pull away from her he backed further into the knife blade, which now actually hurt.

"My mind is fine, dear brother," she said, still continuing to whisper. "I am glad I could see you before you leave."

Julius gasped from the pain of the blade. "What has come over you, Aelia? Your mind has become sickened by your experience. I will fetch a doctor for you."

"You will stand very quietly, my dear brother, or I will drive this knife into your kidney. It is a painful way to die they tell me. You will stand here until a slave fetches you a litter, and then you will leave. The estate in Tarraco is far," she said, her head pressed against his chest.

"You cannot banish me from my own house, Aelia, the city will not stand for it," blustered Julius.

"They will stand for it when I show them the evidence of your treachery, dear brother," whispered Aelia.

"Treachery? What treachery do you...," he started, but stopped when the knife went deeper. He could feel a thin trickle of blood running down the small of his back. Then he noticed the three men in the yard. One was vaguely familiar and wore a centurion's transverse crest on his helmet. Next to him was a stocky, stone-faced officer with a phylum. The third officer—a Greek—stepped forward, opened a box, and spilled a pile of silver coins out on the ground.

"That is not the ransom I sent. I sent gold. This Greek has stolen it, Aelia. Greek are all thieves," Julius said in as outraged a tone as one could muster up with a knife in his back.

The Greek said nothing, just stared. It was not a comforting stare.

Julius started to struggle, but the woman to his left put a hand on his arm. "I have seen your sister butcher a Mauri warrior with that knife, brother of Aelia. You resist at your peril. Call a slave."

"I will raise the house is what I will do, and..., " started Julius. The stocky officer with the phylum was pointing it at him and slowly shaking his head. Julius swallowed. "You can't just take a man's house from him," he ended weakly.

"If he is a treacherous dog who bribed a governor to keep his sister in slavery, I think a man would do more than lose his house, dear brother," said Aelia quietly, still keeping Julius in her firm embrace.

"I never did such a thing," protested Julius, stumbling on the words.

"We know you did, dear brother, we know you did. Now be a good boy and call a slave. The day is early. You can get a good start," said Aelia tilting her head up toward him but keeping the knife firmly pressed against his back.

He considered trying to break loose and raising the household, but even if every slave in the house armed himself, and his bodyguards were to come to his aid, how long would they stand against the three soldiers? Would they even fight? How did Aelia find out about the bribe? It could be just a guess and a bluff on her part, but could he take the chance? He could try to raise the town, but Julius knew that while he was feared in Corduba, he was not liked. Aelia was well liked. Corduba would be more likely to side with his sister.

"The slave?" prompted the dark woman on Aelia's left.

Julius was quiet for a moment, and then sighed. "Aemilius" he called out.

"Sir," said a voice behind him. The man had been standing there most of the time.

"Call for a litter," he said, and then to Aelia, "I will have to pack."

"You wear what you have on your back, dear brother, just like I did when I was taken a slave," said Aelia.

Julius said nothing. He took on the appearance of the defeated, although he was already thinking of ways he could avenge himself.

The minutes stretched out, but Aelia seemed relaxed, smiling up at him with eyes of pure ice. Finally, a litter handled by eight slaves arrived. Aelia pressed the knife in a little deeper, prodding him towards it. He strode down and stepped into it. He glared at them all and closed the curtains. The slaves stepped briskly out the front enclosure.

The litter had not gone far when it came to a halt. "Why have you stopped?" bellowed Julius.

The curtain parted and the Greek stood looking at him. Julius recoiled. The man stared for a long time, and then pulled from his belt a long-bladed knife and flicked it at Julius. It sliced open his toga and opened a long, shallow cut across his chest.

"How dare you, you," sputtered Julius.

"'Thieving Greek'? Do you wish to repeat that, Dasumi?" said the man quietly.

Julius looked up into the Greek's eyes and decided that to do so would almost surely be fatal. He said nothing.

The Greek leaned into the litter until he was nose to nose with Julius. "Hear me, Dasumi. If something should happen to Aelia, I will come for you. All the bodyguards in the world will not save you. And when I find you I will cut your belly open, extract your intestines, and strangle you. Do you understand, Dasumi?"

Julius nodded mutely, paralyzed by the vivid image.

The Greek stood, sheathed his knife, and waved the litter on.

Aelia stood in the atrium surrounded by household staff. They eyed her curiously, what with her ragged and stained dress. All had heard at least some version of Julius' expulsion from the house. Aelia's brother was not an easy man to serve, but Aelia's bizarre attire and the presence of the three soldiers made them wary.

She waited until there was silence. "Over the next few days, you will hear my story and the story of all those who were taken at Ambis by the Mauri. It is a tale worth telling, and we have here," she gestured to Marcus, Flavius, and Demaratus standing near a side wall, "the men who rescued us from bondage." The slaves and few freemen craned their necks to look. Marcus and Flavius looked embarrassed, Demaratus expressionless.

"We have a new addition to the household," and Aelia reached her hand out to Rachel. "This is Rachel. She was a slave. Now she is my sister." Rachel came forward looking uncomfortable. Aelia entwined her arms into Rachel's. The household members stirred, some whispering back and forth.

"My sister and I have seen many things over the past month, things which have made me think about the world in a different way," said Aelia. "I am not clear what all these experiences mean, but things will be different in the Dasumi household in the coming weeks."

The household members glanced at one another and waited. They were suspicious of change. Slaves could hide in routine. Anything that broke routine held potential danger.

"Go about your duties now," said Aelia, and the slaves scattered. Aelia and Rachel immediately put their heads together and whispered for several minutes. Finally, both turned, their arms still linked, and came over to where the three men stood. With some amusement, Marcus noted that Flavius was doing his best not to look at Rachel. Instead, the optio fidgeted, shuffled his feet, and pretended to look closely at the frescos and wall hangings. Demaratus must have noticed the same thing because his visage shifted from expressionless to amused. He was careful not to make it obvious.

"Gentlemen," said Aelia. "Will you make my home your home while my sister and I bathe and change our clothes? I know that you must leave in a few days, but for now you will have proper food, a decent bath, and wine that is worth remembering."

Flavius begged off for himself and Demaratus. "We thank you for your generosity, Lady Dasumi, but we have a century to organize before we sail north."

"I cannot persuade you?" she beseeched.

"Duty is even more persuasive, my Lady," said Demaratus, "but I fear you have not seen the last of us."

"May the gods make that so, Demaratus," answered Aelia, "You, however," she said, turning to Marcus, "are not allowed to leave until tomorrow. If I judge my brother correctly, this matter is not over, and until I can procure proper protection, your presence will ensure my safety." Placing her hand on his chest, she asked, "Will you do this for me, Marcus?"

He bowed. "Of course." Turning to Flavius and Demaratus he said, "I will meet you in Gedes tomorrow night.'

Following a kiss from Aelia, both saluted and left.

"Now come, my centurion. I will leave you in the library for a short time. I will have wine and food brought to you and I promise not to be long," she said.

He was neither thirsty nor hungry, but it was a wondrous library, and he soon lost track of time. When Aelia finally reappeared, he was surrounded by books and scrolls, the wine and bread untouched.

Aelia was dressed in a simple sheath, belted at the waist. Her hair, still damp and cascading down her back, was pulled back and held in place by a silver clasp. She had just a hint of makeup. Marcus had to stop himself from staring. He had forgotten what a beautiful woman she was.

"Oh, good," she said with a dazzling smile. "You are speechless. Women love to make men speechless." She came forward and took both his hands. "Come with me, Marcus. We have unfinished business."

She led him across the atrium and down a corridor to a carved double door. Pushing it open, she led him in. "Do you remember this room, Marcus?"

"Of course," he smiled. It was here Aelia had shown him the ancient Greek helmet, and where the two had first—what? What had passed between them? Marcus had felt a connection, but Julius had disturbed the moment, and Marcus was not sure the moment had been his alone, or both of theirs.

Holding his hand, she slowly looked around the room. "I dreamed of this room, Marcus. I dreamed of you. I remembered when you quoted the Iliad. Say it to me again."

"I too shall lie in the dust when I am dead, but for now let me win noble renown," he recited softly.

"Yes," she said, looking up at him. "And you have won noble renown, my centurion. Do you remember what I said to you before my brother barged in?"

He did—how could he forget—but he was too embarrassed to say, so he stood mute.

"My awkward hero," she said run her hand up his cheek. "I said that I had learned something from you, and that I wished to return the favor. Do you remember that?"

His chest felt tight. He nodded.

"It is time to return that favor," she whispered softly, pulling his head down to her.

Acknowledgments

This book could not have been written without the careful copy editing of Anne Bernstein, Betsy Wootten, John Isbister and Roz Spafford, as well as their critiques and suggestions. Danny Hallinan was the book's historical editor and Jack Radey gave valuable advice on the Roman Army and ancient warfare. I am deeply grateful to readers like Susan Watrous, Antonio Hallinan, Danny Beagle and Linda Williams who gave me practical suggestions on how to make the book better, plus invaluable encouragement. My thanks go to Ann Higgins for the cover design and to Caroline Jennings for interior formatting and final editing.

Glossary and Notes

Ala. Auxiliary cavalry unit, roughly the size of a infantry cohort.
Century. Basic administrative and military unit of a legion.
Centurion. Commander of a century.
Cohort. Basic tactical unit of the legion.
Cornus. Roman war horn.
Contubernium. The smallest unit in a century.
Curia. Meeting place for municipal councils.
Dolabra. Basic infantry entrenching tool, a sort of pick-axe.
Gladius. Short stabbing sword of the Roman infantry.
Intervallum. Border inside of a fort or marching camp.
Latafundia. Landowner.
Legate. Commands a legion.
Optio. Second in command of a century.
Paenula. Cloak with a hood.
Pilum (pl. pila). Heavy spear of the Roman army.
Praetorians. Emperor's personal legion, and the only legion allowed in Rome.
Prefect. Third in command of a legion.
Principia. Army headquarters.
Pugio. Short dagger.
Quingeniaery. Cavalry unit. It is composed of 16 turmae of 30 men each. Normally from 480 to 500 men.
Sacramentum. Oath of loyalty to the Emperor.
Sagum. Cloak used by soldiers, fastened at the right shoulder.
Scutum. The basic rectangle shield of a legionnaire. It was 4 ft long, 2' 6"

wide, and curved to deflect blows.

Signifer. Officer who carries the century standard, and also oversees the unit's books and the men's pay.

Signum. A century's standard.

Spatha. Long sword used by Roman cavalry.

Taberna. Tavern.

Tesserarius. Most junior officer in a century, oversees assigning guard duty.

Testudo. "The tortoise," an infantry maneuver that forms a wall and roof of shields. It is effective for attacking towns and protecting against archers.

Tribune. Senior staff officer in a legion.

Turmae. Basic cavalry unit, normally 30 men.

Valetudinarium. Hospital.

Vexilla. A detachment of troops operating away from their parent body.

Vigiles. Served as police and firemen in cities.

The Structure of a Roman Legion

A Roman legion was designed to be a tactically flexible fighting force. To enhance that flexibility, it was divided into discrete units. In that way, a legion resembled a modern infantry division, which is divided into brigades, battalions, regiments, companies and squads. The legion's units could act independently of one another so that they could reinforce a unit that was in trouble, exploit a weakness in the enemy's line, or block an attempt to out-flank the legion. Mobility was the essence of a legion's tactics and made it virtually invincible for almost 700 years. Modern armies owe much of their organizational structure to the Roman legion.

A legion was constructed as follows:

Contubernium: An eight-man squad, the smallest unit in a legion.

Century: Comprising 10 contuberniums. A century is normally 80 men, commanded by a centurion.

Cohort (regular): Composed of six centuries, approximately 480 men.

First Cohort: Composed of five centuries, but each century has160 men. A First Cohort would be approximately 800 men.

Legion: Made up of 10 cohorts normally deployed in three lines.

When Headquarters units, plus specialists, are included, a legion would be approximately 5,400 men.

Legate: Legion commander.

Tribune: Senior legion staff officer (normally three per legion).

Prefect (Praefectus castrorum): Third-in-command.

The Structure of a Century

The century was the smallest tactical unit in a legion. That is, it was the smallest unit capable of fighting on its own. It was closest to a modern infantry company, although smaller. In the case of a century from the first cohort, however, it was somewhat larger than a modern infantry company.

A century had four officers:

Centurion: Commander.

Optio: Second-in-command.

Signifer: Holds century standard during battle and keeps the unit's books.

Tesserarius: Junior officer, who also sets sentry duty and oversees camp construction.

Centurions, in order of seniority:

First Cohort
Primus Pilus
Princeps
Princeps Posterior
Hastatus
Hastatus Posterior
Hastatus Posterior
(The five centurions
of the First Cohort
make up the *Primi Ordines,*
a group of the most senior
centurions)
Regular Cohort
Pilus Prior
Pilus Posterior

Princeps Prior
Princeps Posterior
Hastatus

Place names

Mauretania names/ Modern names
Ambis
Capera
Carthago Nova/ Cartagena
Corduba/ Cordoba
Barcino/ Barcelona
Emerita Augusta/ Merida
Elmantica/ Salamanca
Baetica/ Andalusia
Emporiae/ Ampurias
Gades/ Cadiz
Gaul/ France
Hippo Regius/ Annaba
Sala/ Chellah
Legio/ Leon
Tarraco/ Tarragona
Tingis/ Tangiers
Tortosa/ Tortosa
Valentia/ Valencia
Volublis

Bibliography

Adkins, Lesley and Roy A. Adkins. *Handbook to Life in Ancient Rome*, Oxford University Press, 1994.

Appian. *Wars of the Romans in Iberia*. Translated by J.S. Richardson, Aris & Phillips LTD, 2000.

Armstrong, Karen. *A History of God: The 4,000-Year Quest of Judaism, Christianity and Islam*, Ballantine Books, 1993.

Breem, Walter. *Eagle in the Snow*, Rugged Land, 2004.

Campbell, Brian. *War and Society in Imperial Rome: 31 BC-284 AD*, Routledge, 2002.

Casson, Lionell. *Ships and Seafaring in Ancient Times*, University of Texas Press, 1994.

Goldsworthy, Adrian. *The Complete Roman Army*, Thames & Hudson, 2003.

Grant, Michael. *The Army of the Caesars*, Charles Scribner's Sons, 1974.

Griess, Thomas E. Ancient and Medieval Warfare: The West Point Military History Series, Avery Publishing Group, Inc., 1984.

Hadas, Moses. *Imperial Rome*, Time-Life Books, 1965.

Hamey, L.A., and J.A. Hamey. *The Roman Engineers*, Cambridge University Press, 1981.

Hopkins, Keith. *A World Full of Gods: The Strange Triumph of Christianity*, The Free Press, 1999.

Keppie, Lawrence. *The Making of the Roman Army: From Republic to Empire*, University of Oklahoma Press, 1984.

Le Glay, Marcel, Jean-Louis Voisin and Yann Le Bohec. *A History of Rome*, Blackwell, 2001.

Lewis, Jon E., editor. *The Mammoth Book of Eyewitness Ancient Rome*, Carrol & Graff Publishers, 2003.

Luttwak, Edward N. *The Grand Strategy of the Roman Empire: From the First Century AD to the Third*, Johns Hopkins University Press, 1979.

MacMullen, Ramsey. *Roman Social Relations*, Yale University Press. 1974.

Richardson, John S. *The Romans in Spain*, Blackwell, 1998.

Scarre, Chris. *The Penguin Historical Atlas of Ancient Rome*, Penguin, 1995.

Southern, Pat. *The Roman Empire: From Severus to Constantine*, Routledge, 2001.

Strauss, Barry. *The Battle of Salamis*, Simon & Schuster, 2004.

Wells, Peter. *The Barbarians Speak: How the Conquered Peoples Shaped Roman Europe*, Princeton University Press, 1999.

Conn M. Hallinan was a long-time columnist for Foreign Policy in Focus, "A Think Tank Without Walls," and an independent journalist. He holds a PhD in Anthropology from the University of California, Berkeley. For 23 years he oversaw the journalism program at the University of California at Santa Cruz, where he won the UCSC Alumni Association's Distinguished Teaching Award, as well as UCSC's Innovations in Teaching Award and its Excellence in Teaching Award. He also served as Provost at Kresge College of UCSC, retiring in 2004. He is a winner of a Project Censored "Real News Award," and lives in Berkeley, California. The Middle Empire books are his first works of fiction.

Preview of Book III: Tarraco

Centurion Antonius Crispus, hastatus posterior, Third Century, 10th Cohort of the VII Legion Hispania Gemina Pia, stood at the center of the Via Augusta leading into Tarraco. To his north, a great army moved inexorably toward the city of Scipio. The late afternoon sun flashed off of weapons and shields, and two blocks of cavalry flanked the vanguard. Behind the wall of shields was an enormous cloud of dust kicked up by horses and wagons.

The man beside him fidgeted. "Sir? Your orders?" asked the man.

Antonius turned to look at Tiberius Cicero, his tesserarius. He was a bright young man who had yet to draw a sword in anger. He was scared and doing his best to conceal it. That was fine with Antonius. Any man who could look at the army marching on Tarraco and not be scared was a fool, and foolish men were much more likely to get you killed than fearful ones.

"What do you say we march out and teach that Frankish rabble a lesson, Tiberius?" said the centurion with a smile.

"Sir? Shall I prepare the century?"

Antonius chuckled. "Tiberius Cicero, an officer's duty is to the Empire and his men. What would happen if the Third Century marched out to fight that army over there?"

The optio swallowed but said nothing.

"We would all die, Tiberius. Would that help the Empire? "

Tiberius fidgeted some more, looking increasingly unhappy. Antonius resisted the urge to tease him. "It would not, optio. We would have our honor, but the city would fall."

"Umm. Isn't it going to fall anyhow, sir?" asked the optio.

"Yes," answered the centurion.

"Then what is our duty, sir?" asked Tiberius.

Antonius had turned back to look at the human avalanche descending on Tarraco. "Our duty, optio, is to be a thorn in their side," he answered quietly. "Did you send the riders out?" he asked.

"Yes, sir. Two, by different roads to Legio," answered Tiberius.

"Good. The VII Legion will come," said Antonius, turning to go back into the city. "The trick, tessararius, will be staying alive long enough to greet them."

www.ingramcontent.com/pod-product-compliance
Lightning Source LLC
Chambersburg PA
CBHW071236300726
48975CB00002B/442